MARIGOLD TEMPLE
CYGNI SEA
MORF MOUNTAINS
LOVER'S LIGHT
ELEMENTROPOLIS
MUDDY BAY
ABANDONED CITADEL
OSPHERIA
ROYAL PHILOSOPHERS ACADEMY
AVELMORE CASTLE
MAP OF DENEB

ISBN 979-8-9956510-6-2

Edited by:
Lauren Baker, Tea and Tales Publishing LLC
Sabrina Stapleton, Inkfall Editing LLC

Cover Design by Louise Devismes

FORSAKEN FLOWERS

THEOPHANY JUHN

For the ones whose existence is hated, and still showed up despite the efforts to be forsaken. For those who have ever felt like weeds among flowers.

Crowning Clown
THE QUEEN

"ONE IS NOT BORN A QUEEN. One must become queen. To become queen, she must be worthy." The voice of the High Priestess resounds through the throne room. The traditionally ornate room glitters with the kaleidoscopic colors of Elemental folks from noble and common lineage.

The High Priestess presses the end of a white cotton string to the princess's forehead and wraps it around her head. With small golden scissors, she snips the string.

The High Priestess echoes, "This represents your worth of carrying the crown." The priestess pulls another end from the ball of string, places it to the princess's throat, and pulls the ball down to her navel, snipping the yarn. "This represents your worth of carrying the future." The priestess measures the string down each of the princess's arms. "The weight in which you shall carry the Elements of this Crownship." The priestess cuts the length of the string to each of the princess's legs. "The balance in which you must walk for the realm."

The High Priestess takes all the cut strings and braids them together. After securing the end of the braid, the

High Priestess opens her hands towards the princess standing before her. The princess picks up the gold scissors and snips a winding wave of her dark hellebores hair. The cut petals flow like droplets onto the High Priestess's extended palm. The High Priestess paints the braided strings with the princess's hair petals.

She hands the princess an unlit candle with her free hand, and the princess blows against the barren wick. The wick ignites into a tall pillar of fire. The High Priestess takes an end of the braided strings and welcomes them to the flame. The braid sparks into flying stars. The stars fall down, combusting into flames as they crash into the bowl below.

The High Priestess nests the fiery braid into a large ancient bowl made of gold that is filled with clear water and representations of the realm. Star Jasmine flowers for the Floral Elementals, Funeral Bell mushrooms for the Fungal Elementals, and butterfly wings for the Insectal Elementals.

With a small wooden stick, she gongs the side of the golden bowl. *Gong, gong.* The flames devour the braided strings.

With each hit of the stick, the resonance thrums through the princess. At first, a ringing pulses in her ears. With each gong, the ringing overlaps with the last echo. Sending a wave from her head, down her spine, and circling back upward. The sensation runs back up her spine to the top of her head, as if ready for bearing the crown.

The fire snaps and spits into a fiery swirling cyclone reaching out from the ancient bowl. Sparks fly like falling stars fluttering at first. The closer the sparks reach the top gape of the fiery cyclone, the stars are pulled into the vortex.

Once the braided strings touch the water, the bowl bursts into a thunderous black flame, roaring high into the face of the High Priestess.

The priestess continues to gong the side of the bowl as the monstrous fire overcomes the rest of the braided strings until only a sliver of smoke leaves the bowl, sizzling whatever is left in the water.

Her golden silk cape flows into the air as the High Priestess lowers onto her knees, gesturing to the princess to do the same on the other side of the bowl. They both bow their heads, their foreheads touching the rim.

A glow forms with soft lines through the princess's veins. The High Priestess chants and the glow brightens into sharp lightning of gold across her skin. The priestess lifts her head and rises, taking the princess's hand, lifting her from the ground.

Still gripping the princess's hand, the High Priestess pulls her close and whispers, "You know as well as I that this is not the way of tradition, may you walk from this room with protection." Louder for the entire throne room she said, "On this day, the last day of the frost season, the Princess thaws from the dead of winter. She is not only at the rightful age to inherit the crown and throne, but her skin glows with her worth to take on the Crownship. On this last chilling day before the solar season begins, the Princess performs before you her Rite of Divinity. In the name of the Goddess Ko'nkiun and the Blessed Descendants, Princess Aelyta Aurelianus is now ready to be crowned Queen of Ospheria."

The princess faces the common folks sitting below the noble seats and bows her head. Her father's nostrils flare towards the dais. He leaps from his seat and gestures the Richards family and Ronanbrands for the dining hall before anyone notices. The Royal Advisers, ambassadors of the Crownship, so many guests, including her ladies-in-waiting. The nobles make their way for the dining hall. The common folk's cheers and rejoices rebound through the throne room as Aelyta waves to them from the head of the large, long room.

Stepping towards the edge of the dais, lifting her chin so her voice carries over the cheers. Silencing the large room, Aelyta addresses the public:

"Thank you, Elementals of Ospheria. Thank you for your cheers and your pride. I am truly honored to be bestowed the worth of becoming your queen that I know my mother, the late Queen Jane, would have wanted to see. My role has been set forth before my forthcoming. I uphold the traditions of the many queens who have stood in this very place with bright eyes and bright visions for Ospheria. I stand here before you now, blessed by the elements to honor the Blessed Descendants of our past. I stand here before you now to honor all of us, and may I walk the line of Crownship in your honor. May thou be blessed by the Blessed Descendants. Queen Aelyta, first bloom of the season and first to winter, Beacon of thine Crown."

A funneled light fumes on, the spotlight glaring over Aelyta. Voices ring through the throne room, "Queen Aelyta, Beacon of thine Crown."

Aelyta descends from the dais. One step at a time, she walks down the throne room. The light burning through her. Her neck stiff, though her head barren.

Whispers resound beside her as she creeps past the

rows of Elementals, "Blessed Queen." They bow their bodies.

Her eyes burn with the urge to look, to thank them, to acknowledge their presence. But one wrong move—Aelyta's face burns at the thought. One wrong move will guarantee her fate sealed the same as her mother's.

The Elementals cry out as they bow at her passing, "Blessed Queen." The urge ticks at her neck. Look, acknowledge them. Her head snaps to the side and she is greeted with the colorful rows of Elements.

"Thank you," she whispers. "Thank you. I see you all, and I thank you." Blended descendants of long history, a relief relaxes her back. But the spotlight following her cuts off.

Darkness consumes the castle, as if before the sun dives over the horizon. Aelyta prefers specific parts of the castle far more than the dining hall. The high, vaulted ceilings covered in gilded paintings of the old descendants dance above them. Tonight, in particular, Aelyta despises the idea of celebration.

The Rite of Divinity caught her off guard, and her father, nor the Royal Advisors have given her an explanation as to why her coronation ceremony had changed. Rejoice is not something she feels. No, at this moment, Aelyta feels her Crownship is being undermined. She glances at her father with a proud smile on his face, clasping hands with his two favorite men.

A sneer almost slips onto her face before she notices Minister Nyup approaching. She gives a smile to the Fungal Minister from Elementropolis. He extends his hand

and she gives a firm shake. "Beautiful ceremony," is all he had to say to her.

"Thank you, Minister." She watches as he awkwardly shuffles off.

Aelyta's stomach churns with an emptiness carving into her sides. She hadn't eaten all day. The idea of eating in front of all the noblemen, all the Elementals with power at their fingertips, causes her stomach to twist like a knife in her guts. She discerns one of them to be behind the change of events.

Gently shuffling through the crowd funneling into the door of the dining hall, she rounds the group and nearly slips through the door.

Kyanston Richard pulls her arm, stopping her. "Why aren't you seated yet? You're the Beacon tonight."

"I feel it my duty to let the kingdom come before the queen," she recites. Her eyes falling forward, neutral. She steadies her gaze towards Kyanston's right ear. Her eyes focusing on the darkness of the hall outside the doorway as he continues.

"If you choose me, you'll have more than all of Deneb's riches. You like the sciences. I will grant you all-access to what the Richards' have been brewing as long as you name me king."

"I hope you're playing fair, Kyanston." Cory Ronanbrand walks up to them. "We have to let our future queen decide who she shall choose to accompany her on her journey through the crownhood. I'd hate to find out you cheated your way to the position."

"Thank you, Cory, for that." Aelyta glances to the door. The High Priestess's golden cape flickers barely in sight behind the entrance of the door. "I must speak with someone before the dinner starts. Please begin without me." She quickly curtsies and jets for the High Priestess.

Aelyta ensures they are alone before leaning into the High Priestess. "Never in my twenty-six years have you ever mentioned caution until tonight. Would you care to explain yourself?"

The High Priestess smiles at her, lifting Aelyta's chin. "You look so much like your mother." The priestess tucks a piece of Aelyta's glittering dark hair behind her ear. "Do not let them confuse you with her. There is a darkness that envelopes your family. I have been by your mother's side for as long as she had been queen. I ask you to keep your wits about you." She scans around them, whispering harder, "A storm is brewing in preparation for your coronation, I believe you will take down towers with you." With knitted brows, Aelyta studies the woman's face. "When a storm rolls in, what do birds do?" the High Priestess asks the princess.

"They take shelter," Aelyta answers.

The High Priestess nods before ducking through the door to the dining hall, leaving Aelyta alone in the grand hall. She's left with more questions than answers. The room spins around her as she leans against the wall.

She hears the doors of the dining hall close with a bang. Now she's all alone in the hallway outside the large elaborate room filled with chatter and noise.

Looking up, the room isn't spinning anymore, she can escape to her chambers. Taking a few steps down the hall, the colors around her begin to spin again. This time, not because of a blurry case of the spins, but it's as if the shadows are snuffing out the lights against the walls.

Curious, she pauses in the middle of the hallway. The shadows leap from the walls and slither across the floor.

Aelyta tries to scream, but her voice is caught in her throat.

Shadows swarm her, erasing the light and colors of the hallway. Her breathing hitches as she blinks at nothing. She can't see a thing.

"Hello?" Her voice holds nothing back as she yells into the void.

A hand reaches out from the darkness. Aelyta steps back, but she bumps against a wall. A figure appears, silhouetted in the dark shadows. Their hands grab her throat, but he roars like thunder upon contact. She jumps at the static spark jumping from her skin to his hands.

Through the shadows, she sees him pull out a dagger. He aims it towards her, but she reaches out for his face first, sparking another electric shock between their skin. The weapon drops from his hand.

"Stop shocking me." He grinds his teeth.

He slams his fist beside her head, causing her to lean into the wall harder.

She struggles. "You're the one shocking me."

"Well, you're really bad at dying," he replies, leaning into the side of her head.

"You're really bad at being an assassin," she mutters under her breath.

He tries to grab her jaw but jumps at the static leaping between them. He moves to pick up the dagger, but as soon as he leans down, she kicks him, pushing him down the ground. He grabs her ankle as she attempts to flee.

When she falls to the ground, he climbs on top of her, pinning her as she twists. "What are you?" He pokes the skin of her back, zapping himself again, but this time he was prepared for it.

"The princess, you prick," she spits. "If you're really an assassin, why won't you just kill me already?"

"Why in such a hurry? You don't want to get know each other?" He struggles, jumping at every zap against his skin.

Careful not to touch her, he hurls her onto her back. She coughs at the impact. "You know, not all men enjoy foreplay." She attempts to twist free again.

"Lucky for you," he leans into her once more, "that's my favorite part."

Aelyta's scoffs, but it's cut short when he wields the blade over her head. Screaming, she lifts her head and bites his shoulder. The static lightning bursts from their contact, strobing through the dark shadows. The shadowed figure cries out in pain as he twists himself free from her teeth. The dagger clinks onto the ground.

She yells for help, but he laughs at her. Gripping his shoulder where she bit him, he picks up the dagger with his free hand. "No one can hear you in my Shadow Realm."

"Who are you?" she mumbles through his hand.

"Your death." His voice rumbles like thunder as he plunges the blade into her heart. Electricity bursts from the blade. They're thrown back from the combustion. The dagger clinking to the ground in the distance between them.

Aelyta fumbles to her feet, grabbing the dagger. She lunges for the assassin. Another zap shocks the two of them. "You're supposed to be dead." He grinds his teeth.

He grabs the wrist holding the dagger and flips her around. His other hand around her neck. The touch is so electrifying, he can barely squeeze. The energy burns under his skin and he releases her.

"You can keep that as a souvenir." The shadows evaporate, revealing the dimly lit hallway. The lights flicker as if she'd never left.

The shadowed figure is nowhere to be seen, but the dagger is still in her hand. The dining hall doors are still closed. The sound of the dinner party still ongoing, echoing down the hallway.

Aelyta balances the dagger between both her hands. The chill inside the castle consumes her to the bones. "What just happened?" she whispers, not to interrupt the quiet around her.

She jumps at the sight of movement, but only the flicker of candlelight responds to her paranoia. The shadows taunt her.

She dares a glance down at her chest. Her bodice is ripped, but she's not bleeding.

Her breathing unsettles, hitching at every wave of movement. The firelight flickers, and she turns restless. Her legs move before her thoughts catch on. She runs for her chambers where Sir Jaycub Battonfield greets her with a newly minted knight beside him. Jaycub bows as she approaches. Steadying her breathing and hiding the dagger behind her, Aelyta gives him a warm greeting before pushing past the two of them.

"Your Majesty," he whispers as he rises from his bow.

"Jaycub," she scoffs. "I'm not queen yet," Aelyta shakes her head,"no need to be formal." She pushes the door open and steps through. Her eyes scan for shadows, as if they are waiting for her behind the door. Her hand grips the handle of the dagger tighter.

"But Lyta." He grabs hold of her arm gently, pulling her closer to him. "I have to tell you something," he whispers harder, almost hissing.

"Whatever it is, you can tell me while I kick these shoes

off," she says, slipping off one shoe at a time. Her eyes trained sternly on the task at hand, then back at the knights before her.

He gestures to the new knight awaiting to be acknowledged. She straightens herself. Tucking the dagger into her waist ribbon before clasping her hands in front of her and clears her throat. "Your name, please." Aelyta nods to the knight.

"Itzal Markwardt," he answers promptly. "I have been assigned as your personal guard beginning tonight. Don't mind my saying, but you look as ghastly as a spirit."

___

2

Without Due Process

___

"I LOOK LIKE A GHOST?" Aelyta's scoff turns into a cackle. Her shoulders square up to the new knight. "I look like a ghost to you?" Hysterical laughter pours out of her as she thrusts herself into her chamber, slamming the door shut behind. Her back presses against the cold wood.

She can hear Jaycub from outside say, "Her majesty must have had a long day. Return to your post tomorrow morning." The sound of a metal clicks signaling their salute and footsteps recede from the door. Jaycub's voice softly comes from behind the door. "He's gone. Aelyta? Are you okay? Should I bother bringing up the rip on your dress?"

"No." Her voice louder than intended. "Long day, like you said."

"You know where to find me, uh, whenever and for whatever."

"Keep it in your pants, Jaycub." She rolls her eyes. If a chuckle could be knightly, it came from Jaycub, muffled on the other side.

Aelyta slides off the door and quickly climbs the spiral stairwell up to her bedroom floor. A fire crackles in the

14

fireplace of the first landing's sitting room. She lets out a sigh but doesn't make it into her room. Spreading herself out onto the top-most landing, she stares up at the glass ceiling of the stairwell, the cold stone floor against her back.

The dagger falls from her hand, clinking onto the stone. Her hand presses into her chest where the dagger pierced her heart just moments earlier. Today, she was supposed to be coronated. Instead, she was met with her killer.

Tears overwhelm her eyes. Her hand grips the surface where her beating heart should have stopped. Someone wants her dead, but all she wishes for is her mother to be here again. She was so close to meeting death.

Her tears dry at the realization. Aelyta has been given a second life, a second opportunity, a chance to find answers. She's not going to waste it.

Rising from the landing, she doesn't wipe her tears from her face. They dry, sticking to her skin, as she makes her way to her studies. Someone was hired to have her dead. She was meant to be queen today, but her father surprised her and all of Ospheria with the Rite instead.

Pulling her petals back from her face, she pores through the books and journals inherited from her late mother.

Aelyta recognizes one book in particular: a journal with her own notes from a royal tour to the Alchemadia Committee with her mother, the last event she attended before her mother's passing. Queen Jane left Avelmore Castle alive and returned from the Academy dead.

Aelyta sighs as she flips through her notes. Theories from what felt like a long time ago, yet it was only a year. Useless information weighing against the death of a woman, a Beacon to the Crownship, a queen. What are the uses of Morf Crystals from Morf Mountains, discoveries on the other side of the map from Ospheria?

Between the lines, Aelyta grasps the absurdity of the Alchemadia Theory. The gruesome idea that Elementals could be repurposed into resources suggests that living Elementals are not just living beings, but materials.

For the rest of the night, Aelyta reviews her old written words, filled with optimism despite the weariness in the corners of her eyes. Every flicker in her peripheral results in Aelyta sitting at the edge of her seat.

But she needs answers. Despite her fear, her grief, Aelyta reads on. Morf Crystals are, in another form, Morphenum, a material used to transform Elementals. A material supplied and harvested by none other than the Richards.

Soon enough, morning light welcomes her window. Aelyta quickly gathers herself and does a short wash in her ever-flowing basin. She changes out of her dress from the night before and descends the stairwell.

There are sounds of scuffling coming from the first floor. She turns to look up at the third-floor landing where her bedroom and bathing room are situated. Carefully stepping down the stone stairwell, she peers into the second floor. Her study room opens to a large room lined with bookshelves, a large tabletop surface in the middle of the room, and two armchairs in the back by the large leaded windows. As she makes her way down to the first-floor landing, she peers around the corner. The sitting room is empty and the fireplace hisses with soft smoke from a large log. She makes her way through the sitting room to the dining room where she runs straight into an armored breastplate.

With a loud clang of metal, Itzal bows to Aelyta awkwardly due to the lack of space between them.

Aelyta taps Itzal on the shoulder with the small of her fingertip, releasing him from the bow. "Ready? I've got a full day of meetings." She looks down to the watch on her wrist. There are no numbers, but eight small dots signal the different parts of the day. "Shall we?" She raises her arm towards the spiral stairwell, waiting for him to begin walking with her.

As they make their way through the castle, Itzal scans their forefront and behind them at every hallway and corner. She leads them to the meeting room where she normally meets with the Royal Advisors. It's the same meeting room in which her mother had once held her meetings with them.

She takes a seat by the closed window, directly in the morning sun. Taking a peek at her watch, she glances around the room to find the large hardcover folder she gave the Royal Advisors last week during their meeting. Leaning over, she unwraps the string holding the folder closed.

A servant walks in as she gently pulls a few papers out from the folder. She smiles at him. "Good morning, Branson. How are you this morning?" From the corner of her eye, she glances at Itzal who has tucked himself in a corner where he can keep watch of her and the door at the same time.

"Your Highness." Branson bows his head. "I hate to alarm you"—he jumps at the sight of Itzal—"but I should inform you"—another sideways glance at Itzal—"all your meetings today have been canceled." Branson's hands fumble around each other. "Boreas has cooked you some breakfast with tea. Where would you like to have them?"

Aelyta leaps to her feet. "What do you mean all my meetings are canceled?"

"I was just told." He looks at her nervously.

She throws the papers back into the folder and snaps the folder under her arm. Storming out the room, she hastens to the main hall. Itzal and Branson keep pace behind her.

"Your Highness, where are you going?" Branson cries.

"They made these plans and then cancel on me on the morning of the meeting. All of them today, canceled. And what about tomorrow? Or the day after? I need them to answer for themselves." She picks up her dress as she climbs the large main stairs to the library. "They're in there, right?"

Branson runs up the stairs. "Yes."

Bursting the large stained-glass doors open, she turns to the sound of muttering. There, she finds the four Royal Advisors sitting around a rectangular table.

"What is the meaning of this?" She interrupts.

"Your Highness," one of them scolds, "we're currently in a meeting."

"Canceled on me to have a meeting without me," she replies.

"You have yet to pick a husband from our selected eligible bachelors. We gave you a year to decide, Your Highness," another spoke.

"I have told you all that I have been in preparation for the crown. I will not just marry someone—"

"Your father is not pleased with your lack of contribution and your lack of interest in marrying," a third advisor chimes. "You gave us a folder full of information we already knew prior to picking these two fine men. Kyanston Richards, despite what you think, is from the wealthiest family in the world. Cory Ronanbrand is the son of the most powerful man, besides the current king."

She scoffs, "The Ronanbrands own the Assassin's Guild. That makes a union with Cory Ronanbrand a controversial one, did you not read anything I wrote?"

The fourth advisor walks up to her. "And that, my dear girl, is what makes the Ronanbrand men the most powerful. We detailed everything in the folder we left for you this morning. Review it and we'll discuss at next week's meeting." He lifts an eyebrow at her as if to rub salt to the wound, but he raises his hand to wave her off.

A marriage outlasts her Crownship. Every Crown retires at the age of sixty-five, and the crown is passed down. Or, in her case, Aelyta was to receive the crown at the crowning age of twenty-six. Her mother must forfeit the crown to her once she becomes of age. A queen is not determined by her marriage, and neither should the crown.

Grinding her fingers over the folder in her hand, she turns to leave the library and heaves herself out. "Is tonight's dinner with the King still to occur as planned?" She stops at the end of the hallway near the servants' door.

"I believe so." Branson nods. He pats her back in reassurance. "I will send word if it has been canceled."

"Thank you." She gives him a small smile in return, watching Branson leave through the servants' door. She waits for him to close it before throwing the folder onto the ground. Her hands go up to her face, rubbing the top of her nose and between her eyebrows. Taking in a few breaths, Aelyta's hands fall to her sides. She looks over at the folder, but it's no longer on the ground.

"Ready when you are," Itzal says to her, folder tucked

under his arm. Glancing up at the ceiling, Aelyta sighs, then proceeds to her chambers.

Her face must have given her emotions away, for Sir Malcolm Queninbrett, standing guard for the day shift, welcomes Aelyta back to her chambers with a small hand to her arm. She slips off her shoes, throwing them under the console table next to the mirror hanging at the end of the foyer. Taking the spiral stairs, she pauses at the landing to the sitting room, a fire already roaring for her in the fireplace. Continuing up to the entrance to the second floor, she turns around the corner for her studies. Aelyta finds a servant setting up a corner of the table with breakfast and tea.

"Briley, I miss your face." She runs to him with an arm out. He tucks into her casual embrace.

She never wants to treat servants as beneath her. She saw them as friends, as a functioning team that keeps the system up and running. Decidedly, Aelyta would do everything in her power to treat them as important—if not more—than the position of queen. Most rulers would treat the people as numbers, the servants as slaves. She's not like most, and she refuses to believe otherwise.

"Branson didn't even need to tell me. I had the tea and Boreas already had food made for you—do not forget to eat it. He slaved over it for you." He pokes her cheek.

"Let him know I won't let his food go to waste this time. You all know me too well." She tosses the folder onto the table. Her and a couple servants helped scour for a few stray old dining tables in which they aligned together to make one giant table in her studies.

Since her father had taken the throne in place of her mother, he had her desk removed and nearly had her studies stripped barren. His reason was that women do not own desks, for women do not do important enough work to obtain one.

"Oh." Briley leans towards Aelyta on his way out. "Who's the brawn?"

"New personal guard, disregard him." Aelyta waves her goodbye to Briley, who gives Itzal a look up-down as Briley saunters out of the study.

Itzal awkwardly meanders into the study, stationing himself beside the doorway.

"I'll be here for awhile, just take a seat. Except for that one." She points to the wingback chair by the window. "I might move over there once I'm done here."

And she meant it when she said she'd stay awhile. Aelyta had not moved from her chair since planting herself there. She started the day with four piles of paper, which she had extracted from the hard-covered folder. Now, with all the papers she has added throughout the day, she is crouched behind ten large piles with four or five books laid out to specific pages marked, all detailing Morf Mountain.

Morf Mountain is as old as Deneb itself. The mountain range encases all of Deneb. No one goes out, and hardly anyone ever comes in. It happened, but only once. The tale is as old as the beginning of Ospheria when a human fell from the stars. A mother fell from the clouds and crashed into the mountains that became known as Morf Mountain. She came from another star in search of her youngling stolen by the goblin. The crystals found in the mountain gave the human a magic that defeated the Butterfly Queen, who used the mother's gullibility into believing the youngling was in this realm long after they were safely returned back home. An old fairy tale that was told as far back as the tale of the Goblin King.

She hears the yawn Itzal tries bottling up, but he refuses to sway from his position by the window.

He watches his shadow cast move from one side of the room to the other. The evening light slowly extending his shadow taller.

He clears his throat. "Don't you have plans tonight?"

Aelyta leaps from her chair. "What time is it?" She glances at her watch. "Holy Elementals, you gave me a fright. I have an hour or so to prepare for dinner. Oh, of all Elementals." She takes a deep breath. "I thought I was late!"

She rushes for her bedroom and slams the door to her wardrobe room. A few minutes pass until she exits with a new dress. Cut low in the chest with a square neckline complimenting flutter sleeves ruffling over her shoulders in a fabric embroidered with pastel flowers, mushrooms, and small bugs throughout the dress. Heels in hand, she fixes small gold earring buds to her ears as she runs over to the vanity.

Twirling in the mirror, admiring the embroidery, Aelyta chuckles. "This dress is picturesque."

"Yes, you are." Aelyta's handmaid appears from the stairwell. "I knew you would love this look."

"You have quite the eye for details, Aubree," Aelyta compliments her handmaid.

Aubree claps her hands excitedly. "I had all your dresses swapped out for you. If one is to be queen, one must dress diplomatically and beautifully at that."

"I love it," Aelyta gasps. "I love you for the extra work you've put in. How can I repay you? A raise in salary?"

"As long as you wear the dresses." Aubree swats Aelyta away. Her handmaid turns to Itzal. "Doesn't she look the part of a queen?"

"What in god's name are you wearing?" Aelyta's father gags at the sight of her as she enters her father's wing. "You're already a flower," he gestures to his head as if hers is big, "and you choose to add more on? A plain dress for a Floral is suitable, tameable for the palate. Quick, come in." He flops into an armchair by the fireplace. "For god's sake."

"Ospherians believe in goddesses, not a god."

"I am a human, and you are half human. Humans believe in a god, a man. You're old enough to know that."

"And not all humans believe in a god, either."

Her father hisses at her in response before two knocks come from the door. Branson enters the study, rolling their dinner in on a food trolley.

Her father demands the servant to light a fire. Branson walks to the fireplace, placing a log onto the dying embers.

Her father clicks his tongue at the servant. "Why are you taking so long?" he snaps before turning to Aelyta. "I'm sorry, the room is cold. It'll warm up soon. I should dock the pay of the staff, better to motivate them. Come, sit." He gestures to one of the two large wingback chairs by the fireplace. "It's annoying how still you stand. What has the future queen been up to these days?"

Aelyta gives the nervous servant a soft smile. "Thank you, Branson."

"We do not address the servants!" Miles yells at the top of his lungs. "How could your mother teach you to behave so beneath you?"

Scurrying to the chair, Aelyta takes her seat. Her stems uptight and her hands rest flat on her lap. A pretty princess sits as a pretty flower. She offers her reply, hoping to soothe her father. "I've been studying the history of our people. All of our descendants are related to the Elementals, like the flower descendants are of the Earth Elementals. And my favorite thus far, there are those who are of mixed descendants and Elementals, which can cause a variation of sorts in the genetics."

"Ah, yes. It is an interesting subject," he responds. "This kingdom once started off with five types of descendants, now filled with a multicultural array of people. So full of potential, so full of use."

"Well, the history is quite interesting," she starts. "But the science of it all, it's just as important—"

Her father puts a hand up, signaling for her to stop talking. "So, I assume you still are set to not marry before the coronation, then?" he inquires. "Have you met with the eligible bachelors at least?"

"I have"—she pauses—"not. I would like to offer you my opposing opinion. There are no rules against a queen becoming a wife before taking on the Crownship. Why are you so pressed to having me marry? It's never been a problem before for previous Crowns."

"Hm, well let me advise you." He leans in. "Becoming the new monarch of our kingdom, you must ensure to have an heir to the throne before all else. Your opinion is weak. You have no power to sway me otherwise." A smirk forms on his face.

"Why? Are you set to having a grandchild so eagerly?" she banters, keeping her petals from quivering. Keep it light, keep it silly.

"Because as queen, you will have to play both roles of the crown. I should've had your mother train you better as a female, but she insisted that one in leadership must study the role of leadership. That lazy woman leaves me to do all the work. But, alas, you passed the Rite of Divinity. And now, I may retire sooner than later."

"She died," Aelyta corrects.

"Yes, well." Her father looks over at her. "If she were so good a queen, she would still be alive today."

Branson finishes setting the table and moves the trolley to the wall before standing at his post awaiting their approach to the table.

"Come, let's have dinner." Her father takes his seat at the table.

"Aren't you excited for retirement?" she asks as she proceeds to her seat. "I'm sure you'll enjoy your free time."

"There is so much more I'd like to do with my time as king. But as you have turned twenty-six in November, my time as king must cease at some point."

"And the fact that mother died," she mutters, taking the knife to the steak on her plate. "If it satisfies you, I'll set up a meeting with each of the eligible bachelors tomorrow. I hear they're enjoying their time in Avelmore Castle. Would that satisfy you, my King?"

"I'm glad to hear," he answers. "Don't discuss your studies, and remember what your mother taught you about becoming a wife."

"Right, of course," Aelyta states. "I'll ensure to decide on someone you'll approve of."

"Perfect." He gets up from the table. "Then I'll have you start shadowing me next week. Great dinner, my dear. I will send word for you about your transitional onboarding."

Aelyta quickly gets up from her seat, curtsying before making her way out of her father's office. The door closes behind her as she takes a few steps into the hall, her breathing unsteady.

A sour taste fills the back of her mouth. She'd hate to end her evening this way, turning towards the servants' door, running into Briley.

"Lyta." Briley catches her. "I mean, Your Majesty."

"Not Majesty yet, but," Aelyta corrects, "could you lend me a hand?"

"Anything for you." Briley does a silly salute ensuing one chuckle from Aelyta.

He follows her down to the kitchen where they're greeted with a stern-faced Boreas, the master chef of Avelmore Castle.

Boreas points at the two of them as they maneuver to the pantry. "Sorry, Boreas." Aelyta shrugs. "I barely got a bite at dinner. Would you be able to whip up seven plates for me?"

"Seven?! And you're headed where with all that?" Boreas gestures to her armful of wine bottles. He turns to Briley for an answer.

Briley shakes his head. "Don't look at me! I'm just following the Queen's orders."

"Not queen yet." Aelyta returns with another armful of wine bottles. She gives the two of them a mischievous smile as she places them onto the counter in front of Boreas. "Take the night off, folks." Directing Briley with the food trolley she says, "Alright, you. Come with me."

3

On a Night of a
New Moon

MOMENTS LATER, Aelyta and Briley arrive unannounced to Odetta's chamber door. Odetta appears behind the door. As soon as she sees Aelyta and the food trolley filled with food and wine, Odetta's face lights up.

"I'll gather the others." Odetta rounds the other ladies-in-waiting.

"I'll set the table and leave you ladies to it." Briley excuses himself with the trolley rolling in front of him.

Food and fine wine always assure a good time with Aelyta's ladies-in-waiting. A round of food made by Avelmore's finest chef and wine imported from Elementropolis causes the ladies to extend their intake limits.

Aelyta and her ladies scatter about the sitting room after they have eaten their fill. Each of them armed with a full glass of wine, taking sips in between the chatter. Her colorfully-drunk ladies fill the room with colors of flora and iridescent gleam.

Lyza, one of the younger ladies, shimmers in the soft light next to Aelyta, with skin of starry blue and yellow tint. Aelyta is on the floor between Lyza and Ellsy. Ellsy is a petite elemental figure the color of a smokebush in the depth of summer in a deep burgundy purple. And as she turns from side to side, she glimmers a bright green.

Maurene, hair resembling lilac petals, is shuffling the deck of cards next to Presley and Margaret on the sofa. Presley resembles a yellow tulip, and Margaret a pothos plant, with large eyes and larger glasses to accompany them. Odetta also has yellow hair like Presley, but she resembles white lilies and her skin is a pale green. Odetta is in the chair between the girls on the floor and the sofa, attempting to count the scores that they've finished acquiring thus far.

Maurene taps the shuffled deck of cards onto the table, signaling she's ready to start up the next round. She looks to Odetta for the scores, but she's still scribbling a few calculations on the side of the paper in her hand.

"Presley is in the lead with sixty-eight. Margaret following second with fifty-four. Ellsy, third, with forty-two—and everyone else are losers," Odetta exclaims, sticking her tongue out at everyone.

"You're a loser with the rest of us too, silly." Lyza pokes fun at her.

Ellsy attempts to peer over at the paper. "What score do you have?"

"You do not need to know." Odetta tries to brush off.

"Are you in last place?" Aelyta props up on her knees along with everyone in peak interest.

"No..." Odetta quickly tries to get Maurene to start up the next round.

Presley blocks Odetta from the deck of cards. "Losers chug their glasses. You all know the rules!"

Four groans sound through the room before being replaced by the sounds of gulps and cheers. Presley flutters about the room with the canister, refilling the emptied glasses.

"Another round!" yells Lyza.

"We just drank our round." Maurene slaps the table.

"No, the game," Margaret cries. "You can't be drunk yet!"

Maurene laughs. "We're all drunk!"

"You're the one dealing our cards." Ellsy leans onto the table.

Margaret rises from sofa. "I think we should call it a night. All your faces are red. Lyta's red down to her neck!"

They all turn to Aelyta who's using Lyza to prop herself up, which Lyza, in turn, is doing the same to Aelyta.

"Last round, then," Aelyta slurs. "Then, we call it."

Ellsy nods ferociously up at Margaret, who's laughing wholeheartedly. Raising her own glass she says, "Last glass and we chug." She points to them.

They all scream in excitement, chugging, before they all gasp for air once done.

Odetta hugs each of them. "Get back to your chambers safely." She waves to them from her chamber door, watching them leave.

Aelyta watches her ladies hug one another before they disappear to their chambers. She waits a few moments before descending to her own. Something she can't quite remember, itching away at her. Did she forget something? Whatever it was, she had left all her worries with her sober self hours ago.

She bops her way down the small hallway and turns in the direction of her chambers. She salutes Jaycub with a giggle and he helps open the door for her. Her shoulder against the wall, she glides her way up the stairs.

She takes the steps slowly, trying to avoid the long hem of her dress. Her heels slip out from her feet, causing her to trip up a step. A hand grabs under her arm. She looks up, only to be reminded of what it was she had forgotten, or *who* it was.

"Ah, that's what I had forgotten." She taps Itzal on the nose. "Pity, you found me alas."

"You had fun," he replies sarcastically. Helping her take each step, stopping every now and then for her to kick a shoe off and fling them down the stairwell.

"You don't need to help me." She pushes him off her. "I'm almost up the stairs anyways."

She didn't push as hard as she thought, Itzal barely budged. "You've only made it four steps."

Glancing down, she learns that she really didn't make it around the bend to the first landing and sighs. "Please be quiet, I can't even hear myself losing the will to live."

"Says the drunkard I will have to drag up the stairs." He pulls her up the next set of steps, practically dragging. "You get drunk so easily."

She laughs. "Remember when I asked for your opinion? Me neither." Laughing harder at herself. "I haven't even slept for almost a week now."

They make it to her bedroom where she unconsciously begins to undress as she makes her way to the wardrobe room. She comes out in a plain silk dress with the waist half-tied behind her back. Waving at Itzal, she walks past him towards the studies.

He yanks on the silk ties dangling on the back of her dress. She scowls at him, but drunkenly trips into his body. A moment in his arms and her irritation falters, replaced by a quiet gaze into his face. An unplaceable awareness of his physical body encompasses her that she quickly dismisses.

"I think I might be a little drunk..." she whispers.

He ties the ribbons together and tugs her to the bed. "Sleep." he says as he drags her.

"No, you can't tell me what to do." She shakes her head. "Besides, I've got work to do."

"You haven't slept for a week. Go to sleep." He heaves her onto the bed. With demand in his voice he says, "Go. To. Sleep."

"You can't give me orders." She props up onto her elbows. "I'll be queen soon," she slurs loudly.

"I." He jabs her shoulder. "Just." Another jab. "Did." A harder jab, pushing her onto the bed.

The way his knee rests beside her hip, his shoulders hovering over her, Aelyta nearly loses composure. If she could lift into his chest, run a hand behind his neck, and pull him into her—no, she is a professional. They are professionals. He's still on royal time, paid to protect her. She's been in this situation before. Not with Itzal but with Jaycub. They have a job to do.

Crying out loud, she crawls over the bed and flops onto the other side. He waits for her to try to pass him, but she darts forward, pivots and climbs up over the bed then swings out towards the landing.

"Why do you care if I sleep?" she yells as he wraps an arm around her waist and pulls her back, her arms crossed across her chest.

"Why do you care to work?" He throws her onto the bed. "You're a drunk, spoiled princess."

"You think I'm spoiled? They're spoiled!" She pouts, lying exasperated and spread out like a star. "I don't want to marry either of those spoiled pieces of feces."

Itzal lifts himself off the bed, sighing. "There are no laws saying a future queen must have a husband. Why are you so fixated on it?"

"Me? It's them. All of them," she groans. "Because I need to please my dad, or he won't begin the on-boarding process, the transition of power." She rolls onto her stomach, burying her face into the mattress. "I have no control over anything as long as my father considers himself the current king." She lifts her face from the bed. "This, I want to be able to control. The person I choose to rule with, my partner in arms. The man I must live with alongside me for the rest of my life. But first and foremost, how I want to be seen as queen is decided by whom I shall choose to share the throne with. Deciding between the two most powerful families is not how I want to take my first steps to becoming queen."

Itzal fidgets on his feet, hand on one hip and the other rubbing the back of his neck. He turns to leave her bedroom.

From under the blankets. "Thanks for bringing me to bed. Sorry for being such a thorn. Tomorrow, same time?"

"Tomorrow, same time." She hears him say. She doesn't see the way his expression softens—only the fading sound of his footsteps as sleep overtakes her.

Night progresses without a moonlit sky. Aelyta gently lulls to sleep to the sound of a crackling fire from the sitting room fireplace. A shadow moves through her bedroom, making its way to her.

Something about the way it slinks from one dark corner to the next, rustles Aelyta in her bed. What should be absolute silence sounds like loud thunder. She sits up like a flash of lightning and the shadow pulls her into its darkness. Her body remembers the tug into the shadows. She's been waiting for him.

The darkness, wiping out any and all forms of light, overcomes her. She sits looking around for something, anything, but all she feels is a familiarity in this pitch noth-ingness. Almost soothing, she lets the sound of thunder roll around her as the shadow moves closer. Closer, and closer. She can feel it barely touching her skin, and she finds herself chasing the feeling.

A voice like thunder in the distance rolls towards her, "Did I wake you?"

There, the feeling of an electric zap nips against her neck and across her shoulder. Familiar, as if every atom in her body has woken up from eons of sleeping.

"You feel it, too." The voice sounds from all around her, yet so close to her ear, she can feel the touch of air against her shoulder.

"Here to try again?" Her hand reaches up, hoping to feel more of the electric touch.

The voice chuckles. "You," the voice rumbles, "are of Lightning of the Ancient Age." A zap flashes in the dark-ness at the touch of her fingertips. More, she wants to light up the darkness with more. "How can I kill you now that I know so much." The voice close enough she feels the breath of air on her cheek.

"By stabbing the heart," Aelyta quips.

A grip around her neck sends a chill down her spine, but the electricity coursing through her skin wakes every-thing within her. Sparks of electric charge sputter from her throat where the contact is. The tighter the grip, the larger the charge.

A face she couldn't quite make out appears in between the whisps of light and the stun of complete darkness. The pressure pulses like a warning rather than a threat.

Whiplashed into a paralysis, the only movement she could muster was a soft gasp for air as the grip loosens. Aelyta freezes as she lets the shadow explore her face the same way she is with his. Wariness keeps her from moving, but curiosity invites him.

"You." The voice grazes against the exposed skin of her neck, a soft kiss sparking a gentle shock. "You were supposed to be asleep," the voice says, like thunder rolling away into the distance.

"You're leaving without finishing your assignment?" Her question quiet as if to not scare away the darkness.

"I never left." His thunder gently dissipates.

The shadows dissolve, revealing the outlines of her walls and the edge of her bed. The fire crackles in the fireplace downstairs.

Her breath held tight, she loosens a soft breath onto her fingertip where the zap had just lit up the darkness. The electric feeling still lingers even after she blows gently against it.

An emptiness is all that is left. No longer sleepy, Aelyta climbs out of bed and meanders down the stairs. She gravitates to her studies.

Grabbing a blanket hanging off the back of a chair, she wraps her shoulders, settling into the table, her mind racing. Who is the strange Element?

4

Shadow Meets the Light
THE SHADOW

HE WATCHES her from the shadows. Her light glows in lines across her skin in the barely lit study. A picture of divinity sits in his presence, distant but present. The way her hair petals curl at the ends, the colors a gradient from dark to light.

His hands clench at the urge to paint her as she is, forever encapsulate the image before him. The way the light shines from beside her, casting a shadow over her pile of books.

Nearing her, he peers over her shoulder to observe her feverish reading. He watches her make the connection to the lack of magic in the realm of powerful Elementals. The magic-less are the ones who are in positions to behold the head over all those with unique magic. He's familiar with the concept. Too familiar.

Holding in a scoff, he wants to make it known to her. Humans are tricksters, but that's always been his conspiracy theory. One human fell into the world and tricked the Elementals into believing they are useful. This idea grew into the larger known present he sees today. The magic Elementals are slaves to the magic-less. They use and take, and they rise to create laws and more propaganda to make the rest of Deneb believe this is all worth something.

He doesn't have any proof or evidence, of course. As a specific ghost tells him often, this theory of his is baseless if he can't back it up. The thing his friends don't know, though, is that his life is the most direct, living proof of this enslavement.

She scribbles "shadow demon" and circles it. A smile reaches his eyes. She's trying to learn who he is. That's cute.

Only a few know of his true name. The anonymity comforts him like slinking through the darkness where shadows cling to the edge of light. It makes his job easier and is the reason his clients hire him. An assassin's job is accomplished cleanly, crisply, and precisely. But hiding in a blanket of darkness, his natural state is put at ease. Until that first night, everything was going as planned, then he touched her. His dagger deeply kissed her, and yet, she walks away alive.

By his second attempt, he knew better, or so he thought. Pulling her into the Shadow Realm where sound is muted, she fell into the darkness without cowering. Her lightning flashed through his shadows. He's never experienced anything like it. How could one be capable of such potential within his shadows? And yet, it felt as if he had done it before, in a dream or another time, another life. Every sensation craved her as if to say, "I've waited lifetimes to find you."

Every day after that night, he's watched her every move within his humanoid disguise and his natural form.

Hoping there will be a chance to strike, but he finds he could never advance on her. Why is that? How is that?

He's an assassin. He never hesitates. Clean and precise was what he has been known for. But with her, things became complicated.

She senses his presence in the shadows. Curious, he needs to know why, or how.

The worse is that every part of him craves her. He can't stay away, but he must keep a distance not to be found again.

He watches her sit at the table in her studies for hours on end. He watches her having dinners with her ladies. And some evenings, he watches her having wine with her friends in the large castle kitchen. He watches the way she tucks her dark umber petals of hair behind her ears when she's fixated, focused, or no longer masking.

But this specific job, this job not only is worth the pay—this job, by far, has more stakes he's not willing to risk.

Most of his targets don't sense his shadows like she does. When one is used to being invisible for so long, he was unaware of what to do when it came to being noticed, being felt, being heard.

The way she knows prickles the skin on his neck. Could he risk it all?

Every night, he makes his way to her during the darkest hour. Shadows do not make sounds. And yet, she wakes every time he gets near. It's as if she can hear him approaching. At first, he assumed it was mere coincidence, the fact that she stirs awake each and every time. He no longer believes in coincidences.

He follows her to her chambers, greeted by Jaycub, and he wishes he no longer had to hide. He craves the way she mindlessly pokes at the lit log in the fireplace, the way she reaches for a blanket to wrap around her as she sits in her studies mumbling different law descriptions to herself, the way she forgets the hours exist altogether.

"I can feel you lingering, yet again." She doesn't look up from her book. "Ready to kill me yet?"

She feels his shadows pool from the bookshelf behind her. She looks out the corner of her eye with a smirk. His dagger slides out from under her dress skirt, and she slides it across the table. The dagger stops with a thump against a pile of books.

"I'm not used to being noticed," he says, voice low. He slinks past her. "With your kind of power, why beg for death?"

He settles into one of the armchairs next to the wing-back by the window, a book open in his hand.

"I've felt you around for a week now, give or take." She pauses. "With my kind of power," she scoffs, leaning back into the wooden chair at the table. "As if I don't have to fight for my seat on the throne?" She slams her book closed. The sound echoes through the study.

"Tsk," he clicks. "I hit a nerve there."

Her eyes roll. "You can kill me now."

"As if I haven't tried." He drops the book onto the ground and crosses his legs. His arms slump over the armrests.

"Then why are you here? Instead of killing me, you're now spying, and for who?"

"I like books too, you know. This one in particular is interesting." He points to the book dropped by his feet. "I've read it in different editions, from different authors. But this one, this one is very unique."

Her elbows press into the table, hands to her forehead. "Why are you even here?"

"Books." He swirls the shadows fiercely around his head. "Why are you here? Don't you ever sleep?"

A laugh forms from the back of her throat. "You're ridiculous."

"Not I, it's you." He picks a piece of lint off the top of his pants. "Why don't you read anything outside these sources? Other subjects?"

Aelyta scans the books piled before her. Her lips scrunch in thought. "I'm dissecting them." She shrugs. "Your job is to gather information and assassinate, right? Then you'll know that I'm gathering intel from the very people who are fighting against me. There's something here that will give me insight on their motive, their reasoning for going up against my Crownship. So yes, I will read these very sources, written *by* these very sources. Once I assume the crown, I will know what I am fully up against."

His turn to laugh, his head shakes slightly. "See." He throws his hands over the armrests of his chair. "Now how can I dispose of someone with a brain like that?" He rises from the armchair.

"Hey, shadow face." She looks up at his figure cloaked in darkness in the dim of the light. "Stop by more often. I like the stroke to the ego."

He approaches her, a hand to her cheek inflicting a zap between their touch. He runs his thumb down her jawline.

"I'm never that far away," he whispers. His hand departs, leaving an empty feeling in his palm.

He slinks back into the shadows of the walls and watches as she notices his leaving. Her face drops back to her books as he slithers through the darkness, leaving her chambers.

He heads for the King's Wing. Reaching with the pull of

the shadows, he climbs through keyholes with ease. He makes his way into the King's study. With the help of the dark of night, he reads through the papers splayed out on the desk without touching anything.

A piece of paper tucked into a book titled, *The Political Evolution of the Elementals*, authored by Pyerre Loso Riverkin. He gently opens the book to where the paper is tucked. The page of the book didn't catch his attention, but the contents of the paper did. It's a binding contract with two signatures. One of which he recognizes as King Miles's, but the other he can't make out except for the fancy *R* in the surname. He picks up the paper to find that there are two sheets. The bottom paper is also a contract with two names. King Miles's signature and Julius Ronanbrand's, he recognizes both. The contracts are the exact same, but with two different recipients from King Miles. Each contract will grant the recipient a guaranteed marriage to Aelyta if they provide a specific service. Here's where the contracts differ. On the contract with Ronanbrand, King Miles asks Julius to provide Miles Dedrick an assassination service of Queen Jane and Aelyta. And on the other contract, King Miles asks Thelonius Richard to provide him with mined blue-crystalline rocks that Thelonius found in Morf Mountain. That's the fancy *R*, for Richard.

The Richards family has owned a mining establishment since the age of the Goblin King. The Ronanbrands are the leading ownership of the largest assassin's league in Avelmore Castle region. They are the ones who own him and, as he just found out, the ones pulling his strings the morning he killed Aelyta's mother. The same ones who also hired him to kill Aelyta.

He checks the date of the contracts. These were signed a few years ago.

Grabbing the two sheets of paper, he traces the exact typography of each word. Once both pages are exactly copied, he holds his breath as he puts the copies back in the order in which he found them. And the other two pages, he carefully folds into his pockets.

Slinking with haste out of the room, it's his turn to search for answers. He climbs through another keyhole.

He finds the older man crawling into his bed. Stepping into the light, he pulls the man around to face him.

"It's not bedtime for you yet." He confronts the man in a nightgown.

Julius sneers. "What is with you? What do you want?"

"Answers, Father," he spits.

The man's eyebrow furrows. "About what? You're late on your assignment and we need this done. You do not need answers. You need to get back to work."

"The assignment isn't done because—"

"I don't need excuses from you. Get back to work, and do not call me father until it is done."

"What if it isn't?"

"Then you don't get to have the Ronanbrand empire like you ever so wanted."

Shadows swirl a tornado around the room in response. "What if that changes?"

"I thought you wanted freedom for you and your poor enslaved mother from all this darkness?"

Malo grinds his teeth. "I have to get back to work."

"Good."

He returns to the shadows before morning breaks. He travels through the Shadow Realm, leaving the castle as fast as he can, timing how long it will take to get to the peninsula of Elementropolis. Time is of the essence, and morning is soon approaching before he has to return to the castle. No one must know who he is and where he has been.

Groaning from the sight of the sun over the eastern sky, Malo glances at the house jutting from the large rock off the peninsula attached to the land by a covered bridge.

Two people approach him before he whisks away into the shadows.

The woman with large glasses and a frantic voice, shouts a command, "Do not question me. Take Kody. Trust."

Together, the two of them turn back in the direction of the castle through Malo's Shadow Realm. A pit sits in his stomach. Morning came too soon and he doesn't want to know why he's taking the alchemist to the castle with him. But he trusts his friends like they are family, and when Lorraine's antennae go off, he listens.

5

Throwing Dices
THE QUEEN

AELYTA LETS the morning light pass into the study. She didn't rush to leave her books, her table. But as the light turns orange, she rips herself from the words on the pages describing nothing but old notes. Old notes from an old time when her mother had once lived and walked, breathed.

She makes her way to the bathing room, taking her time, hoping Aubree would yell from the stairwell any moment now.

Aelyta contemplates two dresses in her changing room between the bedroom and the bathing room. From behind the door, she hears footsteps rushing down the stairs. Aelyta quickly dresses as more footsteps climb up the stairs and back down.

"Aubree?" she yells from the dressing room. "Where have you been? I've been waiting for your assistance all morning."

Aelyta pauses for a response, but only the sound of footsteps echoes the stairwell. Aelyta quickens, buttoning her dress as fast as her fingers can muster.

She rushes out to the landing to see who is hastening about her chambers. Pausing barely out of her doorway, she finds Itzal dragging Kyanston's limp body up the stairs to her sitting room.

"Would you like to explain?" Aelyta narrows her eyes. "Why?" She gestures to the scene before her.

"He tried to get into your chambers." Itzal flops Kyanston's body onto the ground.

She glances over to the door left open with the use of Jaycub's unconscious body. "What happened to Jaycub?" Aelyta gasps.

"I told you," Itzal squawks. "Kyanston tried to get into your chambers."

Aubree arrives with a man, dressed in an Alchemadia uniform Aelyta's never seen before.

"Your Majesty." He bows his head. "I'm Kody, an alchemist on contract."

"Lyta." Aubree rushes over to where Aelyta's still standing in the stairwell.

She rubs Aelyta's hand with her own before she ushers her into the sitting room. They stare at Itzal tying up Kyanston.

Itzal nods in approval before him and Kody haul Jaycub out of the doorway.

Aubree and Aelyta hear the open and close of the door.

Aelyta slowly meanders through the sitting room to the dining room, towards the small kitchenette tucked away in the corner between the two rooms. Aubree follows fast behind her. "My dear." Aubree's hand reaches out for her. "If you need anything, I've got you covered."

Aelyta simply shakes her head. "Why would Kyanston try to break into my chambers?" Her hands refuse to stop shivering.

"Are you cold? I can start you a fire in the sitting room. I can also get you a pot of tea started. Head to your studies, I'll meet you there." Aubree softly steps in front of her, pushing Aelyta out of the kitchenette.

"I can help," Aelyta's voice small. "Let me make the tea. Could you start the fire?"

Aubree nods, heading for the sitting room. Closing her eyes, Aelyta takes two long, drawn breaths. She hones her focus on warming the water in the kettle.

Letting her focus tunnel on only the tea, Aelyta lets the world blur around her. Her breathing steadies as she pours the hot water into the teapot already filled with tea leaves of her choosing.

Aelyta watches the steam float into the air as if her worries are floating away with them.

A tap on the door brings her back to the kitchenette. Aubree asks if Aelyta needs any assistance with the tea or bringing it to her studies.

"I'd like to have it in the sitting room. I'll wait for Kyanston Richard to wake from whatever deferred him to his current state." Aelyta steps out of the kitchenette. "I will step up to the study for a moment, but only to obtain a book to read while we wait for Kyanston to come to."

Not a moment too soon, Aelyta finds herself immersed in a book with pen and paper pad in hand. Aubree had set the small tea table next to Aelyta's favorite seat on the cream-colored sofa. Kyanston has been wrapped in a bed sheet and moved to the doorway of the sitting room near the landing, but not close enough to roll down.

Stoking the fire, Aubree kneels in front of the fireplace. Aelyta puts her book down, watching Aubree feed the fire more logs. "I guess I should ask Cory to marry me since that one is indisposed." Aelyta sighs.

Aubree pauses. She pulls away from the fireplace, sitting back onto her heels. She looks over at Aelyta, who is staring into the fireplace unblinkingly. Aubree exhales loudly, her eyes roll before she speaks, "The men in this castle, Blessed be Descendants...stupid and messy men. Enlarged toddlers, that's what I think of them."

Returning a soft smile, Aelyta says, "My reign shouldn't last my entire lifetime, but my marriage will. The Royal Advisors don't seem to see it that way. And, it's up to me to change that perspective, right? Me against the institution? That who I choose to marry will have to be with me for my lifetime. But since I retire from the crown as soon as my child reaches twenty-six, I should be the one to decide who to marry, who could help me run the kingdom for the kingdom, for the Elementals, for the people."

"For the Descendants," Aubree repeats. "For the Elementals."

"I thought the queen's job was to lead the institution." Itzal steps in from the landing, tapping Kyanston with his foot on the way to the sofa. He picks up an empty teacup.

"How's Jaycub? Is Kody assisting him now?" Aelyta stands up. "And why is he"—she points to Kyanston—"still out cold?"

"Kody is working on Jaycub, yes. They're under some kind of magical impairment according to him." Itzal pours himself a cup of tea after getting a nod from Aelyta. "I'm not sure who cast it or why they were even in here."

"What are you going to do with him then?" Aubree points to the sheet burrito on the floor.

"I'm going to take him to his room, unwrap him there, and have his people figure it out." Itzal places his empty teacup down. Cracking his fingers he says, "Alright, round two." He hauls Kyanston over his back and disappears down the stairwell.

Aubree quietly waves from the sofa, turns to Aelyta and says, "I think Itzal has a secret."

"Just like that? You have a feeling just like that?" Aelyta sits back onto the sofa, picking up her own teacup. "Are you sure?"

"Yes." Aubree leans over whispering, "He just pops from the shadows. It's mysterious the way he moves."

"He's probably just a lonely lad." Aelyta shakes her head. "I doubt he has a secret beneath that armored exterior."

"I don't know." Aubree tilts her head towards Aelyta. "Him, Kyanston, and Cory, they give me a weird feeling." Aubree brushes her arms. "I don't like it."

"I don't trust any of them either." Aelyta sets down her tea. "But, what makes you suspicious?"

Aubree shakes her head, waving her hand dismissively. "I'm just being an old maid."

She brushes the idea away. "And if I were you, I wouldn't either. Do you trust Cory enough to ask him to marry you? And for the sake of your coronation?"

Aelyta holds her breath as she stares at Aubree's face, examining the wrinkles forming around her eyes and lips, the way her face is permanently burgundy red. Aelyta nods.

A twitch appears at the nook of Aubree's nose and cheek. "Miles may be your father, but I don't like him and I know I can trust you enough to say it to your face. I don't like him, nor those pompers who use their titles to walk around the kingdom with the confidence that they have—those Royal Advisors are twisting history as we speak."

Aelyta shushes her. "You don't like anyone." Aubree nods with a scowl. She huffs her way to the food pulley, placing the tea tray into the stationed shaft. The world spinning around her like some force of nature only makes her feel how real her naivety of her actual position truly is. Beginning to feel restless, her eyes jump from the landing of the stairwell to the fireplace, then to the book she had attempted to read earlier. She recognizes the author's name as one of the Royal Advisors.

The men in charge of this kingdom have been taking far too much control for far too long. Aelyta finds Aubree tidying up the room. "Aubree, I think it's time to enjoy the spring air. If it is not too much trouble, could we have the lunch today out in the gardens rather than indoors? Could you also send word for Cory to join me as well?"

Aubree smiles. "I'd love to."

Aelyta will not be made the fool. But if that's what everyone thinks of her, she will play along. She'll play along to watch them all fall into their own wind.

As for the meeting with Cory Ronanbrand, she will use the encounter to her advantage. If her father and Royal Advisors want this meeting to occur, she will ensure it goes exactly how she wants it to. She'll give them what they want. They'll never see what she truly has planned, though. Ambition, attention-seeking—or whatever derogatory term they want to call her—wearing a pretty, feminine dress.

Running down the staircase in her chiffon dress, waves of fabric flowing as she descends the stairs, she finds Itzal on the sofa in the sitting room. "Do you know how Jaycub is doing?" She stops in the landing.

"He's awake and he says he's ready for you to see him."

Itzal rises to his feet. "Wow, you look stunning," he blurts, coughing. "Uh, we can have a meeting with Jaycub whenever you're ready. And until he's well enough to return to his post, I will be taking his night shifts." He practically gulps for air towards the end.

"I thought this dress embodied springtime in the garden." Aelyta twirls left to right, letting the fabric flutter around her. "And what of Kyanston?"

"I ran into Aubree this morning. She gave me a note regarding Kyanston Richard," Itzal pulls a folded page from his pocket. Aelyta runs over, snatching it from his hand. Why would Aubree give Itzal the note after she told Aelyta that she didn't trust him?

> *Got wind Kyanston has been revived. He grabbed two servants, they say he had crazy eyes when he told them what happened. Best you ought to know and hear before Rich pays everyone off to silence what they've heard of his son.*

Aelyta hands him back the note. Itzal throws it into the fire, ensuring it catches the flames before turning back to Aelyta.

She sighs. "I have a meeting at ten." She turns towards the landing. "That should leave me enough time to meet with Jaycub. Kyanston's a spoiled brat—he can rot in his chambers a little longer."

Itzal leads her to the Knight's Keeps where Jaycub takes residence in one of the apartments. "Do you live here as well?" Aelyta steps through the musky hallways.

"No, I don't have residence here." Itzal keeps forward, leading her down to Jaycub's door.

"Where do you reside, if not here?"

"Pretty much wherever you happen to be...getting you to sleep at all is no easy feat."

Aelyta crosses her arms in defense.

He knocks, and a few moments later, Jaycub opens the door. They both enter and find themselves with nowhere to sit, so they stand staring at one another. Jaycub looks around and drags a chest out from a closet, and he offers a stool from his bedroom, which was once holding a pile of dirty clothes. Aelyta takes a seat on the wooden chest instead and Itzal stands near her.

"Thank you, again. Kody has healed me rather quickly." Jaycub nods to Itzal. "I'm sorry it has taken me this long though to reach out to you, Lyta." He turns to look at her. "It's hard to process something that does not have words to describe, but I hope you'll understand my effort."

"Of course." Aelyta reaches out to him.

Jaycub smiles at her, takes a deep breath, and begins. "As you both know, magic is not prevalently used here on the castle grounds. In fact, King Miles prohibits the use of magic altogether. I have no experience in it and have no way of truly describing the nuances as they are. I can only tell you that he was terrifying, absolutely terrifying. He was dressed like one of us knight guards. But instead of a head, hands, or legs, they were made of dark matter. Like a fog of black shadows, mists of pure darkness. His eyes glowed silver. Cory and Kyanston were there. They called him Malo, and the three of them were arguing. Cory and Kyanston were getting physical. They were yelling about something to do with Malo's dagger inside your chambers. I told them off, and Kyanston struck me with a blast of magic. Kody said it was some Elemental magic. I thought Elementals were just elemental people. I didn't know they had magic. I thought that was all a fairy tale. I guess I passed out from Kyanston's blow of..." Jaycub looks to Itzal. "Plant magic? I'm probably not good at talking about it."

Itzal nods.

"I'm sure Itzal can fill in the rest of what happened after I passed out." Jaycub shrugs.

"Oh, Jaycub," Aelyta exasperates. "I'm so glad you're alive from what happened." Her hand to her chest.

"Me too." He hesitates, looking up at her.

"I'll see you tonight then?" Aelyta looks over to him from the doorway.

Jaycub winks. "Same time, same place."

Aelyta chuckles as she closes the door behind her. Itzal follows her as they walk the castle grounds, traveling the gravel path that leads around one of the castle towers. Itzal trails her steps as she walks to a bench behind the gardens where she deflates herself. Aelyta looks up at him from the bench.

"Ready when you are," Itzal simply says.

"So, Cory, Kyanston, and Malo"—Aelyta pauses—"shadow demon. The three of them were in an altercation outside my chambers and busted through my chamber guard, impairing Jaycub and Kyanston. Cory is also somehow involved." Aelyta stares into the distance. I'm about to propose something to Cory at ten this very morning. This proposal requires that I trust him. Should I trust him like I must put my trust in you?"

Itzal bends down on both knees in front Aelyta. His hand to his heart, his head tilted up towards her. "My loyalty lies with you and will always lie with you. I swore into the knight's guard, and I swore to protect you by your side at all costs."

"Your loyalty is like the stars to my darkness." Aelyta

reaches out to pat Itzal, but he slinks away from her touch. "I'm sorry, I should really learn to stay more professional..."

"No, no, that was me. I don't like being...touched."

"On your feet, knight." Aelyta stands. "We must carry on with our duties."

She leads him to the Royal Garden.

The Royal Garden, her second most favorite place in Avelmore Castle. Or at least, it used to be. She's unsure how she feels about the ranking now that her mother is no longer around to signal the beginning of gardening season.

The smell of fragrant florals fills the air as they step out into the courtyard. Aelyta can recognize the smell of honeysuckles and lilacs from outside the gardens. Her senses glitter with excitement at what it must smell like inside the gardens themselves.

A Glimpse of the Spotlight

AELYTA HAS an itch to get her hands into the soil, planting geraniums, begonias, and bulb perennials. She was much too occupied these past couple months, and she had forgotten to check for the last frost to plant any seeds.

She leads Itzal to the large gazebo at the north side of the gardens where they find Aubree laying a tablecloth over the iron table. Aelyta leaves Itzal by the gazebo as she enters the small greenhouse to the east of the gardens. She grabs the harvesting basket with the pruners already placed inside, clipping the flowers in bloom. She clips a few greens and a few bulbed flowers that are not yet bloomed for the aesthetic.

Returning to the gazebo, Aelyta trims the extra leaves and thorns while Aubree leaves to the kitchen for the food trolley. Aelyta loses herself in arranging the flowers, trimming the clipped flowers as she goes.

"Mom, what do you think?" she yells over her shoulder. Aelyta turns around, only to remember where her mom truly was. Blinking hard and fast, she heads for the greenhouse with the basket and pruners in hand. "Why did I do that?" she whispers to herself. She hides her face in her hands.

"Because real love doesn't truly leave even after they do," Itzal says quietly behind her with a wet towel and a napkin in his hands. Keeping her face away from Itzal, she simply waves him away.

He pivots to leave the greenhouse when she reaches her hand out for the wet towel and cleans her hands, whipping the towel over her shoulder once she's done. She grabs the napkin and dabs at her eyes, lifting her face up to prevent the tears from falling.

Aelyta places a hand on his arm. "Thank you." She exits the greenhouse and installs herself in the gazebo as Aubree returns with the food trolley.

Who really is Itzal? What does he know of love?

Aelyta helps set the table as Aubree sets out the food and tea. Not much later, Cory enters the garden with a gasp. He quickly meanders his way over to the gazebo where Aubree whispers "Good luck" to Aelyta before stepping back from the table.

"What a lovely spring day it is." Cory lunges up to the gazebo. "Thank you for the invitation."

"Thank you for joining me at such late notice." She gestures to the food. "Please, help yourself. We have a masterful chef in Avelmore Castle who will take offense if we do not indulge in his cooking."

Cory takes a seat, Aubree steps over and begins pouring the tea for them both. Aelyta waits for him to take a few bites of food before continuing.

"How is your father?" She takes a sip of her tea after stirring in her cream and sugar.

"My father is well." Cory takes a swipe of cheese and butter for his griddles. "He just left this morning, actually. He's a busy man, as am I."

"Running Ospheria's largest assassin's guild is hard work." Aelyta pours snowdrop syrup over her griddles.

Cory swallows his bite. "He owns the largest assassin's guild. There's more to it than just showing up."

She cuts into her griddle. "I struck a chord, again. I apologize. I simply was wondering how you and your father spend your time. What are your interests?"

Cory stops mid-cut. He puts down his fork and knife, and looks up at Aelyta. "I'm going to be honest with you. I feel like you're leading me into something I'm going to regret."

"Could you blame me?" Aelyta hides a chuckle. "We grew up together, but we didn't really, not truly."

Cory sighs. He leans back into his chair with his arms crossed. He takes a second to think. "You want to know about my interests? Music," Cory sighs at his answer. "Yeah, I always wanted to learn how to play an instrument. I'd love to learn to write a song one day, maybe when my dad passes."

"What do you think your father would say to that?"

"I'm sure he'd be more than upset. He's spent my entire life preparing me for taking over his guild. It feels like I'm prepared for his deathbed as well as my own."

"Would you say you have a good relationship with your father?"

"I wouldn't say that. I wouldn't say I don't have a relationship with him. If I follow his direction, he's a great father. If I stray his path, I'm a failure."

Aelyta studies his face, which stayed soft and thoughtful. But people never look hard or rough when they're lying.

"If I give you a proposition, please think it over. I don't need an answer right away, but I would like a response in the end."

"I'm all ears." Cory leans in.

"Want to get married? Not for the reasons our fathers think, of course not. I want to find out what my father has planned for both your father and Thelonius Richard. In order to find out their plans, I propose we play out their whims. I am willing to negotiate compensation for your time and effort."

"You don't know what your dad is doing?" Cory's eyes widen. "Like you have no clue what he's been doing this whole time?"

"That's correct," she slowly says. "Unless you know what it is he's doing, I'd like to know. Again, I can compensate."

"You have that kind of magic and that's how you're getting the answers?" Cory points, his mouth almost drops.

"I don't have magic." Aelyta's eyebrows knit.

"Yes," Cory starts, "you do. And so does she." Cory points to Aubree. "And him." Cory scans his finger to Itzal, who has gone stiff and still, arms tightly straightened to his sides. Cory smirks at Itzal's tense stance.

Aelyta laughs. "I assure you. I do not have an inkling of magic."

"You have like, a magic replication. I have the ability to see who has what kind of magic." Cory looks away. "Which is why my dad wants me to continue his line of work. I'm handy to him. So that even after his death, I may continue to do his work for him. But for you, I can go along with your plan. I wouldn't mind seeing how this affects my dad as well. I want to see if he'll be held accountable for what he's done."

"What has he done?" Aelyta leans in now.

"If your plan works, you'll find that answer for yourself." Cory winks. "Look, if things don't work out, then I'll tell you, because you should know. Until then though, I think this will reveal much, much more than that."

"So, you'll go along with the plan?" Aelyta looks about the gardens. "Then would you like to join me on a walk around the garden?"

Cory swiftly sweeps onto his feet and next to Aelyta with an arm out for her. "It would be my very pleasure to join an alliance with you, Your Highness."

"You make it sound like I am a pawn in a larger game." Aelyta chuckles, tucking her hand under his elbow.

They leave Itzal and Aubree under the gazebo as they follow the gravel pathways circulating around the gardens. As the bell tower strikes noon, Aelyta and Cory stop their walk on the main path between the entrance and the gazebo where they may be seen from the castle balconies.

There, Cory gets down on one knee ceremoniously. Aelyta takes a step back with a gasp, hands clutching her mouth. She waits a few moments, counting one breath, two breaths, three. She steps forward with a large nod. Cory rises to his feet, and with a large sweep of his other arm, he yells, "She has said yes!"

Squeals can be heard from the castle, Aelyta recognizes Presley's and Odetta's screams of excitement, but she could hear a couple more voices. She knew more than half of them would be having their brunch on the terrace balconies above the castle gardens. They will soon spread the news.

Before the sun had risen the next morning, Aelyta

sends a letter to the Avelmore News Printers, ANP for short, to publish her engagement announcement to Cory Ronanbrand, including the date of the wedding to be the first day of summer, no sooner and no later than that. She ends the announcement with the statement that this wedding will follow the events of her coronation that will occur prior to her wed. She asked the ANP to print the submission that very day with enough to compensate the speedy printing and to spread the papers immediately.

By breakfast, she was sipping on her morning tea in her dining room with her exact words printed on the papers laid before her on the table. She turns to Aubree, who is fluttering about the first floor of her chambers. "Was it difficult going into town at such an awful hour this morning?"

"No, miss." Aubree barely pops her head in to answer. "I am already in acquaintance with one of the printers."

"Oh, I didn't know that." Aelyta finishes her tea.

"Yes, my brother." Aubree tidies the table in the dining room. Aelyta nods at her as she flutters out of the room and through the sitting room.

Itzal walks up the stairs as Aubree is wiping down tabletops and dusted surfaces. "How are you both doing this morning?" Not straying his eyes away from the busy body in the sitting room.

From the dining room, Aelyta answers, "Anxious."

Aubree bursts through the room. "We're not sure how the King will take the news printed in the ANP this morning. Dreadful not knowing what the storm's like."

"Well, do I have news for you." Itzal pours himself a cup of tea. Aubree glides into a chair beside Aelyta. They both stare at Itzal, mouths slightly agape as they watch him take a sip of his tea. "Miles, with the Royal Advisors, has agreed to your coronation. They have agreed that your coronation date to be on the last day of spring."

"A day before her wedding date?" Aubree reaches her hand out in a halt.

"Yes," Itzal says over his cup of tea. "A day before her wedding."

"At least we'll have a beautiful, sunny spring."

7

Calm Before the Storm

SPRING TORE through with more rain than Avelmore had seen in decades. But that didn't slow the busybodies that ran the castle, preparing for the two largest events of this generation.

Choosing the event colors took almost a month, and deciding on the fabrics took another month. Aelyta and her ladies-in-waiting were fitted for seventeen different dresses and robes. Colors all coordinating in arrays of lilacs, soft blues, seafoam green, and red. The finalized dresses were barely made in time for the events.

This timeframe excludes the details of the jewels, the fine dining, and the floral arrangements that will decorate the castle during those two days.

The coronation ceremony alone has always taken a couple days, but the King and the Royal Advisors have decided to plan for a short ceremony the evening before the wedding ceremony. Their reasoning being that Aelyta has already completed the Rite of Divinity.

Flowers, live butterflies and dragonflies, and foods exotic to Avelmore were all brought in despite the terrible weather. Time flew by faster than the rate of the raindrops plummeting from the sky. The castle was busy and alive, readying for a new queen and a new ruling couple.

The night before the coronation finally arrives, and there's nothing left for her to do but rest. This night is the night she has looked forward to for months. Tomorrow will be the day she was supposed to have had months ago, instead of the Rite of Divinity.

Playing by the rules is what may have gotten her mother killed. She rises from her bed and paces her bedroom. If Aelyta wants to make it through her Crownship alive, she'll have to play off script, against the rules her father and the advisors have expected of her. She needs to find the Shadow.

Grabbing one of her night robes, she walks out of her chambers and straight for the ballroom.

Only a few staff members linger about the floral decorations by the doorway. Aelyta takes a turn around the room and ends up by the flower arrangements where the staff members have settled on the last details. Aelyta thanks them for their work. She watches them take their leave for the night.

The battering of the rain outside the windows is the only sound in the room. Aelyta dims the light, leaving only four fire lamps lit. Enough for her to see but mostly, it casts longer shadows. Aelyta reaches her hand out to the dimmed room. Running her fingers along the shadows, the emptiness prevalent. She drifts through the edges of the room, hand out before her. The shadows vacant.

Finding herself in the center of the ballroom under the large crystal chandelier, Aelyta regards the blue of the crystals. "Where are you shadow demon?" she whispers.

Behind her, shadows ruffle through the darkness. Aelyta hears the soft rolling thunder of his presence.

"Looking for me?" His voice a low rumble, as deep and thunderous as the thunderstorm outside the windows.

Without turning around, she states, "I have questions for you." Shadows swivel into form in front of her. The shape of a man steps through the darkness, his eyes glowing white, but the shadows only form the silhouette. His smile appears as bright as his eyes. He bows before her, tilting his head to look up at her.

"At your service, Your Majesty." His voice vibrates through her skin.

Aelyta looks down at him. "Who hired you to kill me?"

"Most men are out to kill the new queen," he answers. "They have much to gain from your spilled blood."

"Why were you at my chambers the night two men were found magically impaired?" She paces, one step gently after the other, around the shadow demon.

"You already heard from one of the men themselves." He chuckles, rolling thunder rumbling along with every exhale of sound.

"I need to hear the whole story." She steps up to his left side from behind him.

He doesn't turn to look at her. "You should ask your dearly beloved instead."

She kneels next to him, tilting her head. "I don't trust him."

"You shouldn't trust me, either."

She reaches out to him. Under his shadows, she feels his hair running through her fingers. A soft smile to comfort him before she grips a handful, pulling his head back. Leaning into his ear she says, "I don't care about that right now. Tell me what I ask."

Even through his shadows, she notices a gulp bob down his neck. "I was hired to kill you the first night we met."

She tugs his hair harder. "But, you didn't."

"I didn't, nor the second night."

"In fact, you've failed to kill me at all."

His smile widens. "That's correct. I have a bigger plan for the Ronanbrands and the Richards, even Miles himself."

"Is that why your visits to my chambers stopped?"

"Your Majesty." He attempts to tilt his head towards her with her grip tight in his hair. "I didn't think you'd care."

With her hands still in his hair, she moves his face towards her. "In your dreams," she hums. "I assume you've collected intel while you've been here." Her eyes darken. She can feel his breathing jagged. Tangled in his hair still, her fingers loosen slightly.

He pulls her down and pushes her onto the floor of the ballroom. One knee pressed next to her hip and one hand under her chin. She feels the press of him, the stillness of his hold—controlled, not cruel, but unyielding.

A zap bridges from his fingers to the skin of her neck. Her breath catches as she is pinned to the ground.

"Information comes with a price, but you already know this." His voice sends shivers down her back.

"What do you want?"

"A promise."

Aelyta blinks up at the crystal chandelier dazzling in the dim light above them. She turns her eyes towards him kneeling beside her. He lets her sit up. "What's the promise?"

"Promise me that whatever I do, you know I do for your loyalty. Not the Crown, not the power, not the magic, you. I need you to promise that you put your trust in me.

Promise that you will not imprison me for the things I have done."

"While we're negotiating, I'd like to secure a safe place for my ladies-in-waiting. I don't trust Cory. I don't trust the advisors. I don't even trust my own father."

He chuckles, causing her to scowl. "Sorry, it's just that I already have a safe house for you. I don't have any room for them. Do they not like you? Why care for them?"

"Why do you have a safe house for me? Aren't you an assassin?"

"So, exactly how much intel do you really want to know?" His hand reaches behind his head. Her scowl hardens. Her eyebrows knit and her lips twist tight.

He's laughing now. "Ready when you are."

She rolls her eyes. "Just spill it already."

His hands go up in defense, and he settles with his legs crossed. "I have intel on Thelonius, Julius, and Miles. What they have planned for you began long before the death of Queen Jane. You probably have more questions, I get it." He cracks his neck and continues. "Miles obtained a signature from both Thelonius and Julius for two separate contracts, both ensuring the claim to your marriage and your death."

"Then I think it's a good idea if a separate safe house from the ladies should be in order. If anything goes awry tomorrow, I want their security to a safe place. My mother has an abandoned atrium manor, maybe they can stay there. It still belongs to her, an inheritance of the Aurelianus family, so I guess it belongs to me now, but it's furnished. It simply hasn't been maintained since my mother's death."

"I have recruited assistance. They can escort them there when the time comes."

"I have another request, if you don't mind." Aelyta's eyes

droop. "Could you deliver a note to Cory for me? The timing must be perfect. It must be as soon as I am crowned."

"Are you calling off the engagement?"

"Precisely."

"Then I'll be close by." A glowing eye winks through his shadows. "I love a good drama."

"There's no need for that." She brushes off the idea. "Itzal shall stay close."

"Right." He rises from the spot. "As long as you agree to the promise."

Aelyta also rises from the floor. "I still don't understand what I'm promising."

His hand reaches for her jawline, but he retracts instead. "I don't care for anything in return. Honestly, I don't need anything from this." He evaporates into a mist of shadows. She's left alone in the dimmed ballroom.

"Strange and moody shadow demon." Aelyta stares at the spot he once stood.

She turns the lights off completely and exits the ballroom. She meanders through the castle back to her chambers. Climbing the stairwell, she stops at the landing in front of the sitting room entrance.

Aelyta walks over to the sofa where a fairy tale book lay closed. She begins reading the tale of the beginning of magic.

A goblin, hungry for vengeance, stumbles upon a human who has blue crystalline embedded into her skin. With the aid of the human, a winged creature, and a dragon, the goblin sets forth on a journey to regain his wings from the evil queen who reigns over the winged kingdom founded by the bug descendants. From the water of the river's deep, they bring forth a large flood into the winged kingdom, sprouting forth the flower descendants from the soil. The goblin slays the winged queen, taking her crown and wings. The goblin became known as the Goblin Mushroom King who brought magic to Ospheria.

A child's tale with no real tell of where magic actually comes from. She's spent so much of her time dissecting books, looking for the biological level of magic. Did magic come from the goblin? What happened to the mushroom descendants? Who is the human with the blue crystals embedded in her skin?

Flipping the illustrated book closed, she spots the author as one of the Royal Advisors. Groaning, she tosses the book back onto the sofa and departs from the sitting room. One of the men that wants her to marry despite the laws of Ospheria, despite Ospherian traditions. And they wrote this as if it's objective truth, Aelyta groans. This is far from the truth. No wonder Ospheria has a lack of knowledge. The Advisors are feeding them whatever they deem fit for the public.

The dawn frames distinct storm clouds rolling towards Avelmore Castle.

8

Raining on the Reign

A WALL of cold rain pattered down outside the open window. Aelyta stands up on the dressing podium, watching Aubree and a few more chambermaids fastening all the buttons down the back of her gown. She glances down at the burgundy chiffon overflowing from her waist. As the buttons clasp up her back, the dress tightens against her body and the boning of the corset. Her hand against the side of her waist pulls her back straight.

Her ladies-in-waiting slowly trickle out from the dressing rooms dressed in their pink and lilac dresses. Chosen to match the distinct pink and purple of their hair or skin. She looks down at her watch, eight dots, the hand points down toward the lower right corner. For the amount of time had quickly blown through in preparation for this very evening, it has decidedly slowed to a staggering halt.

With proper attention to the details of the day, they had planned time for their hair and dressing. Aelyta did not want her face made up in any fashion on her coronation day. She wanted to face the crown with the most purest of faces. May this be a testimony to the way she will rule, no cover-ups, no power over the many that has been seen before. Aelyta will face the Crownship with the most honest of faces, the purest of her being. But she didn't want to stop her ladies from getting their faces done.

Margaret was the last of the ladies to exit the dressing room in a deep purple that complimented her hair, green with streams of ivory. For Aelyta, Margaret resembles a pothos plant basking in frosted lights. She watches Margaret approach Lyza, who is just as stunning in her pastel-pink gown that does wonders for her starry luminescent blue and yellow skin.

Aubree clasps the last button at the nape of her neck with a quiet huff and a smile. Holding onto Aelyta's shoulders she says, "Your mother would have done this for you if she was here. She would have been so happy to see you in your coronation gown."

"She has her mother's likeness, especially in the same shade of burgundy as her gown the day she was crowned," King Miles says, hands clasped behind his back, still standing in the doorway.

All the women curtsied before him. He clenches his chest. "Oh, I'm sorry, I didn't mean to intrude, but I simply wanted to let you know that everything in the throne hall is ready for you. And to say"—he clears his throat—"please be careful not to make a jest of yourself from now on. I'd hate to take the crown from you." He chuckles.

They all stare in response. King Miles glares. "Come on, girls. It's just a joke. I know the females here don't know how to joke, but come on, that was a good one. What a waste." He holds the door open, over his shoulder towards Aelyta he says, "I'll see you in the throne hall no later than ten minutes tops." He shuts the door, leaving the women gaping between the door and Aelyta.

She steps down from the dressing podium. Her bare feet touching the cold stone of the ground. Aubree and two other chambermaids help with the train of her gown, carefully holding it flat and off the ground. Aelyta looks to her ladies-in-waiting. With one firm nod, she stands before the door. Her ladies line up behind Aubree and the chambermaids with her train in hand. She gives one look over shoulder at the women behind her then opens the door.

Two knights stand to the left of the door. Aelyta gently reaches her hand out for them, her guards, Jaycob and Malcom. They will be positioned there until the procession makes their way through the hallway. After the last ladies in the back walk into the hallway, the two guards will walk down the aisle of the throne hall with the procession.

To her left, Aelyta almost reaches her hand out, but retracts her arm. Itzal gives her a small bow of the head. He will lead her through the throne hall and down to the ceremony at the head of the room where the throne and crown wait for her. They proceed down the hallway.

Pausing before the doorway to the throne hall, the chambermaids hand over the train to the ladies-in-waiting, each lady with a small piece of her gown in hand. Aubree walks over to Aelyta, they quickly clasp their hands, and Aubree heads back to the room as Aelyta ascends the throne hall.

She walks a few steps to where King Miles stands behind the pews filled with Elemental folks. The ladies gently place down her train. The king ascends the aisle with a scepter and an orb in his hands. Aelyta follows behind him with her ladies trailing behind, Itzal walking beside her. As she passes the pews, the Elementals blow butterflies and dragonflies into the aisle. Those sitting beside the aisle throw lilacs, jasmines, and gardenias. And those sitting up in the balconies lift up their lit torches.

King Miles reaches the top of the aisle and turns to wait for Aelyta. Beside him, the High Priestess stands dressed in her golden cloak. She approaches the High Priestess, the same priestess who had performed her Rite of Divinity, aiming for the mound of dirt piled next to her. King Miles hands Aelyta the scepter and the orb. He steps away and Aelyta steps onto the mound and curtsies, bowing her head to the High Priestess.

The smell of fresh soil beneath her barren feet emboldens her as she stands upon the mound. The High Priestess presses a hand on the back of her head, mumbling incantations Aelyta does not understand. Her voice cries through the throne hall along with the sound of the torrential rain battering against the side of the windows.

Outside, the dark lets shadows enter the hall. The pews of Elementals are no longer visible in the dark cast of night. The High Priestess lifts Aelyta's chin up to face her. The glow of the torches' halos around the throne hall. With a gentle touch, the priestess places her fingertips under Aelyta's right elbow and leads her up to the throne.

Standing before it, Aelyta gets down onto one knee and the priestess reaches behind her to the table where the royal crown made of jade, adorned with small carnelian flowers, mushroom tops, and pale-cyan butterflies, sits. In the top center of the crown, a large blue crystal gem is crested and nestled along the adornments. The High Priestess lifts the crown from the golden pillow and gently turns to Aelyta.

She hovers the crown above Aelyta's head. Red lines like lightning crawl across Aelyta's skin, and she begins to radiate in brilliant gold. Aelyta closes her eyes as the priestess places the crown upon her. With her eyes still cast down to the ground, the High Priestess places her hand under Aelyta's elbow and lifts her up to stand before the throne hall.

Aelyta looks out towards the shadowed Elemental people. Gasps sound through the throne hall when she casts up her eyes towards them. Her eyes glow like white orbs in the dimmed hall. She takes a small step back, feeling her heel press against the bottom of the throne. Aelyta slowly sits herself onto the seat.

The thumping of feet rumble through the hall. "Here, here, Queen Aelyta," from all around the throne hall. A flash of lightning bursts outside the windows, lighting up the hall before the shadows encase all again. Thunder roars a mere second later.

Fire emerges from the torches lit to enlighten the hall. Aelyta recites aloud her oath and promise to the kingdom. Her voice echoes against the walls, competing with the sound of the thunder rolling outside. Once she finishes, silence rings through the hall before cheers are heard throughout the castle.

Aelyta descends from the throne. As she steps down from the podium, Cory rushes up to her side, assisting her down the step with one hand. There's something in his other hand.

Itzal, standing by the side of the podium, closes in towards them. Sitting in the front row, Kyanston bursts up from his seat. He lunges for Aelyta. "No, she's mine!" Kyanston cries.

Cory blocks him with his body. "She chose me. She's mine to take." Cory elbows Kyanston.

A dagger in his hand, Cory lunges for Aelyta. Caught off guard by both men, she stumbles backward, tripping on the step and the long train of her gown. She drops onto the podium behind her. Itzal appears before her, but Cory's dagger was too quick for Itzal to stop. Aelyta gives a groggy grunt at the realization; the dagger protrudes from her right shoulder. Her eyes meet Itzal's before their attention is on the back of the throne room. Itzal reaches behind his back, gripping hold of Aelyta.

A line of knights in formation move towards them. They're not wearing Ospherian uniforms. Printed on the front, the side of a man's face is silhouetted. An order is shouted from the balconies where the nobles are seated. Standing with his arm pointed down, Miles shouts.

The knights stop advancing. In one simultaneous conducted row, they each pull a large mechanical hornet from their backs, a mechanism that Aelyta's never seen before. Stingers pointed at Itzal and Aelyta.

Aelyta feels Itzal's grip tighten, tugging her dress.

Shadows flow from Itzal's feet, climbing up to his hands, consuming the room. A flash of lightning crashes against the windows. The click and hiss of the mechanical hornets ring through the gasps of Elementals. The stingers fly towards them. Blink. A clash of blinding darkness.

Stumbling, grasping her hand out for Itzal, Aelyta is unable to see in the dark. His hand entangles hers and she grips it like a tether in the shadows.

"You're the shadow demon?" her voice rasps. Itzal doesn't answer. "Are you hurt?"

"No, but you are. We need to hurry," he says, his voice like rolling thunder. His hand tugs her forward. "Now!" he yells. He grabs her arms and pulls her to follow him. "Jaycub and Malcolm have your ladies just as planned."

"Itzal," she says.

He doesn't reply and they run through the shadows. She can't seem to see where they're going, but he does. The sound of rain, silent. The sounds of the Elemental folks screaming are gone. The voices of her ladies-in-waiting have disappeared.

"Shadow demon," Aelyta cries.

Silence.

"Malo," she mumbles.

His feet stop moving.

She almost wants to laugh, tears wanting to pour down her face. Every gulp of breath, painstaking. Her arm grips her right shoulder where the dagger protrudes. Realization cuts into her. Aelyta hiccups gasps of air. The boning of her dress bites into her sides as she almost plummets to her knees. An arm scoops her up.

He takes a knife out from its sheath. "Hold still," he advises.

"I swear," Aelyta sighs. "If you also want to kill me, can you at least wait until I get out of this dress?"

He pulls her into him and grips her bodice. His face so close to hers, even if his is covered in shadows. She can feel the electricity of his skin against the tip of her nose. His grip tightens and he cuts through the fabric. As soon as the cloth breaks, air fully fills her lungs. He reaches down to the hem of her immense dress and tears off a long piece of fabric. Aelyta watches as he wraps her shoulder where her flesh meets the dagger, keeping the dagger in place.

Stashing his own knife away, he doesn't step back from her. His lips trace her cheek, causing little zaps to dance across her skin. "Can you walk on your own?" he growls.

"Yes," she murmurs.

He releases her from his arms. "Ready when you are."

Aelyta takes a step back, tripping on the train of her dress. He groans, pulling the train and tucking the fabric into his arms. She gives him a nod.

They run through the shadows. Her feet aching as she runs barefoot, but her legs don't stop moving. Her arms are full of the fabric of her skirt. The dagger a thorn in the crook of her shoulder. The shadow demon carries the rest of her gown. She doesn't know how long they have been running for, but they have yet to stop since her dress was cut.

The shadows swirl behind her and in front of her. The path she's running towards, dark and unknown. The pain from within her and the pain physically encompassing her progresses as she proceeds through the darkness.

9

Suspended in Time

AELYTA'S EYES have now adjusted to the dark shadows, unsure of how long they have been walking. She notices the way the shadows swirl like dark water into a tunnel that they're walking through. She looks down to see what they're walking on, and she finds large stepping stones tiled one after the other through the darkness. Her steps move like a boat on the water. She bumps into Itzal beside her, who grabs her waist, hoisting her up.

"We're here," he grumbles.

With a sweep of his other arm, the darkness surrounding them dissipates to reveal the starry night sky. The sound of crashing waves hits Aelyta first before she smells the scent of salt in the air. They're surrounded by rocks and old trees on what looks to be a peninsula off a coast. Before them, a small bridge that leads to the door of a tall house built straight into rock on the side of a cliff. The house sits alone as the waves crash into the cliff face where the house is wedged into.

"Do you think my ladies made it to their safe house by

now?" Aelyta hugs the fabric of her skirt still wrapped in her arms. Warmth puddles in the cloth around the base of the dagger in her shoulder.

"They made it a while ago," he answers. "I have had the Shadow Realm giving them cover."

Aelyta lets out a breath, smiling softly to herself. Her knees give out and Itzal scoops her up with a grunt. The stars above her spin too fast for her and bile rises in her chest. Itzal hastens through the bridge.

"Someone's inside," he murmurs. "No one is supposed to be here." He sets her down and she grabs hold of one of the bridge trusses.

She watches him quietly open the door when it swings out of his hand.

"Took you guys long enough," a female voice says from the entrance.

"What are you doing here?" The shadow man is taken aback. "No one is supposed to be here tonight."

"The winds forecasted what you were planning," a young woman with chromatic iridescent hair and large round glasses shrugs as she steps aside for them to enter the house.

"I don't like your wind sensitivity." The shadow man glares at the woman swinging the door open as wide as her eyes when she notices Aelyta struggling to keep herself up behind Itzal.

The woman jokes, "It's not my fault you don't understand the language of the winds." But immediately gasps once she sees the state Aelyta's in. "What happened?"

More footsteps sound from inside the house, Itzal already scooping Aelyta into his arms. The woman ushers them in.

From inside the foyer, a group of people bombard them with shuffling and yelling.

A ghost with fluffy hair resembling a dandelion cries hovering from above them. "Grab Kody!"

"Where's Kody?" An older woman, with similar features as the dandelion ghost, runs around the foyer.

"Kitchen, kitchen!" a little girl yells over the bustling adults.

Itzal pushes through the group. "Everyone move out of the way," he attempts over the clamor. Screaming through the rooms, "Why are you all in my house?"

"'Tis was Lorraine's idea." Kody appears from a corner, wiping his hand on a hand towel. Itzal huffs as he awkwardly carries Aelyta a few steps up the stairs. Kody takes an excess of dress material and helps the two of them up.

The stairs open up to a large landing with three doors, one on each wall. They pass the first two doors as Kody rushes in front of Itzal and opens the third door.

Kody runs back down the stairs as Itzal plops Aelyta onto the bed. His hands grip the straps at her shoulders and stop moving, hesitating. "We're going to need to take off the dress," Itzal describes. "Do you need me to do it or can you?"

Aelyta's world is still spinning, flashing white light blurring her vision. She murmurs inaudibly.

Itzal asks her again, "Do you need help removing your dress or do you need me to do it for you?"

Her only response is her head lulling back onto the pillow.

"I'm going to take the dress off for you," Itzal instructs. The dandelion ghost appears beside them. Itzal doesn't turn to look at her. "Edithe, grab something comfortable for her to wear." He points with one hand to the closet.

The dandelion ghost disappears. The sound of rustling echoes from the walk-in closet in the corner of the room. Kody bursts back through the door. The large-eyed woman with iridescent hair following behind him.

"Lorraine." Kody turns to her small figure. "You ready?"

"Ready," Lorraine chimes, handing him one of the tackleboxes in her arms.

The little girl adds behind them, "Ready, too."

"Not you, Luella." The living dandelion woman pulls the girl back out of the room.

She fumbles out of the older woman's grasps. "Aunt Edin!" the little girl exclaims.

Itzal undressed Aelyta while she's tucked under the blanket during the commotion. "Don't worry, Luella. We're definitely going to need more hands on deck." He gives her a salute. "Wait for our signal by the supplies in the kitchen?"

"Yessir." She nods and runs back down the stairs. Edin follows behind the little girl.

Itzal returns his attention to Kody and Lorraine. The ghost folded a set of linen clothes by the desk in front of the double doors leading out to the small terrace.

"Here we go." Kody has a hand on the pommel of the dagger. Lorraine stood ready with a handful of rags. "Malo, hold her still."

Itzal nods at the request and leans onto the bed, gripping Aelyta's unconscious body tightly. Kody tugs gently at the dagger, and it glides out of Aelyta's shoulder. Warm yellow liquid oozes from the gaping hole in her shoulder.

Lorraine jumps in with a rag and applies all her weight onto the wound. Kody tosses the dagger off to the side. From his tacklebox, he grabs a bottle of blue and gold glittering powder and a thick padding. Lorraine unveils the wound for Kody. She moves back to the tacklebox and grabs a roll of sticky ribbon.

Uncapping the bottle with his thumb, Kody dusts a thin layer of the glittery powder onto Aelyta's wound. He places the padding over the entirety of the gaping hole. Lorraine pushes him out of the way as she wraps Aelyta's shoulder with the sticky ribbon.

Kody closes the bottle and tucks it away into the tacklebox. Lorraine sighs in relief as she settles herself down on the bed beside Aelyta's body.

Pointing at the shadow demon's leg, Kody gestures. "Your turn."

"I'm good." Itzal shakes his head.

"Malo." Lorraine places a hand on his back. "Since he already has his supplies out."

"Fine." He plops onto the corner of the bed. He watches the ghost drift over to Lorraine with the folded clothes they picked out from the closet. Without thinking, he blurts, "Make sure they're warm clothes. She likes to be warm."

The ghost pauses, arms stopped mid-air. Lorraine also freezes, arms mid-air as well to receive the clothes. The ghost gives him a sly look and Lorraine chuckles softly.

"What?" He glances between the two of them.

They shrug at the exact same time. Lorraine takes the clothes from the ghost and works them under the blanket. The ghost slowly floats back over to the closet, maintaining eye contact with Itzal. She disappears into the closet.

"Edithe..." Itzal grumbles. "Ow! Kody!"

"Stop moving," Kody grumbles from Itzal's leg. "I'm assuming you didn't feel this 'thing' in your leg."

Kody pulls out the giant stinger from the mechanical hornet used against them.

Snarling, Itzal snaps, "Miles."

Lorraine gasps from behind them. "Malo, her arm."

They turn to find a large gash through Aelyta's right arm. Itzal leans over to look, but Kody pulls him back. "Let me at least check if you've been poisoned. Fungi have already been stolen away by knights in the night."

Edithe, the ghost, mumbles softly from Aelyta's right hand, "There are also Insectals disappearing as well."

Lorraine slumps. "Not just any kind of Insectals. Known to be descendants of Insectals that have toxins."

"Like wasps?" Kody gestures to the stinger he had just tossed aside.

"Or hornets," Itzal adds.

Loud metal clangs ring from downstairs. The shrieks of Luella and Edin echo up to the bedroom. "What are they doing to my house?" Itzal cries.

"Sit, don't move," Kody demands as he rushes out of the bedroom. The sound of his footsteps pounding the wood of the stairs.

"There," Lorraine exclaims proudly. She rises from the bed, grabbing the tacklebox and dirtied rags. "The Queen is all patched up and dressed. I'll see you two later." Winking at Itzal before closing the door behind her. Edithe giggles and winks at him too before evaporating into the air.

Itzal turns to Aelyta. Her umber-purple petals creased under her head, spilling over the pillow. "She bears hell like a hellebore," he murmurs aloud. Pausing at the end of his statement, he notices her eyebrows knit in a wince. "Careful," his voice soft.

"My body feels so sore," Aelyta mumbles. Her veins awaken as her eyes open. Taking in golden-and-blue hues up and down her skin. "I feel funny."

"It might be from the powdered crystal Kody put on your wound."

"I don't like it." She smacks her lips. "I don't feel..."

"You don't have to feel anything right now," he hushes her. "Just rest."

"Itzal." Aelyta sits up. "You're the shadow demon." Her eyes widen at the sight of blood spilling from the gauze on his leg. "You're injured."

"I prefer Malo, and I don't feel it." His hand rests on her uninjured shoulder. He relaxes it once Aelyta lays her head back down onto the pillow.

"Malo," Aelyta tests. "Malo?" She watches his eyes lull back and his body goes limp. "Malo!"

Kody bursts into the room, causing Aelyta to jump. "Ah, I've been waiting for him to do that." Kody rolls his sleeves. He glances at the queen. "You shouldn't be awake either." He taps once in the middle of her forehead. Twice. Her eyes go heavy.

Darkness softly caresses around Aelyta's shoulders before a cold draft breezes through her. The cold cuts into her skin and burrows into her bones.

Her breath catches in her throat. Death must feel as cold as the dead. Gripping her arms, the cold exposes her barren and vulnerable.

A woman chuckles through the darkness. Aelyta whips

around for the woman. "You're not afraid of me?" The voice resounds from everywhere.

"You have come to take me to the other side."

A hearty laugh ignites around Aelyta. "My dear." A face appears in the darkness. A woman with golden skin and black waves of hair ebbing and flowing like the shorelines of the ocean. "I am not here for you. I am here to ask something of you."

"Me? But I—"

"You have been transplanted, yes. You have always weathered your winter season. But winter is soon approaching, this coming winter is a deadly one. A cold reset to all of which you and your kind have ever known. You must prepare them."

"Why me?"

"It is your duty as queen. It is your duty like the queens before you. You must guide them through the storm."

"But you are Death, why save souls you want to take?"

The golden moon face laughs a laugh that reaches her eyes. "I am not Death. I am connected to death, but I am not death itself. I am Ratri, Goddess of the Night."

Aelyta gasps. "Goddess Ratri, I apologize." Aelyta puts her hand over her chest. "I beg for your forgiveness."

"Come, child. I am not heartless like the stories make me seem. You are a true Beacon, a star brighter than I have ever seen and I am glad to meet. You understand what information is given and you understand the lack of information that is hidden. Ko'nkiun is the Goddess of light. She shines a light on what must be shown. I, on the contrary, keep what must be kept. We work as one, and as one we work. A balance that holds the stars in the sky. So, I ask of you, as keeper of shadows, you must guide your people."

Opening her mouth, Aelyta gawks like a seagull. She tries to speak, but her voice blares like a large boat horn. A bright light overwhelms her. Aelyta remembers what warmth feels like. She feels it under her skin and in her bones.

Looking around for Goddess Ratri, the bright light around her blinds her eyes. Foghorns intrude the quiet.

10

Language of the Winds

FAR OFF IN THE DISTANCE, Aelyta can see the sails of the boats floating by. The morning is already warm and the smell of salt strong. She wonders how far from the castle she must be to feel such warmth here, and how cold it usually is in there.

Her hand reaches up to her shoulder where Cory had stabbed her. She should have died twice now. Greeted by a goddess herself, she should have been summoned by Death. Aelyta replays the face of the goddess in her mind. The glow of the moon face swirling over and over.

What was it that Goddess Ratri told her?

She must guide the Elementals into winter.

The seagulls scream by her balcony, the doors to the terrace were left open all night. She steps out onto the wooden planks for a better view now that the sun is out. The breeze coming from the ocean hits her, chilling, but the crispness wakes her fully.

Winter is far into the distance. The solar season cemented in the air, the sun's warmth in the height of morning.

Her hands on the balcony railing, she looks down at the water below her. The gentle waves were caressing up against the side of the rock where the house is embedded. There's a cave diagonally below the balcony to her left, to her right is a dock with a boat attached by ropes.

Groaning grumbles sound from inside the bedroom making Aelyta jump. She whirls around to find Itzal swirling in shadows on the bed she had just risen from.

She gasps. "You were—we shared a bed?" Her voice more an exclamation than a question.

His eyes open, honing straight on her. His face cloaked in shadows.

"You blushed, I saw it." She points.

"Why are you staring at me while I sleep?"

"Me? Stare? That's what you've been doing for the past, how many months?" She steps into the room. "Shadow demon."

Shadows grip Aelyta's arms and the room disappears, darkness surrounding her. Close to her left ear she hears, "And you missed me when I was gone."

Turning towards his voice, Aelyta pushes to her left, but he wasn't there. He was to her right, and she fell right into him. They both tumble and the shadows evaporate, revealing the sunlit bedroom.

With a grunt, he falls off her. Both his hands grasp his leg.

He's curled across the bed with Aelyta splayed across him.

"Are you hurt?" She leaps into a hover over his leg.

"No." He swats her away.

In the attempt, his hand slips. Aelyta notices the large circular scar where the stinger had impaled him. Her arms go limp at the sight of the injury.

A loud clamoring of doors slamming closed echoes from downstairs. They both jump up and away as quickly as they could. "Itzal," Aelyta mutters, gesturing to the door. "You first."

"I prefer Malo. And you can go first. You got up first."

"No, I suggested it first. You go."

"That doesn't really matter, go."

"No."

"Yes."

"Ugh." Aelyta turns for the balcony. "Malo, then." She softly mutters to herself.

"Malo Eldongarey," he states from behind her.

Aelyta nods without looking back towards him. Her eyes taking in the view of the Cygni Sea. "She's a beauty." She leans against the balcony banister.

"Yes, she is," Malo whispers directly behind her.

"How close am I to my ladies?"

"You're on the far edge of Elementropolis and your Ladies are..."—he hesitates—"the other side of Muddy Bay."

"Why here?"

"Why did I bring you here?"

"Yes." Aelyta fully turns to face him.

"I know the route from here to Avelmore Castle. If you need me to take you back, I can—"

"That's a puddle of piss," Aelyta swears. "What's the real reason?"

Malo scoffs, "You still don't trust me, do you?"

It's Aelyta's turn to scoff, and she scoffs dramatically. "Well, let's take a small flashback to when we first met. Remember when you stabbed me in the heart?" She jabs the place where the dagger's hilt had jutted from her chest. "And we must remember the time you came in the night, after you told me to go to sleep. You came back and tried to choke me to death."

"Ooh, right..." He scratches the back of his neck. "Hey, in my defense, I *am* a career assassin." His shoulder partially shrugs. His hands still tucked behind his neck.

"Okay then, why do you still cover your face?"

"I—"

Scratch. Scratch. They both turn towards the sound. *Scratch.* Malo chuckles as he glides the door slightly open. Too occupied on the balcony, Aelyta doesn't see her, but she feels her.

A flurry of fluff skitters across her ankle. Aelyta yelps at the movement of black fur disappearing under the bed.

It pops back out and stares at her. A charcoal rabbit with a white stripe from its neck to its chin, a white nose, and two white sock-like front paws.

The rabbit stomps its back foot at her and runs back out of the door.

"What did you do to Misty?" Malo laughs, still standing by the door.

"I didn't do anything," she scoffs.

"She's mad at you," he says before heading down the stairs.

"What did I do?" Aelyta yells from the bedroom door.

"She probably just likes you," he hollers from the landing.

She throws on a pair of matching pants and top, this time the pants are soft and billowy, which is not to be confused with baggy. They blew gently in the ocean breeze.

The top is gauzy and light. The set is perfect for a

coastal summer day. Aelyta hurries down to the smell of brewing tea and something dark, bitter.

The bottom of the staircase opens to the living room. The room resembles an octagon with four doorways leading out of the room, and each are accompanied by an angled wall on either side. The top of the octagon leads to the stairs and a library nook tucked underneath the stair-well. The next is a large, windowed door that opens out to an expansive terrace facing the ocean. Following along the angled wall, the next doorway leads to where Malo disap-pears, and the last doorway was where they had walked in from the foyer.

Sounds of chatter float through the living room. Aelyta hesitates. She hovers in the living room, staring the direc-tion Malo took.

The house is too foreign, like unsettled soil packed away under new roots. The voices are unfamiliar. The laughter unrecognizable.

Lorraine pops out from a corner. "Why are you just standing there?"

"I'm not sure..."

"Silly, we're just waiting for Kody to finish cooking. That's the alchemist. He loves to cook, and Malo loves to bake. I like making everyone drunk, I mean drinks." Lorraine gives her a wink behind her massively, large glasses. Her large eyes don't amount to the size of her glasses. Lorraine makes her way towards the sound. Turning back she says, "Well, whenever you're ready, come join us."

Aelyta softly pads the path Lorraine took and turns the corner. She finds herself in an airy kitchen. The high ceil-ings and large windows overlooking the glittering endless sea brings in all the morning light. Wood cabinets line the kitchen, and the bottom of the kitchen island is stained in cyan. The room is cornered by marble pillars, except for one corner where the basin sits between the countertops.

Lorraine, Luella, and Edin are seated in the breakfast nook attached to the outside of the island. They greet her warmly, beckoning her to take a seat with them. Malo and Kody are on the other side of the island. Kody busying away with the stovetop. Malo carries over a large, strange carafe filled with a dark-brown liquid.

"What's that?" She points.

"Coffee." The dandelion ghost appears through the wall, causing Malo and Aelyta to jump. Malo nearly drops the carafe, but Aelyta saves it. The entire room stares at them. Aelyta is hugging not only the carafe, but she's embracing Malo.

Large grins plaster across Lorraine and Edithe's faces. Luella's eyes are wide. Even Kody stops cooking to turn around and glance at the two of them.

Awkwardly trying to disengage from each other, Aelyta helps carry the coffee carafe to the breakfast nook while Malo throws cups at everyone. "You guys are still in my house, huh?" Malo takes a seat on the edge of the booth, opposite of Aelyta.

"You can't get rid of us that easily," Lorraine jests. "You also had like twenty-some years to try that."

"Of course, he didn't think to try." Edin shakes her head. "The dear is barely able to hold himself together this morning." She winks at him from the depths of the semi-circular booth.

A squeal of laughter escapes from Luella before her hands fly up to her face.

Malo ignores them all. "Remind me again why you're all here?"

From the other side of the island Kody chimes, "Lorraine let us in."

Malo squints at the iridescent-haired woman with large bug eyes and even larger glasses. She shrugs. "I blame the wind." Lorraine takes a sip of her cup of coffee. Aelyta glances at her from across the table.

"All Insectal descendants understand the language of the wind," Lorraine explains.

"But not everyone can understand the language like you do." Malo glares from over his cup.

"I have yet to meet another Insectal who can see the wind's patterns." Lorraine nods. "Most Insectal these days are not fully Insectal. Most of us are mixed Elementals. Those who do understand the language of the winds can only hear the wind speak."

Luella adds, "But Lorraine is special! She can see the wind's patterns so clearly, she can forecast what the winds will say before they speak."

Turning back to the Malo, Lorraine sheepishly smiles. "So, don't be mad." Lorraine takes another sip from her coffee.

"He's not mad." Edithe floats through the table. Everyone at the table leaps into the booth, far away from the table, as the ghost floats past them. Edithe sits atop the island, above the breakfast nook. She is wearing a librarian's uniform with round glasses. Her dandelion-white hairs are like ivory curls atop her small face. She looks identical to Edin sitting below her in the nook. Unlike Edithe, Edin isn't wearing a uniform.

The ghost's eyes meet Aelyta's. Aelyta tries to turn away, but she smiles instead. "I guess we should all formally meet the Queen of Ospheria." The ghost smiles back. "I'm Edithe Earline. That's my daughter over there,

Luella Earline. She's my little sproutling. My sister, Edin, has been taking care of her in the physical realm as I'm— you know. And this is Lorraine Fenton." She kicks towards the iridescent-haired Insectal. "Kody Flower." Edithe points behind her back. "I'm pretty certain you've already met."

"Oh, we stocked the closet full of clothes." Lorraine's eyes sparkle. "It looks like you've gotten a chance to go through them this morning."

Aelyta looks down at her outfit. "I did. Thank you for that. They fit nicely."

"Thank Malo." Lorraine chucks her shoulder against him. "He told us your size."

Sipping her coffee, Aelyta hides her face behind the cup. Her cheeks warm.

Kody, from the around the island, gestures with his chin to Aelyta. "Are you feeling alright, there? Your face is turning colors."

"I think...it's my cup, it's warm...warming my face."

Placing the cup back down on the table, they're all still staring at her. She couldn't help but chuckle. "It's so warm here. It already feels like the solar season."

"Yeah, it's hot here most of the year," Edin replies first. "Avelmore must be cold and dreary all year round."

"Enough of the weather, I want to hear about the coronation." Luella leans her chest against table. "We have the literal queen sitting amongst us."

"Luella." Edithe's tone hardens. "Give her time. She's been transplanted, you know how plants need time after transplanting."

Luella slumps her back against the booth. "I just wanna show her off at school."

Lorraine chuckles. "What are you going to do while

you're here? I'm sure you'll get to really spread your wings now that you're outside of Avelmore."

"You can come work with me at my bookbinding shop." Edin straightens.

Edithe slaps her sister's arm. "Or with me at Pyerre's Library. We're in desperate need of more volunteers. We're lacking enchantments, so now everything must be done by hand. But Pyerre is a keeper of all Deneb's knowledge. He's Deneb's last dragon who's willing to accommodate as long as you have skills that will help benefit knowledge—in case you didn't know. Of course, you probably know. You're the Queen of Ospheria."

Aelyta's face brightens in interest.

"Talking about lacking enchantments. My entire cafe is based on enchanted drinks," Lorraine exclaims. "I'd love to have you at my cafe in the city." Lorraine raises her hand at Aelyta.

"You could come teach at my school," Luella chimes. "Since we're brainstorming ideas."

"Or she can recover from the coup." Malo's voice rumbles like thunder in the summer storms.

The table falls quiet. Aelyta breaks the silence. "Thank you." She smiles. "I love all your ideas."

"Wanna hear mine?" Kody leans against the island behind them.

"What's your idea?" Edithe turns slightly towards him.

"I think"—Kody pauses dramatically—"we should eat out on the terrace. Florals do enjoy their sunlight."

"I do enjoy a good ray of sun." Aelyta smiles even brighter at the suggestion.

"Food's done?" Luella asks Kody from the nook. He nods. "Thank the Elementals." Luella pushes her way through Aelyta. "I'm starving."

The group shuffles out of the kitchen, through the living room, and out the terrace doors. Aelyta follows along as they walk onto the terrace and around the corner where a large wooden table is shaded under a canopy of vines. Iron chairs laden with cushions line the sides of the tables.

Kody catches Aelyta's arm gently. "How's your shoulder feeling?"

Aelyta turns to face him, testing out her right arm and shoulder. "I still feel funny, but I'm no longer in pain."

"Good, good," Kody answers. "That specific powder, Morf Blue, is new to Elementropolis. The Morphenum has not been in stock these days. This one is sold by the same company, so the Alchemadia is using it as a replacement. Sorry I had to knock you back to sleep. Wanted to make sure the new stuff works, you know." He shrugs. "And look at you, all healed and ready to mingle...uh, Your Majesty."

Aelyta stares at his face. "You're the alchemist who helped heal Jaycub back to health." Aelyta clasps his hand. "Kody!" She's now filled with the realization. "I am so grateful for your attentiveness. Thank you for helping Jaycub!"

"It's an honor to serve the Queen of Ospheria." Kody smiles at her as he leads her to an empty chair at the table. Laid out before them are an assortment of foods Aelyta has never seen before. Kody points to each platter, naming them one by one. "This one is pollen peas, soil-fried blue cheese, curdled fertilizer—Malo has a large planter of these so there's a bountiful amount here—let's see, there's also curried onions from our local spices. Oh, and my personal favorite, banana soup. Please, everyone, dig in."

Aelyta watches the group talking and laughing over stories of their busy day, while the clatter of utensils to plates sound around her. She takes a bite of each food Kody listed. Each one tastes of ocean life and the smell of flowers and salty air. She continues to clear the plate, adding more of what she enjoyed most, surprising herself to find she enjoys the taste of fish and spices from the curry. Accompanied with the creamy, curdled fertilizer, the banana soup delighted her. Taking a sip from the pink bottle, the smell of floral and fruit fumes into her face. The taste of sparkling peach and jasmine refreshing and light.

She's left Avelmore Castle more times than she can count, but she's never experienced cuisine quite like this. She listens to the group describing their days, and she realizes; food and drinks taste much better in good company. Aelyta's throat tightens at the thought of trusting them so easily, but nothing about them seems off-putting to her. In fact, she finds herself laughing along to Lorraine's recollection of a customer walking in with a long request for a drink. Aelyta may have no clue what the requests mean, but she knew the absurdity it was to have contradictories that Lorraine must submit to at the face of service.

Kody joins in. "You think that's bad. I had an ancient toad-man come in today requesting an ailment for his eyes, but also, as I'm measuring his vision, I ask him if he wears glasses. He tells me he doesn't, so I continue on fitting him. This man gets so upset with me. I ask him what's wrong. You won't believe it! He pulls out a pair of glasses from nowhere and throws them at me and claims I'm the one taking money from him!"

They all burst out at the same time. There's laughter and remarks. When they've all subsided, Lorraine turns to Aelyta. "I bet you have ridiculous stories you're keeping from us."

Aelyta chuckles. "I doubt you'll find them entertaining. Politics may sound like a game that's worth playing, but it really lacks where it actually counts." Her eyes cast towards the table.

"I know what can pick you up." The shadow man claps his hand.

"Oh, I know." Luella leaps to her feet. "Dessert!" she screams and squeals.

The shadow man holds his hand out and Luella takes it with gusto. They swing their arms towards the door.

Kody leans towards Aelyta. "Malo was really excited for you to try his biscuits."

Aelyta hesitates. "Is that an innuendo?"

Laughter erupts from the table. Aelyta even covers her mouth as if she's said something absurd.

"Malo is an amazing baker." Edithe puts a hand on her arm for reassurance.

Malo and Luella return to the terrace. Luella's arms are full with a large basket of photosynthesized varieties of baked goods like biscuits, cookies, and croissants. The shadowed man carries a tub of something wet or frozen.

They place their goods onto the table and Malo disappears again around the corner. A moment later, he hands Aelyta a light sweater before opening the tub. "Have you tried frozen cream before?" He turns to Aelyta.

"Never." She shakes her head. "What should I expect?" She smiles at Luella who's handing her handfuls of cookies.

"It's sugar!" Luella roars. Everyone laughs at the response.

After frozen cream, Aelyta finds herself in need of a bath. She stands in the bathing room, hesitating to move. The walls of the room are a pale blue that matches the bathing basin. The ceiling is tall, with a large arched window behind the bathing basin with more views of the ocean. Palm-like trees are in the corners, framing the tall arched window. The late afternoon sun invades the window.

The bathroom is admirable, flawless, unlike her skin. She unwraps herself from her clothes. Reflecting from the mirror, Aelyta doesn't recognize herself. Her eyes linger on her right shoulder. The large, gaping scar resembles a chip on her shoulder.

On her left arm, a scar streaks a line where the hornet's stinger chipped away her flesh. Despite the scars though, her face is plumper than normal, and her eyes lack the rim of darkness. Boreas, Briley, and Aubree would be proud of her for eating and sleeping.

Aelyta unveils the ache in the center of her back. The tension holding her upright unfolds as she sinks herself into the bath. There are an array of different potion bottles lining the mantle between the window and the basin. She picks up one with a rose bud tied to the rim, opening the top to the scent of roses and a hint of lemon.

As she finishes her bath, she turns to the pile of plush towels when she realizes there's a small rabbit sitting atop them staring at her.

"Hi, Misty. May I have one of those towels, please?" Aelyta asks.

The rabbit blinks back at her. She tries to peel one from under it. Finally able to get one of the towels free, the rabbit stomps its back paw at her.

"I asked nicely," she replies. "You've still got plenty to sit on if I take one." The rabbit leans over the edge of the tub and begins drinking the bath water. Aelyta leaps out of the bath squealing. The rabbit leaps away and behind the bathing basin.

Back in the bedroom, Aelyta finds a pair of white linen pants and a matching flowy top with thin shoulder straps. The pants flow like a skirt but without the bulk of one. She pulls on the top and the band under the straps stretched enough to move around, but tight enough above her breasts that she felt confident it wouldn't slip.

Hanging on the inside of the closet door are a few ribbons and small scarves. She reaches for a beautiful silk scarf in a navy-and-yellow pattern, gathering her hair and tying it off with the silk.

Standing before the gilded mirror tucked inside the closet, Aelyta nods at herself in approval before she steps out of the bedroom.

Muffled chatter floats up the stairs. Aelyta catches specific words. She pauses at the top landing, listening.

"You have the chance to get rid of the queen," Kody's voice in the distance.

A woman's voice follows, "But we don't know if the downfall of Deneb is because of her, we don't know anything coming out of Ospheria."

"She was supposed to be queen, and she took forever to start her Crownship," another woman responds. "If Elementropolis is caught in Ospherian problems, it's definitely because of her."

Malo's voice is stern. "The downfall of Deneb began even before the death of Queen Jane. I found this in Miles's study." A pause and footsteps walk across the room. "Can you read the dust on it?"

Edithe's voice is a murmur from the top of the stairs before she yells out, "Aelyta, dear. You can come down and join us."

Aelyta's face burns being caught eavesdropping. She carries herself down the stairs to the rest of the group.

11

Death Counts Down for Cut Flowers

THE CREAK of the stairs at Aelyta's descent into the first floor only adds to the awkward air. The group refuses to meet her eyes, except for Edithe, who greets her with a knowing smile.

Finally reaching the last step, she attempts to explain, "I didn't want to intrude."

"Don't say anything." Edithe points to her daughter whose mouth had just opened. "Since you're here, might as well join the conversation. You are the Queen of Ospheria, you should know what people have to say about you outside of your realm." The ghost hands Aelyta a folded paper.

Opening the page, Aelyta discovers it's two folded papers, both contracts. "I don't know if I want to read this in front of everyone. I don't know you all well enough..."

Malo approaches. "I was keeping that from her for a reason."

"I've read the dust, Malo. I can see that you've pocketed the originals, and I can also see that these have been given to each without the other knowing."

"I figured that, but what is Miles planning?"

"Oh, Miles wasn't the one to write these contracts. He was given the contracts to serve to Julius and Thelonius."

Aelyta steps forward. "By whom? Who's pulling the strings? I've been trying to figure it out. I have spent nights, days, going over my mother's old notes to narrow it down."

"I don't know who." Edithe's hands to her hips.

"There will be unrepairable damage to all of Deneb if they are not stopped." Lorraine pushes her glasses up her nose. "The winds have been forecasting patterns of pretty much Deneb's self-destruction. I don't think we have any control of what's to come."

"Let's not scare ourselves into pacification now," Edin remarks. "I think we have some say as folks of Elementropolis."

"Go take it up with Minister Nyup," Luella barks. The girl crosses her arms and tucks her legs under her on the couch cushion. "If only you had taken the crown sooner."

"My father and the Royal Advisors refused. They stepped into power and couldn't let it go."

"Maybe that's where we should be looking." Kody glances around the room.

Sighing, Aelyta meanders to the library nook. A large window, from floor to ceiling, faces out towards a lighthouse on a rock some distance away. On both sides of the window are bookcases built into the walls. In the center of the library nook are two large chairs overflowing with throw blankets and cushions. Along the bottom of the large window, is a massively larger cushion for laying against the window for reading. She could only assume, judging by how cozy the idea is to her. Running her hand across the back of the armchair, she looks out the window, the sunset warm through the glass panes.

The group rustles behind her in the living room. Aelyta turns around to find Edithe floating towards her. "Malo mentioned you don't read the news, but I think you should stay informed about what is going on with your realm and your sovereignty. I'll come back tomorrow with the latest. He mentioned that you like studying. If you're going to try and outsmart the person who's trying to steal your reign, you should start with the people. We are here, and we like to have our voices heard."

"Even as a spirit, you really are political." Lorraine approaches them. She turns to Aelyta. "It was nice meeting you. We're all heading out now. Wanted to say my good-byes before I go."

Aelyta gestures to her chest. "Thank you. All of you. I owe you all my life."

Waving to the group as they leave for the door, Aelyta watches Malo in the midst of his own farewells to his friends. She's left alone in the living room, and yet, Aelyta feels exposed and vulnerable. Mulling over Edithe's words, she realizes the ghost was right.

Her privilege and the position she was born into are what kept her in the dark about what was happening outside of Avelmore, outside of Ospheria. She ran into Minister Nyup the night of her Rite of Divinity and she didn't even think to ask him how the state of Elementrop- olis was. What kind of queen doesn't think diplomatically?

The walls close in on her. Aelyta walks out onto the terrace. The ocean air breathes new life, a new form of comfort.

Up against the stone railing, a large daybed welcomes the doorway. Curtains drape the posts that hold up the sun cover, entwined in pearl vines. To her left, the large dining table where everyone had lunch hours earlier, sits picturesque. On the wall behind the dining area, a large wisteria plant clings and climbs up the house.

Pivoting to the right side of the doorway, a large magenta bougainvillea bows over a stairwell leading down towards the water.

Enticed, Aelyta takes the stairs. The steps lead her inside the rock in which the house is embedded into. It's not dark inside due to the light at the bottom of the stairs. The last three steps open to a furnished alcove. The waves softly kiss the lip of the alcove edge. Another daybed that can sleep four or five people takes up the back wall. At the foot of the daybed, a firepit is centered in a semi-circle of lounge chairs facing the water.

Where the water meets the rocky edge of the alcove, Aelyta lines her toes up against it, feeling the water lap over, lightly splashing her skin. The water isn't warm, but it isn't cold either. She rolls her pant legs up and sits down. Gently, one leg at a time, she dangles them into the water. She's unsure of the depth, but it seems the water is deep.

Aelyta watches the boats in the distance gliding from left to right or right to left. Farther out, she sees a coastline with tall, skinny buildings covered in green, lush and tall trees filling the gaps between.

Turning her head to the side, she finds more coastline. On this side, the sandy shores are glittering with golden sand. The waves curling up and pulling away only to roll up onto the sand again. Neverending. Roll. Recede. Roll. Recede. An endless lull.

Watching the beach sands and the waves, the sun—once up high—is now angling down. The evening shadows wake up for the night. Footsteps sound through the stairs of the alcove.

"This is where you've been." Malo steps into the opening with her.

She gives him a soft smile over her shoulder. He joins her at the edge, dunking his legs beside her. His left leg catches her attention. The hole where the hornet's stinger was is now a large scar on his shin.

Looking away, Aelyta rubs her cheek against her left shoulder. Her eyes meet the scar on her arm from a different stinger.

"What's the matter? Hungry?" He pokes her right elbow.

She shakes her head, still looking away.

"Are you upset about last night? I promise, I was completely out cold."

She chuckles, but she doesn't budge.

"Is it...the event at your coronation? I swear, if I get my hands on either that filth of a brat or the older filth of a brat..."

"The scar on your leg," Aelyta clears the air. "I gave you that scar. It symbolizes my failure to protect and guide a whole kingdom, the Crownship."

"Pft, please." Malo waves the comment away. "Your father was the one who gave the order—not you."

"He wouldn't have done it if I didn't follow the rules—"

"There were no rules or laws that you broke," Malo corrects. "You're getting stuck in that restless head of yours." He scoots closer to her. "Miles would have attacked you even if you sat and did nothing at all. Even if you hid away from all of Deneb, he would still try to attack. He's just that kind of... Well, he's human."

"And I'm half." Aelyta kicks the water. "I would have attacked unprovoked at some point in my position as queen. Power would do that."

"I know that is not what you truly believe. That is too naive of a perspective for someone training her whole life to lead a Crownship."

Her face falls into her hands. "I *am* in my own head."

"Be honest with yourself." He hesitates. His hand hovers over her back. "That's why you're in your head. The "you" in there needs to come to terms with what happened to you." He pulls his hand away as Aelyta lifts her eyes to his.

Aelyta tensed momentarily as he neared her, her mind racing as all of her senses collided—wondering whether she should accept it. But she knew she couldn't resist. Everything about him screamed to be closer.

When he cups her cheek, she melts into him. A zap sings from his fingers to her skin. She chuckles at the feeling. His hand runs down her neck to the scar on her right shoulder, sending more zips across her skin. Leaning into her, a bolt of lightning jumps from his lips to her skin as he hovers over the scar. A kiss, on the flesh healed over the crater. "You smell like lemon and roses." His lips remain on her skin.

"Mhmm," she hums.

Pulling away, Malo's hand returns to her jawline. She's watching his lips as his eyes watch hers. His thumb tests her bottom lip. Electric shock jumps from his skin to the soft curves of her mouth. His forehead leans against hers. Her chin lifts up to welcome his lips, only to hear rustling coming from inside the house.

Malo pulls away. The sound of chewing echoes from the living room above them. "Misty! Stop chewing on the baseboards!" Malo hesitates. The chewing gets louder; he clicks his cheek before rising to his feet. "Misty, girl! We've talked about this! We don't ask for treats by eating the house."

Aelyta giggles at his remarks to the rabbit. Her smile drops when she remembers she almost kissed the shadow demon. The shadow demon, who put a dagger to her heart, who has a reason to shadow his face from her. What else could he be hiding?

12

Ars Longa, Vita Brevis
ART IS LONG, LIFE IS SHORT

THE NEXT DAY, Edithe hands Aelyta a copy of the most recent print of the ANP just as the ghost promised. Avelmore News Printers, Avelmore's prestigious reports directly from the castle. The news cycle printed on the front page is the reason Edithe is floating directly in front of Aelyta. The queen's grip on the edges of the papers tighten and tense.

> Almost-crowned Queen of Ospheria, Her Highness, Aelyta Aurelianus, is declared dead as of today. Due to the indisposition, Miles Dedrick will receive the crown by the hands of Avelmore's Royal Advisors on the height of the solar season. All are expected. Further details on page 5.
>
> Authored and Edited by RA Constantine, RA Columba, RA Menecrates, RA Ansaldo

Flipping the page, she needs more. Anything more. On the next page, Richards' merchants are describing the new substance of crystal that will replace the Morphenum, the crystal every Elemental knows that powers enchantments, with a gold spice that will adhere to better Alchemadia's desires.

She flips the page. Mysterious disappearances of Florals and Fungi are causing Elementropolis to question Minister Nyup and security. The Minister responds with his full cooperation with the city. Investigation is under way, hired and directed by the Ronanbrands.

The next report states the Avelmore News Printers have been revoked from Avelmore due to the new King's order. The prints will continue until they are physically dragged from the facility.

Finally, on page five, Aelyta skims the report. The Royal Advisors did not go into Aelyta's supposed time of death nor the cause. Instead, the four of them have detailed instructions on Miles's coronation and the plans he has for Ospheria as the new King.

> First order of King Miles: revoke the lies of the Avelmore News Printers. Second order of King Miles: a better, cleaner Deneb. Third order of King Miles: provide a better and richer source of alchemy.
> Long May He Reign.

With the rolled-up printed papers in her hand, Aelyta twists them between her grip. She doesn't look up at the ghost who has provided the news. Edithe stares, but doesn't follow Aelyta as she paces around the edge of the living room. She ends up walking the perimeter of the library nook. Turning back to the ghost, Aelyta tightens her smile. "Thank you for providing me with the news. I appreciate the sentiment. Give my regards to Pyerre as well. This news print is also partly from him, I can only assume."

Edithe nods. "We both wanted you to know what's happened in Ospheria since your escape two nights ago."

Aelyta nods, then nods some more. She's never truly felt more resigned. Acceptance is easy when she knows the way her father is, but she most ardently isn't surprised.

Her father's finally gotten what he wanted, and she fell right into his trap. Edithe floats over to her in the library nook. "I know you don't need me to tell you how to feel, but may I offer some advice?" Aelyta glances towards the transparent dandelion woman. "You have spent your entire life preparing to lead. You must have been *led* to lead. The answer you're looking for isn't in someone else. I'm sure you must feel aimless after your mother's passing, I see it in your face. Luella was the exact same way. It's the reason she clings to Edin. The same reason I'm still haunting around Pyerre's Library. You have been anointed by the Elements, the High Priestess, and the Goddess Ko'nkiun."

"Because I am queen, I should know what to do next," Aelyta offers. Edithe shrugs and evaporates into thin air.

Sighing, Aelyta turns back towards the library shelves. Her eyes aiming for the books as she scans the collections. The titles pique her interest, but she's not in the mood. An ire grows in her chest. Her arms clench. She tosses the rolled papers onto one of the armchairs in the center of the nook.

Promptly up the stairwell, Aelyta examines the entire room behind her before making her way up the stairs to the second floor. On the landing, she hears Malo in the bathing room.

She pivots towards the bedroom, but she spies the doorknob to the door directly on the right of the landing.

Her hand reaches out and the knob fully turns. The door opens to a cluttered room filled with paint cans and canvases. The floor is splattered with paint. A large table is pushed up against the back wall.

An easel is erected in front of the large arched window. There's a canvas painting nestled in place. Another canvas on the floor, propped up against the easel's leg.

She recognizes the scene of the painting on the easel. Taking a step closer, Aelyta sees her ladies-in-waiting. They're blurry, but still distinct. In the center of the painting, Aelyta is painted with such vibrancy and texture.

She's having dinner with her ladies on the canvas. The girls are not as rendered as Aelyta is, but she recognizes they're laughing.

An uneasiness rattles her chest. What did she just discover?

She picks up the second painting. Was Malo hiding in the shadows that night? Why paint her and her ladies?

Just as intricately painted as the first, Aelyta and her ladies are playing cards with their glasses of wine.

They're surrounding the coffee table, Aelyta in the center again. Lyza on one side, Ellsy on the other. Maurene and Odetta pointing fingers at each other from their side of the table. Margaret seated on the couch, crouching over laughing. Presley with the glass fully tilted over her face, but her golden hair gives her away.

The anger in her veins solidifies into tears, now streaming her face. Despite how they are towards her, Aelyta will always believe they are what is left of family to her. Her last remaining family. She knows how adverse they are to her position, and yet, they were always around when she needed them.

How are they faring? Are they warm? Food and wine enough for the six ladies? Will she have to wait—but that's all she's had to do, wait. Aelyta's tired of waiting. Waiting for her father to give her the crown. Waiting for someone to tell her what to do. Waiting on being waited on.

Her legs restless, she throws herself from the room. The paintings left behind. Running down the stairs, she pivots to the living room. Bursting towards a direction, she finds herself in the foyer facing the front door. Nothing's holding her back. She leaps through the door and pounces through the bridge onto the peninsula.

The sunbaked gravel under her bare feet is warm. The breeze whistles through the petals of her hair.

Run.

Her legs carry her forward. Aimless, but restless. Aelyta runs until there is sand kicking beneath her. She runs for the ocean. The Cygni Sea, a vast glittering blue before her. The closer she reaches the waters, the breeze nips her skin. Goosebumps dance along her arms. From the shoreline, the house embedded in rock is still in view.

The water kisses her toes, engulfing her ankles. She laughs as she sinks into the sand as the ocean says good-bye. The water is cold. The sand warm. The smell of seaweed and salt ignites as the wind carries into her petals. The same way the waves lap up her legs.

She rolls her pant legs up and walks farther into the water. More. She wants more. The cold water. The warm sun. The sand rustling beneath her bare feet. Seagulls screaming overhead.

Lifting her chin to the sun, she stares into the cloudless sky. Movement in her peripheral catches her attention.

Malo is walking down the path towards the beach. Guilt strikes her core.

How could she approach him after what she found when she shouldn't have been snooping around? She bites her lip, as if a cat caught her own tongue. But it's not her fault is it, what else has he been hiding from her?

He approaches, handing her a thick knitted cardigan. Pulling the sweater up over her bare shoulders, the warmth comes back to her.

"I should have mentioned that it's much colder by the water." Malo puts his hands in his pockets.

"Thank you for the sweater." Aelyta joins him as he walks back to the house.

"So, um," he stutters, "you found my art room?" He kicks softly at the sand beneath his bare feet. "I saw you run out of it as I was coming from the bathing room..."

"I did," she adds, looking to him for an explanation.

"It's weird, isn't it—"

"You paint beautifully." She didn't mean to talk over him.

"Thank you," he mutters. "I know it's weird to have paintings of people. I don't *normally* paint people." He didn't know how to stop himself from over speaking. "I normally paint objects, landscapes, scenery, but I don't know. I really liked the way the lighting gave your petals a purple umber."

Aelyta laughs. "I like that you enjoy painting."

Malo chuckles. "Thank you," he tries again. "What was the news that Edithe had for you? Whatever it is, you can trust. Pyerre is adamant about having his library collection be accurate, and he will not accept anything else."

Sighing, Aelyta announces the news that has been biting away at her. "The Royal Advisors have announced that I am officially dead, and King Miles has already announced his order of decree."

"He hasn't even been crowned King of Ospheria." Malo grimaces.

Aelyta nods. "I know exactly how bad this will turn for Ospheria. I don't believe my anger is about my control over the situation. Ospheria does not deserve to be taken advantage of. Ospherians should not be manipulated. And, and..."

Malo's intent on her. It throws her in a spin. "I'm still listening," he urges her to continue. Her anger has lost its taste. It's now tinged with worry, sickness, and confusion. But she knows better, she was trained for better.

"And," Aelyta remembers. "I think I need to get back into Avelmore Castle. But first, I need to annoy Edithe about something trivial."

They walk back into the house and Malo claps three times. "Edithe refuses to touch the Goddess of Death." He claps three more times.

The air goes cold. Goosebumps climb Aelyta's skin. In the middle of the room, a small cyclone spirals and evaporates, revealing Edithe in the center.

"Dramatic entrance." Malo rolls his eyes. "She normally doesn't do all that."

"Nonsense." Edithe shushes him away. "What's the reason for my summons?"

"How busy are you at Pyerre's Library?" Aelyta starts, but brushes it away. "Could you go check on my ladies-in-waiting for us?"

"I can do that. All I do is haunt the library. I mean, I do the tasks I did while I was living, because—you know, it's boring. I'd have to let Luella and Edin know before I do, and I'll pop back over when I'm done. Is that all?"

"Well, there's that, and I need to get back into the castle." Aelyta adds, "I was studying quite a few subjects before being transplanted, but there are a couple books that my mother left behind. She had certain annotations I couldn't understand, but I think I do now. If you could send word to my handmaid, Aubree, she's seen me study. I trust her to be thorough with my notes."

Edithe nods. "Stay here until I return. It makes it easier for me to know where you are exactly. Haunting is not easy business." She waves at both Aelyta and Malo before disappearing into the air.

13

Scattered Souls
A GREENHOUSE IN THE
ABANDONED CITADEL

MARGARET, Jaycub, Malcolm, Ellsy, and Lyza sit in a circle in the main sitting room. Odetta, Presley, and Maurene are upstairs in their respective bedrooms asleep.

"We haven't gotten word from Aelyta," Ellsy cries.

Jaycub shakes his head. "We need to stay in one central location, together."

Lyza leans in. "I think we should head back to Avelmore Castle."

"Well, I think we should go to Muddy Bay," Ellsy quips.

"And I think we should try Elementropolis," Jaycub adds. "But we still have to wait for Aelyta and Malo to send a message that it is safe to go out."

The three turn to Margaret and Malcolm who have been sitting silently on diagonal sides of the circle.

"I agree with Jaycub." She doesn't give him a glance. "I trust Aelyta to send word when it's time."

Malcolm clears his throat. "I'd hate to stay in one place for *too* long."

"The point, though, is that we need to wait for Aelyta and Malo," Jaycub emphasizes.

"I'm tired of waiting," Lyza whines.

Malcolm raises his hand. "Me, too."

"We've waited so long now," Ellsy groans.

Margaret glances at Jaycub, who has a twitch in his eyebrow. She turns to the others. "Tomorrow morning. We can discuss with Odetta, Presley, and Maurene in the morning what our next steps should be. I'd hate to leave the three of them out of this conversation, especially if we're deciding whether to wait or to leave."

The others nod, but Ellsy gives Lyza a look.

A scream emanates from above them. Footsteps thump down the stairs. Odetta looks as if she's seen a ghost, the group says.

"I have." Odetta's hair flops around her face.

"Hi, so, sorry to scare you all." A voice comes from behind them.

Odetta screams again. More thumping coming from the stairs reveals Presley and Maurene entering the main sitting room. "Why in all the Elements are you screaming?" They also look as disheveled as Odetta.

"My name is Edithe," the ghost chimes in. "I've been sent by Her Majesty."

"Is she..." Margaret gasps. "Is she dead?"

Edithe laughs, but answers, "The ANP states so, but no. She's well and alive. Angry, but breathing."

Odetta, as far away from Edithe as the room can limit, yells over to the group, "Why did you have to scare me though?"

Edithe shrugs. "I don't know the answer to that. You were the one to happen to be awake. I was in the wrong room. You got scared. Any other questions?"

Jaycub jumps at the opportunity. "Let me get this straight." He blinks. "The papers printed that Aelyta is dead?"

Edithe nods. "That's correct. And Miles made himself king without a coronation. Anything else?"

"What a hypocrite." Ellsy sneers.

Malcolm chimes, "So, what do we do now? Do we still have to stay here? Do we stay here forever?"

"Slow down there," Margaret remarks. Malcolm paces the room. Margaret adds, "If she's believed to be dead, then wouldn't Miles have sent someone out to finish the job because she's clearly not dead?"

Jaycub and Malcolm both perk up. Jaycub answers first. "So, if she's still in danger, then so are you lot." He looks to Malcolm. "And if Miles takes the throne, so are we."

"My work here is done," Edithe interrupts. "I shall depart now."

"No!" they all cry out.

"We still have more questions for you," Margaret plunders.

"Well, hurry up." Edithe crosses her arms. "I need to report back to Aelyta so she can sneak back into the castle."

They all perk up at that. Lyza, silent the entire time, says, "Tell us more."

"She only said in passing that she needs to find something she learned. She's the only one who knows where to look and what to find." Edithe shrugs, arms still crossed.

"I want to go back to Avelmore." Lyza raises her hand.

"Me, too." Malcolm also raises his hand.

"I'll go with you." Ellsy elbows Lyza.

"Count me in," says a sleepy Maurene stumbling through the sitting area.

Malcolm asks, "Do you need a recap?"

Maurene shakes her head. "Don't need one. The girls

need someone to watch them." She gestures to the duo with their hands raised.

"I guess I'll tag along with you four." Edithe nods. "Before I leave for the night, can one of you"—she points to the four volunteers—"give me something so I may find you again?"

Lyza pulls her arm out from under a blanket. A large crack in her skin reveals swirling galaxies. She breaks off her starlight coating and hands it to the ghost.

"You're made of rock," Edithe comments. "That's interesting."

Maurene explains, "Lyza was born from a rock found in the Morf Mountains."

"But why are you all cracked?" Ellsy exclaims at Lyza.

"I just need to get back into Avelmore." Lyza puts her arm back under the blanket.

Ellsy shrugs.

Edithe claps her hands. "When are you going to transplant? Are we going to start traveling tomorrow, maybe?"

Lyza nods aggressively. Malcolm glances at the others. They nod sleepily. "Tomorrow, then," Malcolm confirms.

"Goodnight," Edithe sings as she evaporates. She's returned to the Liminal space, the line between both the living and the dead.

The air is thick with hunger. Edithe moves through the Liminal. Wrong. Something's coming and it's wrong. Lorraine mentioned that, didn't she? If the winds and the Liminal are restless, then something this way comes.

There was also the girl with the crack in her arm like a

porcelain doll. Instead of a hollow inside, she was filled with galaxies.

Rattling her thoughts, Edithe believes this means Lyza must have fallen from the stars the same way the old fairy tales used to say. A youngling was stolen by a goblin in the night, and the mother plunged from the sky into Deneb. The mother fell into the side of the mountains known as Morf Mountains. Of course, this is only a theory Edithe came up with.

She needs to return to Pyerre's Library, and quickly, for all Deneb might very well be in trouble. If the stardust child is cracking like clay, there's something wrong with the balance of the stars and Deneb.

Tugging on the line attaching her to the library, Edithe appears in the spot where her spirit lost its attachment to her material body. She remembers this spot all too well.

Her attachment to this very locale sealed her soul when she felt the cloth cover her face, blocking all her airways. Edithe remembers struggling, before darkness.

The darkness didn't scare her. It was losing Luella that struck a chord.

Luella was only four years old, and she'd lost her only parent. Edithe held onto the material world until the Liminal appeared, guiding her back to her daughter.

Since then, she's learned to use the tug and pull of the Liminal lines that connect the realms between.

As she turns in the spot where she had died, Edithe looks for a book. One specific book. She leans up against the shelf to a spot left empty where the book should be. Who took the book?

Evaporating and reappearing by her desk, Edithe scavenges the files in the documech—an enchanted file searcher mainly used by facilities like the library and the

Alchemadia. She searches for the title in its exact wording, "Human Powders." The results return with the book having been checked out. The date of checkout reads a week after her death.

Her hands fist. She grabs a piece of paper and taps on the dancing quill. It leaps onto her paper, and she whispers the exact pieces of the book she remembers.

From the precise species of plants used to grind to powder by humans, all the way down to the page numbers. Edithe documents as fast as her whispers can carry the quill across the page.

"Angel Wings, page 136. Hellebores, page 304. Marsh Callas, page 588. Roses, page 732." Edithe closes her eyes. Her spirit feels lighter. Her eyes burning from staring at the paper.

There's so much more to do. More, there's always more. The thought weighs her soul down, and she tucks the paper into her pocket.

She blinks around the library, collecting a pile of books. When her arms are too full, she appears in Pyerre's personal chambers at the very deep and dark core of the library. The floor she likes to refer to as the "dragon's depths," as Pyerre is a water-fire dragon.

There are a few bookshelves with space for the books to hide. Edithe busies herself gathering and collecting more books, moving them from the library's top floors to its dark, bottom depths.

Dawn soon approaches. But for a ghost, she doesn't register the time. It wasn't until Pyerre's presence awaiting her when she reappears with another pile of books in the pit of his personal chamber, that she pauses. His head tilts at her and again at the shelves now piled with books. "I didn't have time to ask for permission," Edithe explains.

Smoke seeps from the dragon's nostrils. "There is something we're all preparing for." His voice grumbles through the cavernous chamber. "The High Priestess of Ospheria is aware that the Queen of Ospheria is not dead, but alive. Whether the truth or not, she has cast her calls to Queen Aelyta and I to the Marigold Temple. I'm sure you'll relay the message for us or tell me now if the Queen lives."

"Yes, she is alive," Edithe's voice a mere whisper. "When will the meeting take place?"

The dragon, taking his time to turn through the chamber, replies, "On the first daughter of the week."

"Sunday," Edithe confirms.

Pyerre bows his head, but Edithe knows that is how he nods. As an immense dragon, moving is much slower in tight places. "Dawn has approached. Must you be somewhere at this hour?"

Edithe gasps and evaporates into the Liminal, her hand already holding the piece of Lyza's arm. A rock that is not from this world. Edithe tugs along the line attached to the rock, letting it guide her back to the child of another star.

14

See the Day

THE NEXT FEW DAYS, Aelyta has been reserved in her room most of the daytime. She only comes out in the evenings when Malo knocks on her door.

Every day, she sits on the floor in the closet of her bedroom, her red coronation dress folded neatly atop her lap. In her hands, she holds the intricate crown she was sworn to the throne with. Aelyta turns the crown over and over in an endless loop. From the black onyx of the center of the crown, to the little butterflies and mushrooms throughout, she rotates it slowly, as if she was spinning the swirling thoughts in her mind.

Why is her father doing this? If she proves her death is a hoax, will he try to execute her? A transfer of power is a process not to be reckoned with. If he took the power from her, it's not an easy feat to fight back, which is why she needs those books back in Avelmore.

The books passed down from her mother and her grandmother. They were details of a future that Deneb has long lost. History of reigns fighting against this very overtaking.

Her mother must have known that her father had this planned all along. Or else, she would not have left her subliminal messages in fairy tale books.

Aelyta can't fathom the idea that her mother had fallen in love with a man like her father. Her brain rattles with the mere thought of them in love. Her mother isn't even here to answer for herself.

It's probably the same way Aelyta has felt the target on her back since the moment she walked down the dais after her Rite of Divinity. Her father, as she suspected, must be behind her mother's death. This inkling of suspicion is the real reason Aelyta didn't want to marry for the sake of the crown.

If her mother followed the rules, played her cards exactly as they wanted her to, married the man, got the crown, why did she still end up dead in the end?

And now that Aelyta is out of Avelmore Castle, would her father continue to search for her? Seek for death?

Sighing, she places the crown gently onto the ground. Putting the dress back into the bottom drawer of the dresser tucked into her closet, she sits back and stares at the crown again. Rubbing her face, elbows digging into her inner knees, legs crossed. This can't be all just a game to her father. There must be more, more that she's not seeing, not in tune with. But knowing her father, he despises games. He can't play them, refuses to. Why this? Why now?

Aelyta gently places the crown on top of the dress in the drawer. She gently covers them up with the pile of clothes, fluffing them back up as if she hadn't patted them down. She rises from the ground with a guttural ache from her stomach and through her sides. She should eat something, but she doesn't have the energy for it—possibly because she waited too late to realize.

Somberly, she walks out onto the terrace of her bedroom. The sun is anchoring to set below the horizon. She puts a hand up to the sun, feeling the warmth on her palm, the sunlight streaming between her fingers. "I'm sorry." Aelyta's voice soft and reserved. "I have failed." The breeze swirls through her hair, pushing her petals past her face. "I've failed the Elementals, the people, the sovereignty, my mother..." Her voice drifts into the wind. "I am a failed queen."

"You didn't get a chance to be queen," a voice says from behind her. Malo steps up to the terrace banister next to her. "You never got the chance to show what you are truly made of. You're not a failed queen when you never got a chance to make a choice as queen."

"Then why do I feel like this?" She rests her head onto the banister.

"Probably because you waited too long to eat and your body is eating itself from the inside." Malo shrugs. "Besides"—he reaches out his hand—"you're too focused on what has already happened. You always have. It's good, studious. But one day, you'll wake up or—because it's you, you'll already be awake—you'll have a brilliant idea of what to do next. You are Queen whether the King tries to take that from you or not. You lit the candle on your Rite, you burned the strings measured from your very body, you have been dubbed worthy of being queen. Don't let an eager man take that Rite from you. But for now, I do need help with dinner. Would you mind chopping the vegetables? You were a great help last night—just chop them a bit more evenly this time?" Malo places a hand out before her.

A small smile crosses her face. She takes his hand, jolting them both with an electric shock on contact. He gestures towards the door, and she follows him out towards the kitchen.

The kitchen in Malo's house isn't as warm and toasty as the kitchen in Avelmore Castle, but she enjoys hanging out with Malo in the kitchen anyways. Boreas would never have let her pick up a knife. He'd never let her even separate the herbs from the stems, the easy, tedious work she could've helped with. But here, it was just her and Malo, and she felt obligated to help.

Malo taught her how to chop vegetables with a knife without cutting her fingers off. He also taught her how to properly scrub dishes to ensure they're clean. He showed her where everything is in the kitchen, had opened every cabinet, drawer, and pantry door. He taught her every usage and safety of the equipment from the basin to the cooktop.

As she quietly cut the onions in half, her hands were of use. The vegetables she helped prepare were of use. The herbs and flavoring she chose were of use.

It was a rewarding feeling unlike anything she's felt before. The closest might be when she was able to light her own fires in the fireplace in her chambers, but that was more rare and unlikely.

After enjoying the dinner Aelyta prepared with her own hands—a soup that warmed her from inside out—she left Malo with a polite "thank you," while her mind whirled at the way she wanted to look back at him before closing her bedroom door for the night.

When she awoke the next morning, she didn't have any idea on how to obtain her place as queen. Instead, she felt a surge of restlessness. The sun had shone early and bright almost five days in a row now. Something was absolutely eating inside her, and it was unrest for sunshine.

Leaping from the bed, bounding for the front door, Aelyta asked if she could help feed the moss sheep on the peninsula. Before leaving for the day, Malo showed her where the feed was stored for the fern-feathered chickens. For the moss sheep, he brought her a large tub to fill with water. "Oh, and if you ever get lost, the path circles the peninsula head, so no matter which direction you walk, it'll always lead back to the house," he advises before leaving her with a nod.

She rolled up the sleeves of her button-up top and went to work. Malo had showed her where the supplies are stored in the shed outside of the house, beyond the bridge, directly across from the main path. It's hidden in an alcove beneath the shades of trees.

Starting with a bucket, she fills it with chicken feed. The packaging drawn all over with fern-feathered chickens. She lifts the bucket onto the wagon before tossing in the bin for the moss sheep's water. She drags the wagon up the path into the midst of the peninsula where the trees open up to a flat meadow. There she finds the tips of the fern-feathers bouncing everywhere around the grass and wildflowers.

As instructed by Malo, she carries the bucket of feed over to where the chicken coop is hidden under a large mulberry tree. She opens the latch and the chickens bobble fast towards her. Without any time between, she throws the feed at the ground, and the chickens all ignore her instantly. Laughing at the way the chickens' curled ferned-tipped feathers sway as they peck at the feed, she makes her way deeper into the meadow where it opens to the clifftop. There she finds more than a dozen moss sheep lazing around the windblown meadow grass. She places the large empty bin onto the ground and drags the wagon back down to the storage shed. She fills the bucket with water from a spout jutting from the ground next to one of the shed walls.

Placing the bucket back into the wagon, she gently drags it back, albeit rather slower than she'd like. By the time she made it back to the bin, the moss sheep have all surrounded the bin, loudly beckoning for water. They almost trample her as she fills it up.

Aelyta settles on a rock near the cliff's edge, near enough to see the ocean, but far enough away for her safety. She watches the moss sheep meandering the meadow, drinking the water she offered. And on the other side of the cliff, she looks out towards the endless sea where the line splits between water and sky like the edge of the world.

The wind nipping at her warmed skin, she decides to take the long way back to the storage shed. Aelyta drags the wagon, continuing down the path to the far side of the peninsula she has yet to see. It's a downward walk from the clifftop, but from there, she can see the view of a cityscape far off in the distance on the other coastal edge.

That must be Elementropolis, where Malo's friends live and work. She scans the buildings, amazed by the colorful landscape. The mix of vibrant buildings and tall trees. Among the skyline, she spots a spheric copper rooftop with a tall spire.

From where she is, she can make out the shape of a dragon affixed onto the spire. It stands out among the square rooftops of the skyscrapers. That, she remembers, must be Pyerre's Library. A longing lingers inside her.

What must it be like to be among a dragon's collection of books?

As the path flattens out by the neck of the peninsula where the head meets the mainland beach, walled off with large iron gates covered in ivy, she lost herself in her imaginative idea of the library. She reaches the storage shed, storing the wagon away and latching the door closed. Aelyta rushes back into Malo's house and grabs a cup of water.

A piece of bread in hand, she walks over to the large window in the library nook and watches the lighthouse off in the distance. Her eyes linger on the book titles catching the afternoon sunlight. A book with embossed golden stars glittering in the light that catches her attention. She runs her finger down the spine that reads *The Start of Navigating Stars*. At closer examination, the book was written by someone named Sir Lemont Eldongarey. Carefully taking the book out of the slot on the shelf, she looks for any publication information, any published year, editor names, publication company, printer press. She flips through the first few pages, passing the title page and skimming the table of contents.

Her attention lands on chapter five, "Introduction to Astronomy." Chapter six refers to "The Application of Stargazing." She slowly flips through the pages, skimming each one until she reaches the first page of chapter five.

At first read, she couldn't quite comprehend the terms and factors that are acquired in stargazing. She didn't realize how complex the process actually was until she read through chapter six.

Chapter six discusses different stars as different planets, and how different angles in the sky have a specific meaning. In combination with other stars, they become a constellation. And in chapter seven she discovers the specific constellations, the planets and stars that make up those constellations.

By the time she finished rereading chapter five, Aelyta was excited to see the window pitch black. She heard a chuckle as she closed the book and turned to find Malo sitting in the other armchair, his elbow propping him up on the armrest.

"You didn't hear me, did you?" He chuckles more.

She shakes her head. "Sorry."

"Did you want to eat dinner before going out onto the boat tonight? It's more fun to see the stars in the middle of the ocean."

Aelyta jumps from the chair. "Yes. A thousand times, yes."

"Or"—Malo's hand is up to stop her from getting too excited—"we can take dinner out on the boat with us and eat under the stars."

Aelyta gasps for air, nodding with so much aggression as she listens to Malo instructing her on appropriate clothing attire and what to pack. Before he dismissed her, she was already sprinting for the stairs.

An excursion to see the stars? On a boat in the middle of the ocean with a questionably handsome shadow demon? If only he'd just display his jawline more often— nevertheless, Aelyta hasn't felt this excited about something in a long time.

15

Sea's the Night

MALO THROWS a large bag over his shoulders and carries a lantern in his hand. Aelyta follows him down towards the dock to the left of the main path. Throwing all the cargo into the boat, Malo holds out a hand towards Aelyta. She doesn't take it at first. But her initial step onto the deck of the boat, rocking it in the water, changes her mind. She grabs his hand and slowly climbs into the boat, sitting immediately on the seat next to the large wooden steering wheel. Malo climbs in after her and starts up the propeller in the back. With a large bang, the rotor starts. He unties the boat from the dock and settles himself in front of the steering wheel. Throwing a folded blanket onto her lap and turning on the lantern in the bow of the boat, they finally set off into the dark waters.

The moon waxes in a thin slit above them. The gusts build colder as they speed deeper out into the ocean. Aelyta quickly wraps her legs and tucks her arms into the blanket as they bounce over wave after wave. The air is salty, but it's always salty by the water. Now farther into the oceanic water, the salt is invasive. As her eyes adjust to the dimness around them, she can see the rippling of the sea below them and beyond, reflecting the little light of the moon. Although there isn't much moonlight in the darkness, there's enough to glimmer against the water.

Malo shuts off the rotor and drops an anchor down until the tied end of the rope tightens. He opens the bags he brought, taking out coppery spheric metals. Aelyta watches from under the blanket as he twists all the pieces together and opens a three-legged stand, locking the pegs on the bottom of each leg into the deck of the boat. He twists the large telescope onto the top of the stand. With one eye squinted, the other in the peephole, he swivels the telescope until he pauses, peeks up from the eyepiece, and a smile creeps through the shadowy mass covering his face. It was just a glimpse, but Aelyta could tell. From behind his dark facade, he's smiling at his discovery.

His hand reaches out towards her, beckoning her to him. She stands, rocking the boat, and quickly grasping his hand. He steadies her walk towards the telescope, careful not to bump into it. Holding her stable against the rocking, she peers into the peephole to see a resplendent, dancing planet. Aelyta draws herself away to look up at the little twinkling light among so many other twinkling stars. Peering into the telescope again, she sees the planet swirling in blue dust and pink clouds, dancing in the dark, vast space.

"It's beautiful," Aelyta gasps.

"What you're looking at is the Burgeon Nova." Malo flips through the book. "It's part of the floral constellation. See." He points to the page somewhere in chapter seven that Aelyta remembers. "This constellation will help steer you south if you follow the trail of petals it leaves."

Aelyta follows the line of his finger down the trail of

stars, and she backs up to see the floral constellation up above them. Malo flips through the pages again. "This one, here"—his hand keeping the pages open—"is known as the Mushroom King. He sits with his crown pointing north. Some call this point at the very top the North Star, but in Elementropolis, it's known as the King's Crown."

"The one that inspired the black onyx on the coronation crown," Aelyta notes.

"Yes." With his finger, Malo outlines another two sets of constellations in the sky. "And this is called the Insectal Wings. This one points to the east while the eyes point to the west. And with these three, we can navigate which direction we'll need to go. If you see these three stars overlapping, you are directly under the center of the constellational compass. That one is pretty neat to see in real time."

He gently hands her the book. She slowly takes it from him, reading the description on the overlapping stars while Malo peers into the peephole of the telescope. He turns and pivots until pausing with a gasp, looking down from the telescope at her. She looks up at him with his hand out waiting for her. "Whenever you're ready," he says.

Her hand reaches out towards his, her fingers zap at the touch of his skin. They both jump at the jolt of lightning. Aelyta hesitates, but Malo reaches out his hand again, firmly. She takes it. He ignores the shock and helps stabilize her walk towards him. He holds both her hands as she stands before the telescope, then moves one hand to her waist. Aelyta uses her free hand to hold the telescope up to her eye. Her other hand continues holding onto his. Through the peephole, a mass of darkness swirls with sparks of opalescent sparkles leaping around the swirling dark cloud of shadows. She gasps at the sight. "What star is that?" She looks at Malo.

"The North Star," he replies. "The onyx on the crown of the Mushroom King."

Aelyta takes control of the telescope, scanning the sky of stars and planets. Malo digs through the bags he brought with them. The boat rocks gently, but Aelyta has gotten the hang of keeping herself steady. Every now and then she gasps, asking Malo what the star is, paying little attention to what he's doing.

As soon as she looks away from the telescope, up to the sparkling stars above, shooting stars sparkle across the sky. Aelyta squeals, surprising herself. Malo looks up from the canvas, putting down the paintbrush in his hand before realizing the many shooting stars flying above them.

"Right"—he rests his paintbrush—"you can't see the shooting stars from Avelmore Castle."

"Not even from the Royal Academy," she adds. "Nor from the sovereign kingdom."

Curling herself back into her spot next to Malo's steering seat, she leans back to watch the flying stars streaming through the sky. Malo returns to his canvas. The only sound is the water lapping the side of the boat. With her head still resting on the backrest, Aelyta turns to Malo.

She watches his hand flicking the paintbrush in small strokes on the canvas. She looks at his shadow-masked head. A small dip in her chest when she catches the glimpse of recognition, but who is Malo?

"Is it tiring to use your magic as long as you do around me?" Aelyta breaks the silence.

He pauses his paintbrush, and his head tilts in thought. "It's..." he starts. "I guess the best way to describe it to someone who's never used magic before..." he tries again. "It's like using a muscle, like using your lungs to breathe. You wouldn't think about it until it becomes strenuous."

"Is hiding your face worth the strain?"

"No, but using the Shadow Realm to shield the group at your coronation night and bringing you to my house is comparable to running for three hours without end."

"How did you discover that you had magic?"

He softly dabbles the paintbrush onto the canvas. "I was a little kid." His head tilts as he examines his brush work, dabbing the tip of the brush into the paint palette and dragging strokes along the canvas.

"I manipulated the shadows on the walls to form shapes, then proceeded to learn all sorts of things. Lorraine has a unique magic. It's not unique for bug descendants to understand the language of the winds. She can listen to the winds, but she is so in tune, she can even see the movements of the wind. She says it's like weather forecasting. She can forecast the wind's shapes and the way they move through objects and people. I say it's probably because her eyes are so buggy big."

Malo chuckles, before continuing. "Kody is a mix of bug and floral descendants, but he's gotten more floral magic than either side. It's probably what makes him an inquisitive alchemist. But I have an inkling he might also have some shroom in his family line somewhere. Edithe, when she was alive, could do majestic work with the air. She can sense when Elementals are lying. I think she may still have that ability even after death, but that may also be due to her knowing people and elements so well."

"How did you meet them?"

"Lorraine, Kody, and I met when we were still attending Clair O'voyance School for the Elements, uh, grade school. I believe we were as young as five years old. I met Edin and Edithe through Kody. They're his aunts. We would visit Kody, and the twins were there. Kody lost both his parents. So, losing Edithe was pretty rough on him, but he would never show it for the sake of Luella. Edithe was a single mother, and we all helped care for her and Luella when Luella's father refused to step up to the plate."

He lifts the canvas up to eye-level, then lays it back onto his lap.

"I'm not sure what Luella's magic is, but being a part of all sixteen years of her life is already a blessing."

"You care for them." Aelyta tilts her head. Not in curiosity, Aelyta gazes at Malo with eyes of admiration.

They sit in silence for a little while longer. Aelyta tosses the blanket over her legs, pulling it up over her arms.

Interrupting the silence she says, "I would think my magic is to stay as warm as a lizard. I wonder what magic replication means. Cory said I have magic replication right before the proposal. I have no idea what he means. Royals don't have magic."

"That"—Malo points the end of the paintbrush at her—"I don't know, but you're right. A royal rarely ever has magic."

"I know, right?" She turns back to the stars. Vibrant, colorful ribbons stream through the sky. As the boat rocks to and fro, the sound of the water lapping against the sides mixes with Malo's paintbrush against the canvas. Aelyta's eyes grow heavier with every blink until she dreams of dancing among the stars of black dust and blue clouds.

Aelyta startles awake to the rumbling of the rotor starting up. Sitting up in her seat, she turns to Malo, who's pulling the anchor up from the water.

"Sorry." He settles behind the large wooden steering wheel. "I didn't mean to wake you."

"Are we heading back now?" she asks.

"Yes." He directs the boat slow and steady. Aelyta frowns. He glances at her. "Where do you want to go?"

She hesitates before softly answering, "I slightly would like to see the lighthouse."

"Oh!" Malo exclaims. "We can make a short stop there."

Aelyta's face lights up as Malo steers the wheel left instead of right. From their distance, the lighthouse is a small spinning cylinder of light as the beam circles around the top of the tower.

"What's the history of the lighthouse?" Aelyta yells over the speed of the boat soaring through the crashing waves.

"It's called the Lover's Light," he howls back. "It's been said that the lighthouse was built by a woman who wanted to see her husband sail safely home. She built him a lighthouse so he may see the way home to her in the dark of night."

"She lived in that lighthouse by herself?" Aelyta exclaims.

Malo laughs. "No, no. She had children. One of which was my great-grandfather. He's the one that built the house I live in now."

"That's magnificent history!" Aelyta cries. "I don't think my parents or even grandparents were ever close to being that romantic."

"But wasn't Cory's proposal to you romantic enough?" Malo asks. "I mean, the man literally proposed in the garden your mother created by her own hands."

Aelyta chuckles. "It must have sounded like that through word of mouth. But if you were there to witness the entire proposal—"

"I was," Malo blurts.

"And do you think that was out of love?" Aelyta gives him a look of shock.

Malo pauses. "No, you're right. If I were to ask someone to spend a lifetime with me, I would have done things much differently."

"How would you have done it?" She leans against the armrest closest to Malo, pulling herself up on the chair.

"I'd want her to feel seen and listened to, so it depends on who she is," Malo begins. "But if I were to propose to someone like you, I would take you to a place full of history—not bad history like war or destruction—but a history of everlasting love. I'd take you to somewhere like..."

"Lover's Light?" Aelyta finishes his thought.

"Exactly." Malo nods as he slowly reels the boat into the lighthouse harbor. He ties the rope to the dock and aids Aelyta off the boat.

"Would you propose right here on the dock, or...?" Aelyta looks around the small island where the tall hill beholds the spiraling tower of light.

"Hmm." Malo turns about. "Let me show you."

He leads her to the end of the dock where a brick path weaves through tall grass lining sandy beaches. They walk uphill, not up to the lighthouse, but around the hillside overlooking the ocean. Firefly flowers glow in the dark of night as tall as the cattails swaying in the breeze. The sky overflows with flying stars above them.

"What's the history here?" Aelyta asks.

"I've been told that my great-great-grandmother loved firefly flowers because they're like stars among the grass." Malo runs his hands through the uncut grass. "Her husband would bring one home from his voyages. It's been said that he would uproot them so that they may grow wherever she wanted to plant them. He refused to cut them. You know, in case they might die before he got back to her. The story is that he would care for the flowers in pots on his boat until he arrived to her. He would visit multiple places in one trip, so he would arrive here with a crate full of firefly flowers. It kept her busy, planting each one when he'd set off on another voyage."

"So, each of these flowers are from different parts of the world." Aelyta bends down to admire them. The large flower face similar to dinnerplate dahlias, but the petals glow in the night like stars in the sky.

In the center of the circular brick patio, Malo starts a fire in the fire brass. Aelyta walks over to warm her hands.

"What's that sound? It sounds like music." Aelyta looks around the hillside.

Malo chuckles. "That is the sound of the night birds and the crickets."

"Well, it sounds like music." She begins to twirl, mimicking a waltz. She gestures for him to join her and he swoops in, taking her by the hand and waist.

Laughter intermingles with the sounds of the bird song. As their twirling slows, staring deep into his shadows, Aelyta reaches her hand up to touch his face. Her hand disappears into the shadowed mask until her fingers zap at the touch of his skin. He winces, but he doesn't pull away. His hand reaches behind her neck, pulling her closer to him. His palm runs down to catch her chin as he tilts her face up to his shadows. His thumb brushes against the bottom of her lips, fluttering little electric zips along her skin. Her hand trails up his neck until she feels the touch of his hair. She runs her fingers through it as he whispers, "Ready whenever you are."

Her eyes lift up towards the white glow of his through his swirls of shadows.

Hesitating, she holds back. Simply taking in the way the

shadows curl, she studies their pattern over his face. Her eyes land on where she guesses his lips are. Fighting the urge to find out their taste, she bites her own.

She nods once before he presses his lips to hers. Her hand grips the back of his head. His hands hold the back of her neck.

Lightning flashes, but they refuse to let go. Their lips dance with one another, refusing to breach for air. His mouth slides down her jawline, cand he plants a kiss on her neck.

His eyes soften as he stares into hers, illuminated like the firefly flowers surrounding them. "Don't be afraid of your potential," he murmurs. "Your intelligent and ambitious. Don't run from the men who underestimate you."

Her eyes narrow at his glowing brighter. "And you are afraid of your shadows. I can feel it every time you pull me into your Shadow Realm, the way you tense."

"My shadows hide the past I refuse to bring to light," he answers, pulling away from her.

She pulls him back. "Is that why you stopped coming to my chambers? Or is it because I asked Cory to ask me to marry him?"

"See, intelligence," he chuckles. Aelyta rolls her eyes at his comment. He continues, "You were engaged to him. I didn't know if you had feelings for him or..."

"Itzal? Jaycub? I'm surrounded by men," she jokes.

"You being around men doesn't make me nervous. In fact," he jokes back, "I liked that you stormed into the advisors' meeting after they canceled on you."

"And how do you know about that?" She tilts her head, a smile enlarging.

He steps back, his face widening.

"Show me, show me!" she squeals. "Is Itzal your real form or your shadows?"

"Itzal is my human form when I have to disguise among other humanoids. But my natural form is my Elemental form." He gestures to his shadowed head.

"So shadow demon is your natural state?"

"Precisely." The smoky shadows evaporate from his head revealing Itzal's face and brown hair.

"Is it strenuous holding up your unnatural form? You can just keep yourself comfortable in your natural state around me from now on." She steps close to him. "I beg you, don't strain yourself anymore."

"Yes, Your Majesty." He plants a kiss on her lips.

Aelyta pulls away from him with a smile. "Come on, let's go home."

16

Blanket of Darkness

THE LIGHT of the firefly flowers softly dims as the sky awakens with the rising sun. Malo steers the boat into the dock by the house. Aelyta helps unload and Malo helps her step off the boat. Together, they carry the bags up to the house. They drop them in the foyer and Aelyta proceeds to the sitting room, Malo following behind.

He spins her around, his hands locking behind her lower back. With instinct, her hands grip the back of his neck. He brushes the tip of his nose along hers. She leans up, taking his lips. Electric shock runs through their lips, only deepening their kiss.

They clamor up the stairs entangled in each other's hands, hair, and limbs. Refusing to release even for a breath, they burst into Aelyta's bedroom. She turns, pushing him to sit on the bed and climbs on top of him. He pulls her against himself, feeling what he needs beneath her. He looks up at her, she can't see the expression on his face, but she can feel the plea in the way his shadows swirl around his head. She nods and he pulls her down to the bed.

The morning blends into afternoon as they lay in the bed, intertwined limbs and lips. They don't talk, simply being together is enough. Silence turns to the soft hums of snores.

Aelyta faces forward, blinking, the glare of the sun catching her eyes. She blinks harder, squinting. She sees her own gold irises staring straight at her. Her soft black hair petals flowing in the wind, but she doesn't feel it. Aelyta blinks again. Now, she's staring deep into the face of a shimmering being blinking back at her. "Who are you?" Aelyta asks, her voice muffled.

The being shifts into focus. Aelyta notices her white hair, her black eyes, and the golden glow of her skin. Aelyta bows, but the being catches her chin, lifting her up. The being shakes her head. "A queen does not bow to a goddess." The being's voice sings like the songs of winds. Aelyta lulls to the sound of her voice.

"Goddess? Ko'nkian?" Aelyta's eyes widen, her voice even more muffled as she tries to yell.

The goddess takes Aelyta's hands and dips them into warm soil overflowing from the goddess's palm. Aelyta's arms glow gold like the goddess. "The Empress," the goddess's voice melodic, "is made of the soil. She is fertile and soft. But the earth is not weak. Her vulnerability is not weakness. She is a force of nature. She nurtures, but she is also fierce when threatened."

Aelyta stares at the goddess growing into the shimmering being once again. The goddess sings, "Mother of the soil, Mother of the winds, Mother of humanity." The goddess grips Aelyta's chin. She plants a kiss on Aelyta's left eyelid. "We'll meet again soon." The goddess harmonizes with the sound of the ocean waves crashing against rock.

Aelyta leaps up in the bed at the sound of conversation in the distance. The sun leans in the horizon towards sunset. She's sitting in her bed in her room alone. Malo must be talking to someone downstairs. She quickly dresses and heads down. In the living room, she discovers Edithe floating above Malo, who's curled on the sofa. They both turn to her as she enters the room.

Edithe flies towards Aelyta as they hear the sound of the front door slamming closed. The two of them turn to see Lorraine running through the foyer towards them. "You." Lorraine points.

"Me?" Edithe and Aelyta point at themselves.

"Not you." Lorraine brushes. "You." She stalks towards Edithe, getting in between her and Aelyta. "Don't you dare touch her."

"What did I do?" Edithe crosses her arms. "You didn't come all the way from the city to keep her from getting a stomachache, did you?"

"You didn't do anything, yet." Lorraine blocks Aelyta from Edithe.

Aelyta peers over Lorraine's extended arms at Malo, who's slinking away to the kitchen. He catches her glancing over at him and shrugs as he disappears behind the wall.

Edithe rolls her eyes. "I can still float through you." Edithe passes through Lorraine's body. Lorraine scoffs, then her stomach gurgling causes her face to twist into a squeal. Edithe laughs, pointing at Lorraine struggling with her bodily sounds. Lorraine runs up the stairs to the bathing room, squealing and cursing at Edithe.

Aelyta blinks at Edithe as if she carries a disease.

"My spiritual being gives people stomachaches when I

pass through them. It comes in handy a lot." Edithe chuckles.

"That cannot be why she came all this way to warn me." Aelyta shakes her head.

"No, but I came here to tell you." Edithe's demeanor shifts into a darker essence. "Pyerre has disappeared from his library for the first time in almost three centuries. He wants to meet with you at the Marigold Temple. It's the place of worship for the Goddess Ko'nkiun on an island in the Cygni Sea." Edithe turns to Aelyta.

Aelyta nods. "I know of the Marigold Temple. It's where the High Priestess of Ospheria spends her time outside of Ospheria."

"We can use the shadows to travel there, but we'd still have to take the boat," Malo chimes from the archway between the kitchen and the living room with a plate in his hands. He hands Aelyta the plate. "With the dark of night, it would be easier to travel either way."

"That's eventful," Lorraine adds as she descends the stairs. "Pyerre doesn't leave his library—ever."

Malo walks towards the foyer, grabbing a heavy-knitted sweater. He walks back to the three of them, turning to Lorraine. "What brought you here anyways?" He hands Aelyta the sweater, rubbing her fingers under the fabric.

"You know, ignorance is a bliss." Lorraine shrugs. "Let's go." She gestures to the foyer.

They chase Lorraine out the door, through the bridge, and onto the peninsula. Lorraine laughs as they inquire for more information from her. She simply waves her hand, brushing them off. "I'll tell you guys when it's time."

They make their way down the path towards the dock

where the boat bobs along with the waves. They file onto the boat carefully, one after the other. They all install themselves into a seat; Lorraine and Edithe inside the main cabin, with Malo behind the large wooden wheel and beside him, Aelyta.

Malo engulfs them in his shadows. He glances at Aelyta, who's taken in by the Shadow Realm. She turns to look at him, but he faces forward, powering the boat out into the ocean. From their spot at the wheel, they can hear Lorraine and Edithe bantering in the cabin below. Aelyta sticks her tongue out at Malo and joins the other ladies.

Malo steers the boat through his Shadow Realm over the ocean waves. The Shadow Realm is like a cloaking of the real realm, where Malo can control the shadow's ebb and flow.

In the cabin, Aelyta discovers Lorraine and Edithe hovering over a canvas painting. Edithe pushes it into Aelyta's hands. She looks down to see a rendering of her lounging in her favorite wingback chair. Her legs slung over the armrest, dangling in the silver stream of sunlight peeking through the golden curtains. She's been painted with a book held tightly in her hands and a blanket tucked high under her chin.

Unsure which question to ask first, if she should even ask any of them aloud, she stutters, "I have had multiple opportunities to have my likeness painted, but never one so candid."

"You should definitely keep it." Lorraine winks at her. Aelyta smiles softly to herself, placing the canvas down on the bench next to her. They're seated in the dining nook of the cabin. A small kitchenette tucked across from the table and sitting booths. In the back, the sliding doors are open, revealing the sleeping quarters.

Lorraine and Edithe turn to each other. Edithe asks,

"How's your cafe doing these days? I heard there are a few shops closing their doors for an uncertain period of time. Nobody can afford the Morf Blue, and Morf Crystals are all used up."

"Kody had to close his clinic the other day." Lorraine sighs. "I'm serving normal java drinks, but there are a lot less people coming in for enchantional drinks."

"I get it." Edithe shrugs. "At the library, we had to go back to using normal ink and paper. The work has been overwhelming. We have been looking for more help, but everyone else is also looking for more help. The competition has been fierce."

"I had to let a few employees go these past couple days alone." Lorraine exhales, a hand at her temple.

"What are you two discussing?" Aelyta leans in.

"Morphenum, also known as the Morf Crystals," Edithe answers. "It's what powers the enchantments for Elementropolis. It used to be mined on Morf Mountain, but Richards has stopped supplying the material to the city. He's pushing for a new product called Morf Blue, but most Elementals can't stand the way it makes them feel. The post-effect or the come down can be nauseating, even the risk of death is possible."

"The weirder part is that these deaths linked to Morf Blue have not been made public, only through word of mouth."

"That is weird," Aelyta gasps.

"That's not the weirdest part," Lorraine continues. "The bodies of these dead go missing before the reports are even made!"

"If there are deadly side effects, why push for Morf Blue?"

Malo pops his head in. "That's because he's cut a deal

with Miles." Aelyta, Lorraine, and Edithe peer over at him. "We're also approaching Marigold Temple soon, wanted to give you all a heads-up. The Shadow Realm helped speed the travel a bit." He nods to himself as he leaves the cabin. The three of them turn back to each other.

They look out the window to see an island large enough for a golden temple, which is erected in the center, surrounded by bright orange marigolds and swirls of cabbages. A dock juts from the island, long enough for twenty boats. A woman stands with a golden cloak dancing in the wind. Aelyta recognizes the High Priestess awaiting their boat.

Edithe rises from the booth first, Lorraine following behind. Aelyta glides out the other side of the seat engrossed in her thoughts. Lorraine's hand touches her back and Aelyta whips her head up to look at her. Edithe leads the way as they depart from the cabin. Lorraine assists Aelyta out of the cabin, hand gently under Aelyta's elbow and the other on her back.

A chilling numbness crawls up Aelyta's arm where Lorraine's fingers touch the skin of her elbow.

The ocean breeze rushes against her face as they step onto the upper deck of the boat.

Aelyta pulls from Lorraine's touch, the wind nipping and pulling along her skin. Voices surge through her head in every direction the gusts blow.

"Listen, listen," the voices rasp. "*The soil of this earth urges you to listen. The trees, the fauna, the beings, and life. We beg you to listen. The Flower Queen is the kin of Death.*"

The voices deafening, Aelyta looks to Lorraine, her eyes wide. Lorraine's mouth is moving as if she's speaking to Aelyta, but she can't hear what she's saying. The voices of the wind scream louder as the gusts blow harder.

"The death is near. Death is near," the voices bellow. Aelyta covers her ears and drops to the floor. She gapes up at Lorraine and Edithe.

Malo pulls Lorraine back, pointing somewhere in the distance. Aelyta closes her eyes. She feels Malo placing his hands over Aelyta's ears and shadows emerge around them again. The voices break away, silence rings through her ears.

Aelyta opens her eyes. She feels the tears climbing the edges. Malo's thumbs rub her cheeks before he drops his hands down from her ears. He doesn't speak as she pulls him into her embrace. She holds him tight as he rubs her back. He doesn't pull away.

"Magnetic magic," he mutters. "You have magnetic magic."

"I don't think this is magnetic...

What else could it be?"

Malo shrugs. "I don't know. I just know Cory said you have a kind of magic replication. I feel a magnetic pull towards you when we touch as if you're attracting my magic."

Finally, she pulls away from him. "The winds are revolting against my father," she says to him. He doesn't reply. "The earth is angry, and..."

"Ready when you are." Malo bows his head to her.

She lifts his head to face her. "Good." A smile grows, teeth glowing through his shadowy mask, a gleam in his glowing eyes. He rises from the ground, his hand outstretched.

She takes it as she emerges from the shadows first, then Malo. The wind whips across her skin, but the voices no longer yell.

17

Sitting Ducks

As THEY NEAR the old wooden docks, Malo cuts the auto-paddles to steady the boat into the harbor. Lorraine reaches out to Malo, a look of panic in her large insect eyes. "Cloak us!" she screams. "Now! Cloak us!"

Malo takes his hands off the wheel of the boat. Before the shadows swarm them, a buzzing vibrates through the air. A dark cloud covers overhead.

Aelyta and Edithe look up. It's not a cloud but a mass of large mechanically-winged hornets hovering over the temple. The same emblem worn by the knights on the night of her coronation is plastered onto the sides of each hornet cavalry. Unlike the ones she saw at the coronation, these hornets are larger than three knights tall.

The High Priestess runs inside the temple. But no sooner, an immense hornet goes flying towards the building, crashing into its walls, crushing the intricate structure.

Aelyta screams for the priestess, leaping for the dock. Lorraine grabs hold of her, causing Aelyta to hear the screaming winds again. She collapses to the ground. Lorraine yells to Malo, who is struggling with turning the rotor back on. Edithe helps Lorraine as they usher Aelyta back into the boat's shelter. More hornets fly into the temple's remaining structure.

A heart-stopping roar rumbles from inside the building. A blue dragon bursts from the hole in the crumbling temple. Pyerre extends his wings, erupting massive winds towards the mechanical hornets. Only a couple hornets were indisposed from the impact. The dragon whips his wings, blasting more gusts towards the mechanical insects. Pyerre circles the sky, going up higher. Higher, until he is one with the sun. Raining down towards the mass of hornets, bursting from his mouth, not fire, but flames of water and crystal. Little under half the mass of mechanical hornets are left.

Aelyta didn't see the men on the back of the hornets ready to dismount from the mechanical insects. From the other side of the Marigold Temple, she spots four robes she knows all too well. The Royal Advisors glide onto the island from a mechanical floating platform, held by four winged Elementals.

Breaking free from their hold, Aelyta rushes to the edge of the boat. Lorraine and Edithe hold her back before she could jump into the water. Lorraine whips her head around to Malo. "Shadow Realm," she grits through her teeth.

Aelyta quivers to the ground, covering her ears. The winds are screaming, *"The sword!"* Lorraine turns to see the four Royal Advisors disappearing into the temple.

Pyerre continues raining flames of water down onto the mechanical hornets. The hornets spread out around the dragon with their thorax point spraying large needles into the dragon. Some hit the dragon's hard shell, but the needles are small enough to penetrate between the dragon scales. Pyerre swings his tail, and the hornets use their sharp points to sting him. The dragon screams a thunderous cry. He attempts to fly higher, but four men on the backs of hornets shoot a net over him. Pyerre misses two, but the other two tangle around the dragon. He plummets towards the marigolds and cabbages planted around the temple island. The foundation of the temple halts his fall.

The four Royal Advisors step out from the now ruined temple.

Aelyta gasps at the sight of them. A blue gilded sword in the hands of one of the advisors can be seen from the boat.

Aelyta recognizes it. The Goblin Sword. The only sword to have slain the once mighty Butterfly Queen. Is that why they're here? To find a weapon worthy of killing her?

The wind screams around them as Aelyta, Lorraine, and Edithe watch from the boat. The Royal Advisors mount the floating platform. The mechanical hornets take off with Pyerre tangled in the nets attached by metal ropes.

The boat speeds into the coast of the island. Aelyta leaps onto land and runs for the High Priestess still inside the damaged temple. Malo and Lorraine following quickly behind her. The large doorway is no longer an intricate entrance to the temple. Boulders and debris now block the way in, but Aelyta is small enough to slink into the holes made in the wall of the structure.

Edithe appears before her with a hand in front of Aelyta. "I'm a dust reader." Edithe gestures to her. "I read the patterns of the dust that befalls upon things, people, whatever have you. For example, fingerprints left on pages covered in dust. I can read who they are and what they were doing. It makes it a great skill to have while working in the archive industry."

Aelyta nods, giving Edithe the lead as the ghost scans the debris still floating in the air.

"This way." Edithe lunges for an opening on the first floor. "Watch your step!" the ghost yells over her shoulder.

The opening leads up a flight of broken stairs. Edithe scans the room. Her head stops turning at the sight of another archway.

Aelyta follows her through it and up untouched stairs. They make their way down a breezeway.

From above, Aelyta and Edithe can see the amount of damage to the temple structure. Aelyta gasps at the sight as Edithe hurries them along. The breezeway leads to another set of stairs that take them up to a grand room with no walls or windows. The room is a circular shape with pillars holding a pearl-domed roof. In the center of the grand room is a golden statue of a woman.

At the feet of the statue, golden fabric is splayed out onto the stone floor. The golden cloak of the High Priestess. Blood pools around her.

Aelyta rushes to the High Priestess. Malo and Lorraine rush into the grand room as Edithe examines the body.

Aelyta clutches the face of the High Priestess. She doesn't hold in the tears leaping from her eyes. The High Priestess has a wide wound at the crook of her neck, blood covering her body and Aelyta's.

She doesn't look at the others to confirm what her heart already feels.

The High Priestess lies limp as Aelyta clutches the blessed priestess to her chest.

No one rushes her as she mourns.

Edithe stands before the statue. Lorraine gestures to Malo before she leaves the room. Malo walks up to the statue alongside Edithe.

The ghost explains, "Her name is Marigold. The Mother. She is the protector of the goblin and the sword. The Wind Slayer. A legend in an ancient tale that many have long forgotten."

The ghost reaches her hand up to the statue.

The woman holds a braided string of small golden bells in her hand. Edithe runs her hand along the braid up to the woman's hand. The gold bells are soundless as Edithe moves her hand back along the braid.

The string slips from the statue into the ghost's fingers. She hands the bells to Malo before following Lorraine out of the grand room.

He bounces the bells in his hand. No sound comes from the soft, metal material dangling on the braided string. He tucks the bells into his pocket for when the time is right.

Malo waits beside Aelyta as she says her goodbyes to the golden-cloaked priestess. Lorraine and Edithe find a place to build a large kindling for the High Priestess. Once they were finished, they went back up to help the other two carry the priestess to the pile. Lorraine starts a fire and says a blessing as she sets the kindling aflame. Aelyta holds in her tears, crying for the dead will only keep them tied to the material world. She bites her tongue and grits her fingers as she refuses to make a sound. A High Priestess deserves to pass on to the spiritual world as one who has devoted herself to be the messenger of the Goddess Ko'nkiun.

The kindling slowly builds. But as the wind gusts through, the flame ignites, engulfing the entire kindling and the High Priestess, sending a tower of gold smoke into the sky. Before everyone else, Lorraine takes her departure back to the pier to wait for the others on the boat. She rubs Aelyta's back before making her descent.

Malo takes a place behind Aelyta. Refusing to blink despite the heat of the fire, she watches the flames dissolve every material within its power.

When all that is left of the fire is flames, smoke, and ash, Aelyta turns to see Malo still standing behind her. He reaches out a hand. He doesn't say it, but she hears it anyway. *Ready when you are.* The corners of her lips go up as she attempts to smile, but a whimper escapes her instead. Her hand finds his and he pulls her into an embrace. She doesn't let the tears out. Breathing, no matter how staggering. She inhales. Holds. Exhales.

"Ready." She nods against Malo's chest. "I'm ready." Holding her close to him, he wraps her wrist with a braided string dangling with gold bells. He gives her a nod before they walk together down to the boat and climb aboard. Aelyta turns to the other three and says, "Let's go free the dragon."

The four Royal Advisors remove their hoods, their white, thinning hair exposed to the setting sunlight. The platform transportation hovers at the speed of four winged Elementals, making the distance over the open ocean towards Muddy Bay. Ansaldo holds the ancient sword in his hands. Menecrates, his cousin, stands beside him looking out towards the horizon. The brothers, Constantine and Columba behind them, facing each other as the platform buzzes over the coast and over land.

18

Bottom of the Bay

LORRAINE SITS NEXT to Malo on the deck of the boat while Aelyta sits inside the cabin away from the wind. Lorraine turns to Malo and confronts him. "What stopped you from cloaking us in your Shadow Realm?"

Malo shakes his head gently. "I don't want to talk about it."

"No, I need an explanation," Lorraine quips. "We have the Queen of Ospheria crippled with magic she's never experienced before, a dragon was just attacked and captured before our very eyes, and the High Priestess of Ospheria has just been murdered. Explanation, please."

Malo sighs. "I needed her to see it. No more hiding. No more manipulating the elements. No more running from the truth."

"And you think she would have been fine with you becoming one with the High Priestess?"

"Me...becoming one with the High Priestess? How does that work? What does that even mean?"

"I don't know." Lorraine hesitates. "I forecasted that you would take the place of the High Priestess. The patterns have not been what I'm used to reading. You see, when I see the winds surrounding you, I see the face of three. I assume that means the High Priestess and you." Lorraine slaps Malo's arm.

"You know I will always protect you guys. If we had been in line of attack"—Malo keeps his eyes forward as he steers the wheel—"I would have brought us into the Shadow Realm."

"You still can't do what you're told, can you?" Lorraine demands.

"I appreciate that, Malo." Aelyta leans against the doorway of the cabin and the deck. "I also appreciate being looked after." She turns to Lorraine. "But I am tired of these old gas-holes." She steps onto the deck. "I'm fed up with these aging, old men who think they can take control of the Elementals and use them however they please—simply because they believe they hold the power to do so. I don't care if I don't assume the throne, or obtain the crown, or even if the Elementals see me fit to be queen." She turns to Malo. "Ospheria is full of unique equations of the ancient descendants. The Elementals are made of the soil, the air, the fire, and ocean's deep."

"And as our limbs reach the light, we grow towards a better future," Malo recites.

Lorraine continues, "May we interlock our vines together. May we grow from the dirtied soil..."

Aelyta finishes, "Newer, richer, and stronger than those that came before."

"I would have liked you as queen." Lorraine sighs. "You would have wobbled a bit in the beginning. But once your roots were planted, you would be one hell of a queen."

"She is a helleborus Queen." Malo chuckles. He swivels

the wheel. "Oh, we're coming up on Muddy Bay. Hold on, it's going to get mushy."

"Mushy?" Aelyta asks. "What does that mean?"

Edithe, quiet the entire boat ride, chimes in, "Muddy Bay once didn't exist. Pyerre has been living away from the water for so long that the river slowly dried up into a marshy delta known as Muddy Bay."

"Why did Pyerre stay away from the water?"

"I'd hate to talk poorly of Pyerre, but he is a dragon after all. A water-fire dragon to be exact. His line of descendants has kept the water flowing in all of Deneb. He once said that the river was so wide, you couldn't see the other side."

"Is that why he was captured? To bring back the flood?"

"I don't know." The ghost pauses. "Something is calling for me...I think I must go..." With that, Edithe evaporates into the air.

"Bye." Aelyta gawks at the space left empty where Edithe had occupied moments earlier.

The boat no longer glides along the water, sinking and jutting through the marsh-heavy river. Aelyta grips the handles leading into the lower deck. Lorraine, trying to get herself on the deck, bounces around the boat. Aelyta grabs her with one arm and guides her towards the cabin. Together, they grip the table and bench as Malo maneuvers the boat through the dense waters.

"The marsh is too thick!" Malo yells from the wheel. "We'll have to go up and over. I think I know where they're headed."

"Where?" Aelyta returns.

"They didn't fly into Muddy Bay." Malo swivels the wheel. "They went westward."

"Morf Mountain?" Lorraine asks. "That's as far west until Deneb ends. There's nothing else there."

Speeding parallel to the coastline, they head for the edge of the mountain range in the west. Aelyta stares out of the window of the lower deck, watching Muddy Bay disappear out of view.

"What are we going to do once we get to Morf Mountain?" Lorraine asks.

Aelyta looks away from the window and shrugs. "I'm sure it's probably heavily guarded. If the Richards own it, the guards are there. Security will be top-notch, which I suppose is why they're taking Pyerre there."

"Then you'll need me to get through them." Malo ducks belowdecks. "You two ready? I'm going to pull the boat up as far into the shore without damaging her."

"Aye, aye," Lorraine affirms.

The waves are choppier as they reach the shore. The boat bobbing until the bottom catches on shallow land. Aelyta rolls her pant legs up and jumps over the railing along with Lorraine and Malo. The three of them tug the boat behind a cluster of rocks, away from high waves. Malo grabs a bag of supplies he had stored under Lorraine's seat. Lorraine and Aelyta exchange smiles.

"What?" Malo scoffs. "I like being prepared."

"I like that you're prepared." Aelyta pats the back of his head. Malo blushes when Lorraine giggles at the two of them.

Unlike the sandy shores surrounding Elementropolis, the shoreline is rough with rocks. Large pebbles crinkle under their feet.

Towering over them, the canyons of Morf Mountain look to have no way upward. "Do we climb the mountainside?" Aelyta places a hand on the large slab of rock jutting from the earth.

"I think we can use the Shadow Realm until we get past the guards," Lorraine suggests. "Right?" She turns to Malo for confirmation.

Malo looks up and down the foothills of the mountain range. "I think we can walk further down south. The Richards have been excavating materials on Morf Mountain for three generations now. There should be a path leading to the excavation site."

"That's true." Aelyta nods. "Morf Mountain has a long history in Ospheria, even in all of Deneb, that dates back as far as the old fairy tales began."

"The winds are not happy here." Lorraine's hand reaches for her face, covering the bottom half with her hands. Leaving only her large insect eyes glittering at them. "They want us to turn back." Her hands cover her eyes. "I don't think we should go any further."

Aelyta places a hand on Lorraine's arm to comfort her, but the screams spiraling through her catch Aelyta off balance. She stumbles, and Lorraine tumbles with her. The wind screams, *"Away. Stay. Away. Stay. Away..."*

"Pyerre," Aelyta whimpers in response.

The wind relents. *"The flowers at their fullest bloom...will be crops of goods."*

Lorraine stares at Aelyta. "Harvest."

Malo helps them both up. Aelyta's legs are tingling as if waking from sleep. "But it's not yet the harvest season, we're barely at the peak of the solar season."

Shaking her head, Lorraine's voice quivers. "Not that kind of harvest."

"Then we shouldn't enter Morf Mountain," Malo states.

"I'm confused." Aelyta steps back, hands up in defense.

"Who's harvesting? Are the Richards harvesting more crystals from the mountain? Why take Pyerre? And why use the Royal Advisors to bring Pyerre here? I need answers. I am utterly tired of waiting around for them."

Lorraine grabs Aelyta's elbow, pulling her back. Eyebrows knitted, her voice trembling. "Do not. Be. Seen," Lorraine warns.

Malo places a hand on Lorraine's shoulder, "I'll cover us."

Aelyta crosses her arms, exasperated. "Sure you are."

Shaking her head, Lorraine says, "I'm not going in there. I don't know where I'm going, but I'm not going in there."

Malo takes off his bag and hands it to Lorraine. "We won't force you. We'll see you at my house? I'll send word through the winds when we're back."

Lorraine throws the bag over her shoulder. She pulls Malo into a hug. "Be safe." She rubs his back. Pulling Aelyta into an embrace next, she says, "Don't die for reals." In her arms, Aelyta doesn't hear the wind. They've gone silent. The air stagnant.

Aelyta squeezes Lorraine in response. "You'll be okay on your own?"

Lorraine nods as she waves them off. She waits for the two of them to disappear into the shadows before following the coastline towards Muddy Bay. If her memory serves correctly, it should take her a day and a half to reach the marshland town. And from Muddy Bay, without stopping, Elementropolis is two days walk. But from the edge of the city, Elementropolis should have a few trolleys that will take her across the city. That would cut the travel by a quarter, the total amount of travel to be two days.

Whispers into the wind, she sends a message to her Insectal staff the new schedule for the week. They'll know it's her when she uses their full names. She shakes her head. She can worry about work later. For now, Lorraine needs to make her way back to Elementropolis.

With the heat of the solar season, the walk from the Morf Mountains to Muddy Bay took two full days. She stopped to take a break twice—the first to rehydrate, and the second to snack on pollen-powdered chips. Lorraine didn't want to take a third break to sleep. If she reached Muddy Bay, she could find a place to sleep there. Muddy Bay is a unique place where the Fungi folks mostly populate, marshland in central Deneb. The sun is warm, the air humid, and the water is full of life and algae. The Fungi sprawl across the delta.

But upon entering Muddy Bay, the marshland town is desecrated. Life of the delta marshes hanging limp. Goosebumps rise over her neck. The wind whispers the hauntings of what had occurred, and Lorraine could not take staying in a place so full of pain. It hangs in the air as she hastens out of the marshland town. She must cut through and up the bay to get to Elementropolis.

The other side of Muddy Bay, southeast of Elementropolis, is covered in thickets of cypresses. Then, the land turns to sand dunes.

Lorraine moves quickly but quietly. Despite how sleepy she is, her body refuses to relent and her legs carry her through the sand. She doesn't notice the group of four Elementals sneaking up on her from the foliage to her right.

Jaycub launches into her, pinning her to a cypress tree. "Who are you?" he hisses. His face close to hers.

"Me? You're the one who jumped me, knight."

Margaret, Presley, and Odetta approach from behind Jaycub. Margaret speaks first. "Let her go. She's just an Insectal traveler."

"From Muddy Bay?" Jaycub growls. He pins her harder against the cypress.

"Come on, we need to meet up with Edithe's daughter." Margaret persuades.

"Luella?" Lorraine wiggles. She could barely move under Jaycub's weight. "How do you know about Edithe and Luella?"

"Oh, she knows them!" Presley claps.

Close to her ear Jaycub asks, "What's the name of the shadows?"

"Malo—Oh, Itzal." Lorraine struggles. She can feel his breathing against the side of her face. Her glasses were touching his cheek.

She gasps for air as Jaycub releases her from his hold. "Why were you coming from Muddy Bay?"

"I was actually..." Lorraine starts, her breathing heavy. "Coming from Morf Mountain. That's where I separated from Malo and the Queen."

"Why would she be in Morf Mountain?" Odetta glances to Margaret and Presley.

After a large sigh, Lorraine explains, "We were on Malo's boat to Marigold Temple. Edithe said Pyerre and the High Priestess wanted to meet with Aelyta. They were attacked at the temple. We didn't make it to them in time. The High Priestess is dead, and Pyerre has been taken to Morf Mountain by four Royal Advisors of Ospheria."

Jaycub nudges Lorraine. "You still didn't identify yourself."

"Lorraine Fenton from Elementropolis." She looks Jaycub down then up. "I own an enchantment cafe."

"I'm Jaycub Battonfield, and a—"

"A loyal knight from Avelmore? Yeah, I can see that," Lorraine clips his answer. "You three must be the Queen's ladies, then. Why are you all here?"

Margaret looks to her fellow ladies, then at Jaycub, before answering. "We're headed to Elementropolis. We're going to find Luella, Edithe's daughter."

"She lives with her aunt, Edin. She owns the bookbinding shop in downtown Polis."

All four of them stare back at her. Lorraine sighs. "Between the two competing flower shops; Green with Ivy, and The Floral Reef?" She pauses. No response, no movement. Sighing again, "Across from the Clair O'voyance School for the Elements?" Her hands go up. "On Trolley Road, in Caterpillar Square? Have you guys never been outside of Avelmore? Outside Ospheria?" She cracks her back. "I'll take you to Luella as long as you don't touch a single hair on that girl, or I'll—"

"What? Struggle?" Jaycub sneers.

Lorraine shoves her bag into his chest. "You can carry that for me as a thank you." She gestures for them to follow her. "We need to make it to the Elementropolis trolley station before they shut down for the night."

Presley presses, "What about Aelyta? She's in Morf Mountain? The Richards' Morf Mountain?"

Lorraine shrugs. "She's got Malo."

"It's Lyta, she'll be fine," Odetta seconds. "Besides, it's the Richards. She's known them her whole life. She can handle the Richards."

19

Hive of Hidden Secrets

AELYTA NEVER THOUGHT she'd be hiding in the shadows, with the help of Malo, in the ancient mountain. But, here they are.

He uncloaks them from the Shadow Realm after the shadows have elongated among the mountaintops. They're at the opening of the Richards' excavation site. The two of them slip through, hopping from one shadow to another. The mountain is carved from the center into a massive pit in the rocky core.

They continue on, moving inward towards the edge of the pit. Not a single Elemental nor a single guard has walked by, not a single chatter of life.

"Did the Richards abandon Morf Mountain?" Malo waves his arms quietly in confusion.

"And for how long?" Aelyta glances around. "There is no security that I can see. Can you sense anything?"

Malo's hands reach out. Shadows stream from them, snaking away. "I can't feel anything in the shadows," he answers. "Wait"—his eyes get big—"there's something."

Aelyta scans the view of the mountains in the landscape. The tops from Morf Mountain onward, as far west as she can see, are all flattened. The Richards have carved out almost every mountain to the northwest of Deneb. She walks around the pit to look towards the south. As far as the landscape goes, the mountain range is a flat canyon of pitted mountaintops.

"No wonder the Richards stopped excavating," Aelyta says over her shoulder. "They ran out of mountains to carve." She turns around. "Malo?"

But behind her, Malo's face is knitted in concentration. "There's something in the shadows," he grits. "I think,"—he grinds his teeth—"I think we've been caught."

Aelyta runs towards him, but a large mechanical hornet drops in front of her. She didn't hear its wings beating on the wind. Three more mechanical hornets plummet into the flat, rocky mountaintop. She braces herself for the four Royal Advisors to expose themselves. But instead, she faces Kyanston Richard, Thelonius Richard, Cory Ronanbrand, and Julius Ronanbrand.

Malo drops to his knees screaming in pain. Julius and Thelonius both turn to the shadow-dwelling Elemental. Aelyta runs for Malo, but Cory and Kyanston step in the way.

"Look who lost his way," Julius hisses. "Abandoning your assignment and working with the victim."

"And you found him on my property," Thelonius adds. "How are you going to torture your little bastard? Can't send him off to his mommy anymore..." Thelonius chuckles

"I really thought you wanted to prove yourself." Julius treads a circle around a struggling Malo. "You once said that to me, didn't you? You wanted to take over the Ronanbrand business. Use your shadows the way they were intended. Isn't that what you told me? Answer me when I ask you a question." Julius grabs Malo's shirt, tugging him. "You're just a rat like your mother. A trickster she was, and so are you. Come Thel, let's take the bastard of a son to his punishment."

Aelyta looks to Malo for answers. "You're a Ronanbrand?"

Shaking his head, he tries to answer. Julius laughs at Malo's struggle.

"I knew you worked for the Ronanbrands, but to be...his son?" She points to Julius. "Have you been leading me here? Did you just trap me?"

"How could I?"

"How could you, indeed?" Julius mocks his son.

A disgusted look twists her face as Julius laughs at the two of them.

"Don't worry, female. He most definitely lusts for you." Julius kicks Malo to the ground. Aelyta pushes Julius aside. She kneels over Malo. Her body reacting before her thoughts can keep up. Even after knowing who he is, she still can't stop herself from protecting his body with her own.

Thelonius looks over to Kyanston. "Do what you want with that one." Thel lacks the effort of pointing at Aelyta. "We don't need a queen anymore."

Thelonius and Julius drag Malo through the rocks. Julius jumps on the back of the mechanical hornet. The hornet snags Malo from the ground and takes off into the air.

"Malo!" Aelyta screams.

Thelonius jumps on the back of his own mechanical

insect, taking off after Julius and Malo. Aelyta wants to scream again and again, but she's faced with the two men before her.

"You know what?" Kyanston gestures to Cory.

"What?" Cory answers.

"I think flowers look better cut and wilting in a vase. Forgotten and dying."

"Always the morbid one," Aelyta scoffs.

"You're the one to talk." Kyanston sneers.

"Come on." Cory grabs Kyanston's elbow. "Let's put her with the rest of the harvested."

Kyanston whips his arm away from Cory's hold. "No, I think she should have a royal treatment. She can have her own suite in her own little mountain."

"What is wrong with you two?" Aelyta lunges for them.

"Shh, shh," Cory coos. "We were going to have the whole kingdom on bended knees for us, and you couldn't even behave yourself."

"I told you what I wanted from the very beginning!" Aelyta screams into his face.

"No, you were being a little trickster!" Cory yells back.

"And I thought we could have been at least friends."

Cory scoffs, "With you? Be real. I wanted the kingdom the same way your father has now."

"Crownship," Aelyta corrects.

"Not anymore." Cory chortles. "We no longer have a Crownship, Aelyta. You took the crown from Ospheria."

"You shoved a dagger into me, remember?"

"And you didn't die!" Cory yells. "No wonder that shadow slave decided to change tactics and work *with* you instead of against you. You are a trickster."

"Stop calling me that." Her teeth grind. Aelyta lunges at

him. Both her hands squeezing his throat, but she didn't notice Kyanston behind her.

Kyanston hopped onto the back of his mechanical hornet and snatched Aelyta with the hornet's arms. Aelyta whips into the air before she could realize.

Her fingers search for Cory, but she's too far into the sky. The setting sun enlightens the mountains cut down like manicured grass lawns. Unlike grass, mountains do not have the ability to grow back. How could they have ruined so many? Mountains, of all things. Rocks of Deneb's earth. Immovable, impassable titans of rock. Her chest twists at the ache, at the pain the earth must have felt. The wind cries as she mourns the peaks, only confirming the pain in the air.

The feeling escapes her as Kyanston takes the hornet higher, higher, until the mountaintops resemble beeswax. Or even worse, a hornet's hive.

The hornet's arms gripping her, let go. Aelyta doesn't have time to scream as she plummets towards the rocks below. The hornet swoops down and grabs her again, Kyanston's hoots of laughter ringing from above her. He whips them back up into the sky.

The ground below disappears in a mix of colors. He's going to do it again. She braces for the fall as the hornet flies vertically up. A pause against the setting sun, then the hornet releases its arms. Aelyta drops. She doesn't scream. Instead, she whispers to the wind. She whispers her hatred, her pain, the ache in her chest. She whispers the anger, the anguish. There is determination in her voice despite her softness. She's not mad at the wind. Aelyta molds her ire not in her tone, but the specific words she chooses. "May despair fall upon those who are desperate for despair upon the befallen."

Metal arms clasp her middle. She's whisked away under the mechanical hornet. There is laughter in the wind. Kyanston's ill chuckles in the background, but the laughter in the wind is the reason Aelyta smirks at the sun disappearing on the horizon.

20

Poison from Within

WITH THE SUN setting to her right, Aelyta makes note of the southern direction ahead of her. She scans the foothills of the mountains for signs of the abandoned citadel where her mother's greenhouse is located—an oblong curve of the smaller mountains tucked under the foothills distinct against the backdrop of Muddy Bay.

Kyanston continues flying south, following the mountain range. She scans the hives of mountains, searching for the large dragon. Below her are colorful Florals and Fungi at the center of each core of every hive. The Richards have collected so many Elementals. Why?

In the farther distance, Aelyta recognizes the Royal Academy. But Kyanston doesn't take them any farther, the hornet plummets from the sky. Aelyta is dropped into her own separate mountain carved like a bowl.

Kyanston brings over shackles and chains. Aelyta backs herself into the carved wall of rock. He grabs her arm and cuffs her. She swings at him with her other arm, but he catches it and cuffs her wrist. He attaches the end of the chain to a notch in the clay. Walking back to the mechanical hornet, he gives her a sneer over his shoulder. "I could've been a great king, if only you'd picked me over Cory." He spits at her. "I could've been superior."

"You're still a spoiled little rich boy," Aelyta mocked. "How does it feel to always be this pathetic?"

"You piece of dirt." Kyanston swings his fist into her stomach. "You're not much of a queen now, are you?" He pulls her head back by her petals. "You're going to end up like the rest of the Florals. Dust and powder." He cackles. "You know what's going to happen to you? Let me explain, Your Majesty." His face up against hers. "You're going to dry out in the peak of the solar season. When your petals are dried and ready, I'll come fetch you."

"You're sick! Mad! This is unnatural, against all forms of the Elements. Is that what my dad's been doing? Collecting Floral and Fungi for harvest so your dad can make more money? Gain power over the people?"

"You have no idea what it takes to have power over the people." He cackles.

With disgust on her face she asks, "What will you do with me once I'm dried?"

"You'll crumble like the others." He shoves her face into the rock before clamoring back onto the hornet again and flying away, leaving Aelyta struggling on the ground.

Every Elemental knows that if Florals and Fungi remain in the sun for too long with no sugar or water, they'll shrivel and decay, using their own bodies to maintain itself until the inevitable death overtakes their soul.

She lies on the ground feeling the cold clay against her skin. The stars are appearing one by one. But as quickly as they appear, they vanish behind an emerging wave of clouds. A thunderstorm is rolling in, and fast. Aelyta looks around for anything to climb on, but even if the walls had ridges, the chains wouldn't allow her to.

The sound of thunder roars in the distance. Without warning, the rain breaks down into a torrential storm. Water quickly fills the bottom of the small circular space. Lightning flashes above her. The rain quickens its rate, now ankle deep. She can feel the water rising up her legs with every second passing.

She pulls on the chains as the water makes its way up to her knees. The rain doesn't cease as more lightning flares in the sky. The chains are unrelenting, and a rage soars up her throat. She lets out a scream from deep within her core. Lightning strikes down into her dungeon. She opens up her chest to it, feeling the power surge through her very essence. Aelyta thunders another scream. This is no longer a game of politics. This isn't power over Ospheria. This is something else.

The water rises to her waist, but she doesn't panic. Feeling her powers ebb and flow within her, she wants to fight it off. It tugs at her under her skin. Unlike goose-bumps, it's cutting through her arms, legs, an outlet, anywhere. What's the point of holding back?

She channels her magic out with a scream into the pouring rain. Aelyta exerts her magic into the water, allowing it out to air, to swim, to breathe. The water around her waist glows a violet-purple and smells like ire. Magic courses through her veins, escaping wherever it can. Her skin streaks gold, glowing in the dark of the torrential downpour.

The rain is falling harder now. The water rising towards her chest. Aelyta looks up to the sky. Large drops of water run down her face. She closes her eyes, breathing in the smell of the rock, the rain, the nearing death that awaits her.

From the bottom of the carved mountain, Aelyta doesn't feel the wind, but she knows it's there. "Thank you," she says, her voice soft at first. "Give my thanks to the others as well." She opens her eyes. The water is up to her ears. Not wanting to waste her energy wading the waters just yet, she focuses on the pouring sky above her.

The water rising above her head, Aelyta kicks her feet off the bottom, but the chains hold her down. Her head goes under and water fills nostrils and mouth. She's a Floral, it doesn't hurt to drown a little, but she is also half-human. She won't be able to last long. Panic hurtles in her chest.

Lightning streaks the dark sky. One. Two. Thunder rumbles the mountains. Aelyta pulls on the chains. Air. She needs air. The chains weigh heavier under the water. The shackles cut in to her wrists along with the tangled, dangling bells; the forgotten bells on her wrist from the Marigold Temple. Malo must have wrapped it around her wrist after they had the small cremation for the priestess.

She jingles the bells and they glow gold. From her wrist, the gold surges warmth through the veins coursing within her body. She shakes the feeling from her arm. Metal slides down her hand. The bells materialize into the handle of a sword, a sword made of broken winds.

Crashes of lightning flash against the storm clouds. One. Two. Three. Four. Thunder cries and cracks, echoing from every direction within the bottom of the bowl-shaped mountaintop.

She holds the handle of the sword. Aelyta can't see the blade, but she can feel the water rolling away from it.

Gripping tighter, she whips the blade at the chains holding her to the rock.

A dent appears in the stricken metal. Harder this time, Aelyta clashes the sword's winds into the metal links. Repeating again and again. Every time, she gets a better feel of the force of the wind ebbing through the water.

Using both forces to her advantage, she pulls the sword over her head and whips it down at the feel of the water's roll. The chains crumble, freeing her to the top of the water.

Air invades her lungs. Aelyta lets out another cry as lightning cries behind her. Pushing herself towards the rock, she tests the sword again. Shaking her wrist, the blade pulls into the golden glove and returns to the shape of bells at her wrist.

Climbing the rock's face, the rain has made the stone slippery. She has fallen more times than she is able to count. Waiting for the storm to pass is no option. The climate to the east of Deneb is storm-driven. It is the reason why there are no settlements in the east. The Academy situates southeast and even then, they are plagued with storms.

But because of this, they grow strong plants. Florals grow hardier when they're forced to face the storms and rocks. Aelyta digs her fingers into the ridge, depending more on her fingers than her feet to hold her weight.

Strong winds force plants to grow stronger roots. Aelyta takes the face of the rock slow and steady. Rain drips down her back and face. She feels the droplets against her fingers, but she holds firm, climbing one hand at a time. Time's no longer a concept. Only rain, rocks, the ache in her fingers, and her thoughts.

Aelyta's mind races. There are no longer coincidences. There were plans put into place that she never knew existed. Her mother's death took place at the end of her royal tour. It took place the morning the two of them were to leave for Ospheria from the Royal Philosopher's Academy. The day after her mother had met with the Alchemadia Committee.

Remember. Aelyta works her memory as she clings to the rock. That tour was a year ago. Events have happened since then. Appeasing her father for the crown, the trick with Cory, running away with Malo, and all this time her father was teamed up with Thelonius and Julius.

Her fingers feel the flat top of the carved mountain. Aelyta pulls herself up and throws herself over the edge. She lies on her back, her breathing heavy.

She lets out a long sigh and a bubble surrounds her. She floats up into the stormy skies. With a plunk, the bubble pops mid-air. The rain beats against her front. The flat rock is cold against her back. Power surges through her arms, her veins. Her hands fist at her sides.

When plants are faced with predators, enemies against their livelihood, they form a protective mechanism. Magic. But to the enemies, it is poison.

In Ospheria, Maurene, Ellsy, Lyza, and Malcolm have reached Avelmore Castle. Every foot surrounding the outskirts of the castle grounds, Miles has installed guards. Malcolm approaches the knights by the entrance gate, but they refuse to let them in.

Ellsy and Lyza try their wits at the guards but are still refused entrance.

"What do we do now?" Maurene's arms flop at her side.

Malcolm paces. "I don't want to just sit here idly. It's annoying."

"We can always go to Muddy Bay." Ellsy turns to Lyza. "I really want to go to Muddy Bay."

Maurene glances at Ellsy. "Why is that? What's at Muddy Bay that you want to go so badly?"

Ellsy shrugs. "I don't know. I just have a feeling."

"We would have to double our trip back in order to get to Muddy Bay." Malcolm stops his pacing. "The shortest distance from here would be Elementropolis."

Lyza sighs. "I just want to go inside the castle..." She turns to the others. "Is there really no other way inside?"

Malcolm paces again. Ellsy and Maurene plop onto the graveled ground. Lyza loosens the tears she's been holding onto for some time now. They hear galloping from down the road. Lunging for the closest cover behind large redwood trees and large ferns, the four of them dive off the road. The royal carriage stomps past them.

Lyza doesn't wait for the others as she leaps for the back of the carriage. Ellsy jumps up from the ferns, but Maurene and Malcolm pull her down, covering her mouth. Ellsy tries to yell for Lyza, but if she attempts a single sound, she may reveal them all. They watch as Lyza disappears under the large carriage and descends behind the guarded gates. Ellsy slumps onto the ground. Maurene pulls her into an embrace as Ellsy's breathing unsteadies.

Malcolm waits as Ellsy readjusts herself. Maurene gives her a look before Ellsy nods to the both of them. "Let's go to Elementropolis."

"What about Lyza?" Malcolm inquires.

"Forget her," Ellsy spits. "She left us, so we leave her."

Maurene leans her forehead forward. "That's not how this works."

"I know." Ellsy releases herself from Maurene. "I don't want to think about it right now. Let's go to Elementropolis." She stomps down the path. Malcolm gives Maurene a glance before catching up to Ellsy. Maurene follows beside him.

Lyza clings the axle casing as the carriage comes to a halt in front of the valet stop. She recognizes Miles's voice as he commands orders to the two servants that greet him at the door. She rolls her eyes at the way he mispronounces the word *baggage*. Lyza holds on with her full body as she waits for Miles to disappear into the castle. She counts. One. Two. Three. The carriage lugs forward towards the carriage house where the staff will detach the horses and she'll slip away.

But when the carriage parks in the little station house, a pair of feet stop right next to her head. A man bends down and greets her with, "Hi, you're not supposed to be under there."

Lyza chuckles at him as she removes herself from under the carriage. He helps her out from underneath. "It's good to see you, Branson."

"Wanna explain what you were doing under the carriage?"

"As long as you take me to Aubree." She covers her head with a scrap piece of fabric she ripped from her dress.

21

Busy Little Bees

INSIDE THE PANTRY, Lyza waits for Aubree. Branson had brought her to Boreas, the castle's head chef. Boreas directed her to the pantry. Branson has offered her a set of new clothes, maid clothes, and she swapped her old clothes for the uniform. And now, Lyza sits on a scratchy muslin sack of potatoes.

Boreas pops his head in after he hasn't heard from her in a while. "Let's make you look like a maid." He hands her a pair of scissors. She follows him out of the pantry and sits on a stool. Lyza watches him pull out a couple bowls and fills one with greens. "Cut," he orders. She puts her head down and gets to work.

Throughout the day, Lyza notices the staff that comes in and out. And from those that speak of Miles, she focuses harder on the scissors and greens at hand. A servant by the name of Briley, storms into the kitchen and spills complaints to Boreas. Despite how occupied he is, Boreas listens. He stirs a pot with his back to Briley as he listens to Briley complain about Miles no longer hiding his acts of deception. Boreas ran to the sink a few times, and Briley never wavered as he continued complaining. "He's straight up mocking us Elementals, in our faces too." Briley's hand at his hip. "I can't believe we're still here working for this man. He's not even one of us. He's having meetings with Thelonius and Julius in the public hall about churning Elementals into a power source. A power source for what?"

Boreas turns around and his fists rest on the island where Lyza has been quietly working. "He's going to play god." Boreas shakes his head. "And sooner or later, he's going to find out the consequence."

"Like the Goblin King? He's going to play God like the Goblin King?" Briley's eyes widen.

Aubree enters the kitchen from the back butler stairs. "What's happening?" She walks over to Boreas and Briley.

Briley answers before Boreas does, "Miles is planning on changing the laws again this week. On top of that, he's got himself the Bugnott Sword. Isn't that an old fairy tale, like there isn't an actual sword, right? He won't stop talking about it!"

Boreas adds, "Someone is here to see you." He points to Lyza, who quickly and silently slides the scissors into her pocket. "Oh, and I heard that Miles isn't happy with Julius. Something that Ronanbrand did, Miles is upset about it."

Briley gasps at the news. Aubree smacks the back of her hand against his arm as she passes him. She leans into Lyza. "What are you doing here? You shouldn't be here."

"I had to come back." Lyza looks around before leaning into Aubree. "I need to be here in Avelmore."

"No, you don't." Aubree takes her by the shoulder and leads her away to the far corner. "You need to be as far away from Miles as Elementally possible."

"The thing is though"—Lyza breaks away from her grasp—"Aelyta is alive. Ellsy wanted to go to Elementropolis, but I need to be here."

Aubree's eyebrows knit. "Why?"

Revealing her forearm to Aubree, Lyza exposes the cracking in her skin. Aubree gasps loud enough to catch the attention of both Briley and Boreas. Lyza scans Aubree's face. Lyza admits, "The stars are spinning off balance."

Briley walks up from behind Aubree. "This all because your arm is broken?"

"I'm made of another earth," Lyza answers. "Companions of Lyta said that she may have answers in her studies. You all know her studies better than I could ever..."

"We need to hurry before the castle is swarmed with Elementals for the conference later this evening," Aubree whispers.

Lyza glances at her. "What time does the conference start?"

"A few hours before sunset," Briley answers.

"You really just know a lot of things going on in this castle." Branson bounds in from the stairs.

Boreas shushes. "That's his secret weapon." His arms crossed, head down. "The kitchen will be busy with the dinner sequencing after the conference. Best time for distractions." Boreas nods.

Aubree ushers Lyza towards a stairwell only Aubree, Briley, and Branson know exist. It leads to Aelyta's chambers. The four of them find themselves in an abandoned hall. There is no Aelyta, therefore there is no need for knights.

Aubree unlocks the door and the four of them funnel

into the foyer. Branson, the last to enter the chamber, locks the door behind them. Together, they climb the spiraling staircase and spread out as soon as they make it to Aelyta's study room.

Aubree searches one side of the bookshelves. Branson on the other end, while Briley scours the table topped with piles of books. Aubree takes a few books from the shelves and drops them onto the table, causing Briley to yelp in despair. Aubree shushes him as she peels through the pages.

"Lyta enjoys reading about biology," Aubree asserts.

Lyza explains, "Yes, but her mother gave her books. Notes of what her reign will need."

"But wouldn't the advisors, or even her dad, have taken those from her if he wanted the throne?" Branson leans against the bookshelves.

"That's probably why Edithe said that Aelyta would be the one to know where to look and what she's looking for," Lyza says over her shoulder as she enters Aelyta's bedroom.

"How would we know what to look for then?" Branson moans.

Briley adds, "It's very important we don't assume Aelyta doesn't just study one subject." He lifts up a fairy tale book with the late Queen Jane's handwriting in the margins. "She sure loves diversifying her readings."

Branson recognizes the handwriting from where he's standing. They all do. The distinct curl of the *t* and the squiggles of the *n* that any of them can recognize the handwriting.

"That's definitely Jane's writing." Aubree clicks her tongue. "Where's Lyza?"

In Aelyta's bedroom, Lyza isn't searching for books. Lyza is searching for something that belongs to her, and she needs it back. She opens every drawer. She creaks open the jewelry box, but there's only Aelyta's everyday necklaces, bracelets, and rings. Aelyta keeps her earrings in a separate compartment of the drawer. But none of these are what Lyza is looking for, so she closes all the drawers.

Cracking her neck, another sliver of tarnishing breaks near her shoulders. Lyza spots a pile of books on the nightstands and rummages through them. A notebook with scribbles and drawings scattered throughout drops onto the floor.

Picking it up, Lyza learns the book is filled with Aelyta's scribbles and drawings. They're dated last year, at the Alchemadia Committee meetings. Aelyta recorded time, place, and the alchemists' discussion topics. At the time of the meetings, these ideas were mere concepts. The theory is that they may only remain theories to better understand the Elementals. The Morf Crystals will no longer be in supply. One day, they will be used up after being capitalized for generations. The alchemists studied ways to enhance the clinics where the crystals are slimming. This theory is solely to build off of, not to be a full replacement of the Morf Crystals. Resources are resources, and Elementals are still people.

Lyza carries the book into the study room. Her eyes deeply invested in the notes. "Lyza," Briley's voice brings Lyza back to the room. "What did you find?"

"This is either extremely confidential or the immense reason Miles is in power right now." Lyza hands the book over to Briley.

Aubree huffs herself into the armchair by the window, Aelyta's favorite chair. "Every book and piece of writing in these very chambers is important."

22

King of the Dull House
THE TYRANTS

MILES ADDRESSES THE PUBLIC HALL. "Because of me, as your King Miles, we have done great things here." His voice echoes across the large conference room. "I have won and beaten the monsters in their own game, fair and square. Amazing work," he praises. There was a slight pause before an eruption of applauses and cries come from the crowd in the public hall of the castle. He spots the four advisors taking their seats in the corner of his eye.

He gestures to them. "Tell them about my brilliance in Muddy Bay." The four advisors stare unblinkingly at him.

Constantine speaks first. "We should discuss it later."

"Don't be shy." Miles gestures to the crowd. The room erupts in applauds and cheers. "Give them what they want."

"We really should discuss what your next plans are," Menecrates interrupts.

"I asked you so politely if you can tell my audience how supreme the hive is in Muddy Bay," Miles demands.

Columba answers, "Well, there's nothing to report."

"An empty report," Ansaldo adds.

Thelonius gets up from his seat and crosses the podium

to the advisors. They whisper frantically as Miles turns back to the audience with a grin.

"These guys are so hard at work at all times." He points with his thumb. "I want to give my followers the best of the best. Instead of celebrating the Butterfly Festival at the end of this solar season, I want to give you something better. The best way to end the solar season, the best way to end the celestial seasons altogether. I'm going to give you something no queen ever could. And, the best part, I'm going to get rid of the allergens that are taking up Ospheria. We live in a big, beautiful Deneb. Let's clean it up and make it better. Tomorrow will be a great day!" Cheers and hollers of praise ring through the hall.

A rage clenches her jaws tight and deep into her throat. Her eyebrows twitch as her hand grips the scissors concealed in her pocket tightly. She watches as Cory and Kyanston, having arrived from the sky, split directions to their designated chambers.

Lyza crosses the castle grounds, following close behind Cory. He disappears behind his chamber doors.

As a chambermaid, she passes through the castle guards positioned outside Cory's doors. Climbing the stairs, she makes her way up to the bedroom. She doesn't conceal her steps as they echo against the stairwell. Nearing the top floor, her hand stays wrapped firmly around the scissors.

Not pausing at the entrance, Lyza storms into the bedroom. Cory Ronanbrand lies flopped on the bed. His ivory-striped curly hair gives him away from under the blanket. She approaches the bed, scissors now exposed from her pocket. Lifting them over her head, she steadies her aim for the side of his head.

Before she could strike, hands grab her arms, pushing her. She tumbles backward, falling onto her back. The scissors lost somewhere in the fall. Pinning her to the ground, Cory's breathing is heavy on top of her. She screams into his face, but he doesn't budge.

"I just got a chance to lie down. Besides, you're trying to kill the wrong one." He struggles to keep her pinned.

"You're just saying that so you can live to keep your daddy's little money pot." She wriggles.

"If I let go, can we have a nice little chat?"

"No!" she blares into his face.

"I've never met stardust before. You're a fireball, aren't you?"

"No!" she cries again.

He chuckles as he repositions. "I'm going to let you go. But you have to know, I'm not going to fight."

"No!" she yells once more.

He lets go and she leaps for his throat. He wrestles her back onto the ground, struggling to keep her arms and legs pinned again. "What's wrong with you?"

"You!" she screams.

"Go kill Kyanston first!" he yells back at her.

"So you can go run back to your daddy for help?"

"So that Thel's plantation takes the blow from the aftermath," Cory lets her go again. He steps up against the wall, hands up.

She examines him. His throat purple. His eyes both bruised. Giving him a look through the corner of her eye as she sits up, she asks, "What happened to you?"

"Aelyta." He gives her one small chuckle.

Lyza nods approvingly. "Good." She swings the scissors, cutting a large slice against his cheek. "There's more where that came from."

Cory puts both his hands up. "Kill me, but you should know we just left Aelyta in Morf Mountains. She is chained and drying out as we speak. I should mention that before I die."

Twisting the scissors in her hand. "I watched you stab Aelyta in the shoulder. Why should I spare you? Give me one good reason."

"Malo is my brother, half-brother, but he's still my brother. I want to let him know I'm on his side the same way I told you where Aelyta is before you kill me—I want him to know, before my time is up, that I have no resentment towards him."

"You're Malo's half-brother?"

"Yes, and he's in love with Aelyta. Because of it, my father is torturing him this very second."

"Do you know where?"

"I wish I knew, but I don't know where my father and Thel have taken him."

Pinning the tip of the scissors to his throat, Lyza tries to pierce his skin. Her arm tinges with a shiver that she can't shrug off. "Why'd you leave Aelyta to die in Morf Mountain? Why not turn around and go help her if you knew your beloved brother loves her?"

"Timing," he mutters. "I have to return the same time as Kyanston. We're being monitored, watched, tested. If we don't fall in line, we're replaced with metal copies. Mechanical beings are already replacing knights."

Lyza tsks. "I'm killing Kyanston first, then you're next."

She leaves his chamber, Cory following behind her. When they approach Kyanston's chamber door, the both of them notice there are no guards positioned and the door is agape.

"Did his guards get dismissed?" Lyza turns to Cory for an answer.

Cory shrugs. "That's only possible by seven specific

people. My father, Kyanston's father, Miles, and the four advisors."

Holding her breath, Lyza slowly enters Kyanston's chamber. They enter cautiously, quick but quiet.

They make their way up to the bedroom to find a bloodied and dead Kyanston. "I guess we're too late." Lyza steps back to the landing.

Lyza turns the corner and enters the door to the servant's stairwell, Cory sticking close behind her. "Why are you following me?"

"I might die next. You have scissors."

"And that is not my problem right now."

"What is your problem, then?"

She stops walking and spins on the spot. "Did you kill him?"

He shakes his head. "And don't know who did. Maybe one of the many castle staff members."

"No." She shakes her fist at him. "They wouldn't be so sloppy. It was like they wanted him to be found. One of the staff? That would mean the end of their career, their life. This was personal."

"Or political," Cory adds.

"So, you do know who killed him?"

"I know that there are seven people who have that kind of power and privilege to get away with the slop."

"Okay, then why kill Kyanston Richard now?"

"Well, why did you try to kill me as soon as I got back?"

"Only eight people, including you, know where Aelyta is dying?"

Cory nods. Lyza leans against the stairwell railing. She crosses her arms.

"You have intel that no one else has. You're going to have to start escalating the situation for the sake of Aelyta, for Ospheria, for Deneb."

Hesitating, Cory replies, "I'm not sure I can do that."

"Why? Your loyalty lies with your dad?"

He shakes his head. "I don't like taking charge..."

"What is wrong with you? Can't you take your own consequences, reap what you sow, hold yourself account- able? Where does your loyalty lie? Are you for the Elemen- tals or against us all?"

"I don't know." Cory crashes into the stairwell railing.

Lyza grabs his shirt and punches his face. "I can't stand you, for you can't stand for something."

She shakes her hand, crackling at the knuckles, as she walks down the stairwell towards the kitchen.

"Where are we going?" Cory chimes.

They run into Aubree on the way down. She grabs hold of Lyza, but gives her a concerning look after spotting Cory behind her. Aubree pushes Lyza behind her like a protective mother.

Cory puts his hand up defensively.

Edithe pops her head over Aubree's shoulder. "He's clean, you know. I can read the dust on him and this stupid boy is just, stupid—why are we scared of him?"

"He stabbed Aelyta in the neck!" Lyza exclaims.

Nodding, Edithe agrees. "Like I said, stupid. You can't blame a sheep for being a stupid sheep."

"You can blame stupid for being stupid when their consequences led them to stupid results!" She turns to Cory. "I'll kill you if you do any more stupid, stupid."

Aubree hushes Lyza as she pulls her down to the main

center of the kitchen where they find Boreas vexing about rows of ramekins. Branson and Briley stand behind the counter as they watch Boreas throw down plops of goop into each dish. Aubree points to the corner of the kitchen between Boreas's workstation and the pantry. Lyza follows behind her, Cory behind Lyza. The ghost already waiting for them in the corner, causing the other three men to jump.

"Edithe, hi." The ghost points to herself. "I've got a message from Aelyta."

Lyza rises from where she was crouched. Aubree calls for her, but Lyza doesn't turn back. She grabs a scrap of paper, the first writing utensil she finds, and writes a note for Thelonius Richard.

> Look at what you have done. Your son paid the price. He lies dead in his room.

Lyza marches to where Thelonius is having dinner with Miles and Julius. She hands it to one of the guards outside of the grand dining hall. Tucking herself into a dark corner, she pulls her head-covering farther over her hair as she watches the guard walk towards the small circular table towered with food. The guard hands the note to Thelonius and walks back to the door.

Lyza snickers to herself as she walks straight out the front of the castle. She doesn't look back as she takes the path down to Elementropolis.

She hears the crunch of footsteps nearby. Rolling her eyes, Lyza stops walking. "You're still being stupid, stupid."

Cory pops out from behind an alley. His hands twisting in front of him like a schoolkid. "How'd you know I was following you?"

"You haven't stopped following me since I slashed your face."

"And you'd probably do it again if I step out of line."

"Not out of line, just when you need to be humbled."

Back at the table, Thelonius turns to Julius as he slowly unfolds the note in his hands. "Where in god's name are our sons?"

Julius chuckles. "Probably spending all your money."

Thelonius stands abruptly, rereading the note. Once over, twice. He throws it at Miles. Miles quick to his feet, his hand reaches for the Goblin Sword. The sword is larger than the man. With both hands, Miles awkwardly lifts the blade. With the back of the handle against his stomach with both hands, he points it towards Thel. "What's the meaning of this?" Miles yells at Thel.

Thel lunges for Miles, knocking the heavy sword out of Miles's hands. Thelonius grabs fistfuls of Miles's tunic. "You sent someone to kill my son."

"Whoa, now." Julius slowly rises from the table.

Thel points a finger at him. "You're an accomplice. I know it."

"It's not like you liked your son," Miles jokes. "You should thank me."

Thelonius pulls him to his face as he spits, "You killed my son, didn't you? Just like how you killed the Queen. Deal's off. Rip up the contract." Thel turns to Julius. "That's right, I got a contract deal with him to make me richer and more powerful."

"I doubt it's better than mine. Cory just had to marry Aelyta and we're in power." Julius brushes off the comment. "It's too bad she had to die first."

Miles gawks. "The children always get in the way of things."

Thel turns to Miles. "The same damn contract? You gave him the same contract?"

"No, men." Miles chuckles. "I'm smarter than that. I wouldn't play unfair with the both of you. Come, my friends. We were having a nice dinner. You all know how I hate playing games. I simply used the same standards for both parties. Whoever attributes to the cause the most gets to see their contract fulfilled. Easy rules to an easy game with big prizes! I figured you all win in the end anyways."

"That's because you always lose," Thel pushes.

"Someone is just trying to distract us from tomorrow." Miles smiles. "Don't get hasty before our big day."

"That distraction is the death of my son." Thel holds Miles in his grip.

Julius sighs. "He couldn't think of making two separate contracts for us. I doubt he could even figure out how to murder your son. Don't waste your breath and try to be reasonable."

"So, what? We're just going to ignore that my son is dead?"

"That's because they couldn't get to you." Julius sets his knife down beside his plate. "Don't let them get to you now." He slides the fork of cut steak into his mouth.

"But my son," Thelonius whines.

Miles scoffs. "You should have had his mother take better care of him."

"Who do I pass on the Richards business to now?" Thel whimpers into his plate.

"Of course, that's all he cares about."

Miles claps. "We move into the next phase after dinner. A round of drinks while we attend to the Richards' newest equipment."

"Yes, I believe the Richards business will only continue to prosper." Julius sneers at the moping man at the table. "Your money created great things. The people will be devouring themselves over it."

"The scums will be of use." Miles clicks his teeth.

"And you're not worried about your daughter?"

"She's got nothing a man can do. I have no worries about her."

"She might as well be dead by now, too." Thel slams his fist into the table. "My son had made sure of that."

"You may take that hand off the table and torture my bastard instead." Julius swallows his sip of wine. "I have no use of him anymore. I wanted to see the light in his eyes fade, but the bastard still lives."

"It's odd you strung him up on the top of the castle," Miles grumbles over a mouth full of food.

Julius snorts. "For a Shadow Element, the dungeons would be his friend. The sun is his enemy. No shadow wants to be in the light. His mother was the same way." A smirk creeps across his face. "Besides, I heard your daughter took a liking to him. He's our bait."

"A whore? Yes, they're all the same." Miles returns the same smirk but rolls his eyes at the man beside him. "Come on, Thel. Please stop your crying. We're going to be the gods the people will worship. We will fill pages of history with what we will do tonight. We will conquer the written words."

"I'm not hungry." Thel sways in his seat.

"Thirsty, then." Miles wipes his hands on his pants as he rises from the table. "Shall we?"

Julius dabs his mouth with a napkin and drops it onto the floor. "Come on, you men. Let's go see history in the making."

They walk down a set of stairs leading to a room only lit by the large glowing panel on the wall. Glittering buttons and toggles are monitored by the four Royal Advisors. The four of them bow their heads slightly at the arrival of the three men.

The screen behind them showing the metal knights and their metal hornets. In the center of a circle of metal, the Prime Minister of Elementropolis is tied up and blindfolded.

Miles steps in front of the large screen. "How was the torture?"

"Pleasing." Menecrates sighs.

Constantine scoffs, "Better if we kill him."

"You like killing everyone and everything." Ansaldo laughs. "Like that librarian, did you have to kill her?"

The advisor gives the other a smile that doesn't relent. Miles raises his hand to the panel. The advisors stop their quelling.

"Let's begin the next phase." Miles hovers over the button. "I want to see how many tools Thelonius has made for us." He doesn't wait for the others as he presses the button. The sound of beating wings rumbles the screen speakers. "Men, this is delightful. Elementropolis is now ours, which means all of Deneb belongs to us. Congratulations are in order!"

23

Depths of a Dragon's Secret
THE LIBRARY

EDIN, Luella, and Kody sit outside the office door. The hallway of Elementropolis's Capital's second floor is quiet, unlike the first floor. Luella rings her fingers through her pant leg fabric. Kody and Edin stare at the office door. Edin listens as closely as she can to the sounds behind the barrier.

"No one's inside." Edithe reveals herself in front of the door.

Luella jumps from the wooden armchair. "Where'd you come from?"

Edithe points over her shoulder towards the door. "In there." The ghost looks to Edin and Kody. "No one is inside the state room."

"Well, what did you read in the dust?" Edin asks her late sister.

"It's been empty for at least a few months." Edithe reaches her hand out to her daughter. "No one has been in there for that long."

Kody adds, "That means the last time the state room must have been used..."

"Before Queen Jane died," Edithe finishes.

Luella peers over at a window, looking out to the front lane of the Capital. "Guys, I think Prime Minister Nyup is not with us."

"Of course he's not with us," Edin brushes off.

Edithe peers over Luella out the window. "Oh no, he's been arrested."

Kody and Edin join them at the window where the crowd of Elementals gather for a procession. "What happened?" Kody asks.

"You mean what's happening?" Luella pipes. "The Minister's being kidnapped."

Edin's hands cover her mouth. "I think we're witnessing the seige of Elementropolis."

Kody, Edin, Luella, and Edithe stare out the window over the procession cascading into a large crowd in front of the Capital. Edithe gasps at the sight below them. The other three look at her for an explanation. "I see Aelyta's ladies-in-waiting."

But as they turn towards the hallway to head for the main stairwell, humming vibrates from over the roof of the building. They peer out the window again to see the sky darkening with the shadows of mechanical hornets swarming over the crowd of Elementals below. Screams reverberate outside the window. Edithe tries to find the three ladies in the chaos, but Elementals are running in every direction.

The hornets rain down a militant spray of metal stingers into the crowd. Edithe enlarges and covers her daughter, sister, and her friend. Cries thunder.

They run for the stairwell as the first-floor surges with bodies piling in from the chaos outside. Edin pulls Luella close to her. Kody sandwiches Luella beside him and Edin.

Edithe evaporates, leaving behind dust particles in the light.

Luella spots a few Capital employees running towards a back door. She pulls Edin and Kody in that direction. But as they near the bottom of the stairs, the first floor becomes suffocating. The amount of bodies filling the room has become more dangerous even without the hornets. Edin and Kody pull Luella back up the stairs. They run down to the end of the hallway towards the fire escape. Down the stairs, they open the exit door. Hornets fall from the sky.

Edin pulls Luella under her arm and tucks her tight as Kody grabs hold of Edin. Pushing their way through the waves of bodies lost in the turmoil, they notice the firefly lamps that line the streets outside the Capital. Kody yells to Edin and Luella, "Moon Row or Providence Road?"

"Either please," Luella squeals.

Edin tries to answer, but a man with armor slams into the three of them. Edin screams, "Careful, now. We've got a kid here."

"Sorry." The armored man turns his head partially. He recognizes Kody. "Hey, you! The alchemist!"

Kody simply points with his chin. "Moon Row or Providence Road?"

Edithe appears above them. "Neither. Head towards Lilac Lane and go up Cypress Street." The ghost disappears as quickly as she came. The three of them look to the armored man and they all nod.

Malcolm pulls Ellsy under one arm and Maurene in the other. They tuck their heads beneath his armored limbs as he guides them through the crowd. He follows Kody, Edin, and Luella into the depths of the surge. The crowd tightens, then bursts open to a massive patch of grass. The crowd thins, but Elementals are running through the grass towards the road sign, Lilac Lane.

Moving for Cypress Street, everyone follows one after the other.

Edithe reappears in front of Kody and Edin. The dandelion ghost gestures towards a copper-domed building with an ornate spire at the top. She opens the back door from the inside and waves them down from the alleyway.

They file into the door and Malcolm slams it shut, moving the lock into place. He slides down to the ground and passes out. Kody sighs as Edin, Maurene, and Ellsy help drag him deeper into the library.

Pyerre's Library is a seventeen-story collection of books, varying throughout history as one of Ospheria's notorious homes for the written word. The library is open to the public, but you must pass through the arch. The arch is a bias detector, deeming whether one carries in a form of bias or prejudice in their openness to knowledge. The information that Pyerre deems worthy is not meant to be misconstrued or misinterpreted for whatever purpose. It is against the library to spread misinformation. In fact, there are arguments that counter other books and journals. The library contains enough of what has been argued that even the Royal Academy has attempted to remove certain pieces of works. Those books live on the third floor in the gallery directly from the public's front entrance from the arch. It is to welcome everyone, and a reminder to patrons the ebb and flow of academia.

But where Malcolm is being dragged by Ellsy, Edin,

Kody, and Maurene, is the first floor, where Edithe guides them below ground. From the third floor, they take a large flat platform powered by water flames. The fire water decreases in size and the platform drops to the first floor. They step off the platform and into the main area of the first level. Ellsy and Maurene gasp at the sight of the titan-sized pile of books in the very center of the room.

"This is where deposited books get sifted," Edithe explains. "You see, the way Pyerre's Library works is that you trade in a book for a book. Pyerre doesn't like having missing gaps where books once were, so you have to fill in the empty space. At least, that's how he said it started because now it's in this giant pile."

"What's on the second floor?" Ellsy points. There's a circular opening where a banister rings the second floor at the tip of the mountain of books.

"That"—Edithe looks up—"is how the staff can reach the top of the pile."

24

Rock Bottom
THE QUEEN

THE MOUNTAINTOPS ARE CUT FLAT, but the mountainsides are insufferably difficult to walk down. The days and nights no longer exist. Atop the mountains, the sun is at its peak with no cover to hide. The heat beats from straight above Aelyta. She yearns for Malo. Not just for his shadows, but answers. She can only hope he's still alive.

She drops to her knees, scanning the mountain range. What direction was she headed? Which direction is the way out?

Aelyta has forgotten which mountain she's snaking down, only to find she must climb another. Closing her eyes, the strain of the bright sun has her tensing her vision. Remember. She needs to remember. The sun rose to her left. East. The sun casting her shadow behind her, south. She gives out a sigh.

There are Florals and Fungi captives north. And yet, she still has no idea where Pyerre is. When they took the dragon, they went over Morf Mountain in the north. She would have seen them flying towards the south, right? Her

199

head is spinning. Her body limp against the rock underneath her. Her skin scorching as she lies in the heat. Maybe she *will* turn into a dry Floral like Kyanston wanted.

No. She has the answers to stop her father, the Richards, Ronanbrands, and the advisors. She is the only one who knows of the resources and how they're being sourced. It's not about the crown or throne anymore. This is to save lives; Florals and Fungals, Pyerre, Malo. The High Priestess did not die in vain, nor did her mother.

Her hand slams into the rock, jingling the bells on her wrist. She pushes herself up. The waves of heat in the distance glitter in her vision. But mirages wouldn't be pink and green, no? They would be blue, right?

She doesn't question herself anymore as she runs for the carved core of the mountaintop. In the center of the bowled peak, Florals are chained to the sides of the rock.

She peers deeper into the bowl, she can see Florals and Fungi curled into the rock chaining their stems.

This is what Kyanston meant when he said they've been harvested.

Aelyta's knees tremble at the sight of them. They must all be so dehydrated, scared, and hungry. A sickened feeling curdles her stomach. Anger boils there, too.

With a flick of her wrist, the bells jingle, but that's all they do. *Jingle.* She shakes the bells again. *Jingle, jingle.* Why won't it turn into a sword?

Frantically, she jingles the bells over and over. The glances she's getting from the other Florals and Fungi would drive her mad, but the bells had turned into a sword in her hand before.

Now that she wants to transform them on demand, the bells are refusing. This is driving her into a frenzy.

How could she cut the chains? Aelyta glances around for anything, even a large enough rock. She grabs a rock smaller than her hand, but it's sharp. It might not be sharp enough, though. Aelyta slides into the carved core. The first chain she grabs, Aelyta slams the rock against the metal. It doesn't budge. She slams again and again.

The Floral attached to the chain places a hand on Aelyta's arm. The woman shakes her head. The fact that the Floral accepted her fate only riles an anger inside Aelyta. A scream erupts from her, and she slams the rock into the metal chain. Striking the chain again and again, the rock crumbles in her hand.

She stares at her hand, bruised and covered in glittering powdered blue. "Is this Morphenum?"

A Fungal man answers from beside her, "They're in the rocks, Your Majesty. The mountain is literally made of Morf Crystals. It's what makes the blue glint in the light."

Aelyta turns to the Fungal who had just spoken. "So, if the Richards didn't run out of Morf Crystals, why are you all here to dry into powder?"

He shrugs. The Floral chained beside Aelyta whispers, "Too much of something good can be poisoning."

With her head spinning now with more information, Aelyta crumbles against the rock face. "I don't think I have the answers I was looking for," she breathes. "I need...I need to find the dragon."

"I didn't see any dragons fly by," the Floral answers.

The Fungal, too, says, "Neither did I, but there was a whole commotion that way." He gestures with his chained hands northward.

"How many moons ago?" Aelyta climbs back onto her feet.

The Fungal ponders before responding, "The days and nights all seem to blend as one."

Scanning the others all chained to the rock, Aelyta wants to curse, to pain the Richards and her father for this. "I need to find the dragon. And I promise, I will return for you all."

The Fungal scoffs. The Floral holds out her hand for Aelyta. "What's your name?" Aelyta asks her, taking the Floral's hand.

"Anemona." The Floral woman squeezes Aelyta's hand.

"I'll remember that, Anemona."

"Blessed Queen," the Fungal chimes.

"Aelyta," she answers. "Aelyta Aurelianus, and I promise to return with the dragon to free you all. We will walk out of here free and take back our home." Aelyta plants a soft kiss on Anemona's hand.

The Florals and Fungi all chant around her.

She gives them all a bow. As she turns to face the rock and climbs upward out of the bowl-shaped core, their voices echo off the rock-bottom bowl.

"Queen Aelyta, Beacon thine Queen."

Her heart tugs at the sound of their voices reverberating through the rock under her hands.

Shifting her focus back to the task at hand, if that Fungal Elemental was able to hear something, maybe Pyerre isn't that far away. Aelyta refuses the doubt trickling down her back. What if he made it up? What if he was imagining it all? Doubt. There's no time for that. If she presses northward, at least she'll be moving.

Climbing down, the side of this mountain is not as ridged as the others. Aelyta slips and slides down her back. Her fingers search for anything to stop her fall only to scrape her fingertips. She's free falling with only rocks at the bottom to catch her.

A slant in the mountainside launches Aelyta. She's falling midair and drops straight down. No longer resisting the fall, she lands flat on her back. Her shoulder where the dagger struck her aches. The back of her head had slammed into the rock with a thunk. The sky is just a sliver between the mountainsides, swirling and spinning above her. She closes her eyes to steady herself. Her eyes don't open afterwards.

"Aelyta?" A voice surprised to see her. Aelyta opens her eyes with ease. She is shrouded in darkness.

Her voice ringing out, she questions, "Shadow Realm?" She looks around. "Malo?"

"No, just Edithe." The ghost glows before her. "You shouldn't be here." Edithe's voice is tinged with worry.

"I was looking for Pyerre," Aelyta starts. "Then I slipped and fell into the bottom of the mountain somewhere..." Her voice trails. "Where am I?"

"The Liminal," Edithe answers. "The space between the living and the dead."

"What is that?" Aelyta glances down at her hands.

Edithe sighs. "I know what you mean. The Liminal is...how should I put this..." Her face knits in concentration. "The Liminal is alive. But it feels like it's preparing for something."

"Harvest? A big one?"

"Possibly." Edithe shrugs. "It's all a divine response. A checks and balance of Deneb, I suppose."

"Has this happened before?"

Edithe's lips tense. "Not that I've witnessed."

"For someone who's keen to archives and historic knowledge, you seem to not know a lot right now."

"No, and it's hurting my soul—not literally, you know..."

"I know the exact feeling." Aelyta runs her finger across the scar on her right shoulder. "I don't know where Malo is, whether he's alive or not. I don't know any news of my ladies, Pyerre, or the fate of the Florals and Fungals. I don't know a whole lot right now either."

"Oh, my dear, that is what you must bring to light." A soft voice glitters through the darkness. Edithe and Aelyta turn towards the voice.

"Blessed goddess." Aelyta and Edithe bow their heads.

A laught ensues, then another voice. "Ko'nkiun and I are both here to guide you back. You've lost your way, child of the light."

"Yes, she is, isn't she? Child of the light." The Goddess Ko'nkiun ignites into a tender sunlight. She touches Aelyta's cheek, running her hand to Aelyta's forehead. A faint glow runs through Aelyta's vein. Her veins lighting gold against her skin.

"Wait, I have questions." Aelyta glances to the goddesses.

Goddess Ratri softly titters, "The answers are laid out ahead. They're simply in the shadows."

"And you'll find them, child of light." Goddess Ko'nkiun places a hand on the back of Aelyta's head now, where she landed against the rock.

Edithe waves as Aelyta cries out. Her body lunges up. Sitting up from the rock bottom, the sky is a faint blue, pushing aside the navy skies in the distance. Dawn approaches.

"Have you awakened?" A voice rumbles against the walls of rocks surrounding her.

"Pyerre?" Aelyta rises. Her body aches in all the wrong places. "Pyerre? Is that you?"

"Who asks?" He sneers.

"Aelyta." She manages forward, her body depending on the rock face to keep her steady. "I've come to rescue you."

The rocks quake as Pyerre guffaws. "You, in that state, cannot possibly unchain me. Look at me."

"Where are you?"

Pyerre blows a stream of fiery water. The blue brightness almost blinding. "These are chains made to hold a dragon prisoner. Not even I can save myself."

"Oh, hush now." Aelyta approaches. "Did they hurt you at all?"

He huffs, "No."

"Good." She plants herself against the dragon's front leg. "That's good." Aelyta examines the glittery blue powder stuck in the crevice of her hand.

"Mixed with other resources, the Morphenum can be turned into a metal so strong not even a dragon like myself can break," Pyerre grumbles.

Aelyta spins her head towards the dragon. "You mean the metal chains are made of this stuff? And what else?"

"The humans would dry flowers, seeds, herbs, and crush them into powders. They called them spice. Add a little spice and it's flavor. An abundance can be overwhelming, but substance is still resource."

"You're a water-fire dragon. How could they have tested your water flames to this stuff?"

"And they're up there in those vase mountains soaking in rainwater, you don't think it would have melted?"

"That's just soaking in still water under the sun. You are a water-fire dragon. You are the descended from the Mother Dragon of the river, Loso."

"She was not the Mother Dragon. My grandmother was the true Mother Dragon. Loso is my mother. Together, they created the peaceful Deneb that it has been known to be. A place where all Elementals can live amongst one another without worry. A peaceful garden of flowers, fungi, and insects."

"What happened to them?"

"My grandmother gave her last breath to my mother. And with my grandmother's last breath, my mother brought the flood of the Morf Blue to all of Deneb. She woke the Florals and Fungi, and together they fought the war between the mother and the son."

"Mother and son? The human mother that fell from the clouds in search of her youngling?"

"No, time has construed the meanings of words. Connotations reform definitions of terms used of the old scripts. The queen in a fairy tale of the old was a mother to a goblin who then became the Goblin King in some tales. They were in a war. My mother was a large part in the war. She befriended the human, the goblin, and the winged beings. Now, I am the last of my kind."

"Wow, I thought I knew all the answers. I thought if I put my head down and learned everything there was to know about Ospheria, Deneb, and the Elements, I could be a queen who looked after her sovereign."

"You've hit rock bottom. It hurts, but you were sent back here by the divine. You were sent here to fulfill a purpose. Aren't you a queen looking after her sovereign?"

Aelyta stands. Her legs shaking as she lifts herself up. Her back writhing with pain, but she stands before the chained dragon. "As long as I'm alive, so are the forces of nature."

Pyerre raises his head and bows to the Floral Queen. "The bells you wear." His eyes catching on the glittering gold on her wrist. "They are more than just a summon of magic. Do you wonder what they do?"

"Yes, but I don't know..."

"They call upon the winds," he explains. "They summon the air, and you, Queen of Ospheria, Sap of the Ancient Queens before you, Blood of the Humans of the High Heavens, can call upon the winds at your service."

Aelyta glances down at the bells on her wrist. Ancient queens wielded the bells before her? She's not just blessed by the divine descendants. Aelyta takes in the details of the bells. Plain, simple, round bells.

Malo had wrapped it, entangling the braided string around her wrist. But he didn't find them, Edithe did. In the Marigold Temple, Edithe received them from the statue. And Malo gave them to her.

She is a part of the long line of queens from ancient pasts beyond her time, beyond the beginning of Deneb.

Placing her hand to her chest, the bells resting against her torso. What an honor to be part of something larger than the surface of the rocks. Her roots are deep and wide in depths of Deneb history.

"It is an honor to be a queen in the line of ancient queens. Fancy titles, fancy job descriptions. But Pyerre, none of this is helpful in releasing you and the others from these chains. I don't want to use the winds at my whim. I don't want to have power *over* the Elements. I want to stand *beside* the Elements, and return Ospheria and Deneb to what it once was."

"There isn't any returning to what it once was. There is no longer trust in the old ways. As old as I am, I have seen queens rule Ospheria. They have brought comfort and warmth to Ospheria. The Elements may want a queen to lead, but the throne is now tainted with human hands. It will be difficult to trust neighbors, friends, family. It won't be the same as it once was. The Crownship is already scarred."

Her hand reaches for the scar on her right shoulder. "The focus is no longer taking the throne back. This is no longer about politics. This is life or death, and there are Elementals between two countries involved."

25

Wind on Broken Wings
THE INSECT

OUTSIDE OF ELEMENTROPOLIS, the trolley station is usually running throughout the day and closes by sunset. But as Lorraine leads the pack of ladies-in-waiting and a knight from Ospheria, the station is unsettlingly closed. Lorraine runs around the building in search of an unlocked door. It seems the trolley station has been shut down for some time now.

With a plop onto the bench outside the building she says, "Well, that makes sense." Lorraine crosses her arms.

"What makes sense? They're closed." Presley turns to Margaret and Odetta.

Lorraine beckons Jaycub over and grabs her bag from him. "They're open twelve hours a day. It's closed probably due to the state of Muddy Bay. No one is traveling into Elementropolis because there are no people." She pulls a bag of pollen chips to snack on. "Hm, I've got photosynthesized sugar peas for the Queen's lace Florals." Lorraine yanks a few bags of floreted sugar peas.

Odetta gently takes a bag, while Margaret hesitates.

"That's an old term for the Queen's ladies." Presley snatches it from Lorraine's hand. "What do we do now?"

"Rest, because we have about another half-day walk into Elementropolis." Lorraine smacks her lips. "You're awfully quiet, knight." She turns to Jaycub. "Need some fuel?" She gestures her pollen chips towards him.

"What do those taste like?" His face scrunches looking into the bag.

Lorraine shrugs. "Like powdered honey."

Presley meanders around the building eating her sugar peas. Margaret and Odetta lean against the front post. Jaycub is standing in the shade, looking out towards Ospheria. A scream rings into the air. Presley jumps back to the group. "You need to see this." She ushers them to the back of the building.

As they all turn the corner, plumes of smoke rise from the center of the city. They all gasp, but Lorraine is the one to cry out. "That's downtown!" She falls limp to the ground. Her eyes rolling back. Her chest lifts as she lets out a scream.

Jaycub, the closest to her, drops to her side. "What's happening? Lorraine?"

Lorraine whispers, "In the sky." She gulps for air, screaming, "They're everywhere!"

"What is?" Jaycub cups her head.

"There will be no celebration." Lorraine's eyes recenter. "Miles is harvesting Elementropolis."

"We can't go into the city, then." Margaret shakes her head.

"No, but I know a place where we can go." Lorraine's hands fist Jaycub's arms as he helps her rise to her feet. "It's Aelyta's safe house—well, correction—it's Malo's house, but Aelyta has been staying there. I'll send word for Luella if they're not caught in the middle of that." Lorraine gestures to the smoke-filled sky. As soon as she pointed to the sky, a large cloud of hornets flies into Elementropolis from the direction of Ospheria. Lorraine almost screams, but Jaycub covers her mouth, pulling her into the shade of the building. Margaret, Odetta, and Presley all hasten towards the shadows. They watch as the hornet wings vibrate the air as they fly overhead.

Lorraine whispers to Jaycub, "We need to get to the house. Quick."

Jaycub shakes his head. "We need to wait for a clear time."

"No." Lorraine pivots against him. "We need to go now. The winds forecast a terrible, terrible end. We need to go before...before"—Lorraine glances to the ladies—"before they're harvested like the rest of the Florals."

She doesn't wait for Jaycub to answer. Lorraine grabs her bag. The peninsula is a shorter distance than downtown Elementropolis. They will make it. They have to. But the coverage above them is darkening with hornets, if the Floral ladies are seen, they won't make it at all.

Lorraine opens the bag and turns to the three of them. "You need to get in." She gestures the bag to the ladies.

They look at her and at the bag. "What?" Presley scoffs.

"This is Malo's bag," Lorraine explains quickly. "It's pretty much a portal to his Shadow Realm. Get in. They're"—she gestures to the hornets whizzing past over their heads—"looking for Florals and Fungi. Harvesting. They're taking them, you. Get in so we can travel to Malo's house quicker."

"How are we supposed to get in?" Odetta glances at the other two Florals.

Lorraine squeals. "Just step in! Hurry!"

Presley is the first to stick her foot into the bag. The other leg goes in, and she drops in with ease. Margaret's eyes are wide. Odetta jumps in, leaving Margaret frozen in front of Lorraine. Lorraine shakes the bag at her. Margaret slowly steps in and disappears too.

Lorraine doesn't look back as she throws the bag over her shoulder. She sprints towards the west. Lorraine hears the beating footsteps of the knight behind her.

The buzzing of the hornet wings rings louder, but Lorraine refuses to look away from the peninsula. Her legs unrelenting, she pushes forward. A drop vibrates to her right, but she doesn't care. "You," Lorraine hears but she doesn't stop running. The sound of metal clinks and Lorraine turns to look. The sight of Jaycub with his sword unsheathed stops her in her tracks. He's wearing the Ospherian uniform, but the knight he's fighting is wearing a uniform Lorraine has never seen before.

"Keep running!" Jaycub yells to her. "I'll catch up." Lorraine hesitates. "You have to get there first!" he screams, his sword defending a blow.

In the corner of her eye, she notices a few hornets slowing down. Her feet walk backwards towards the peninsula, but they shift. Lorraine runs sideways just as Jaycub slams the hilt of his sword into the knight's face. The face crumbles into pieces of metal and the knight goes limp, heavy in weight due to the amount of metal.

She leaps onto the back of the mechanical hornet. Jaycub rushes and slides up behind her.

Lorraine pushes a lever and the hornet moves forward. She pulls the lever back and the hornet moves backwards.

"Go up," Jaycub grits.

"I'm trying," Lorraine bickers back.

"Well, hurry. I don't like these knights."

"But you're a knight..."

"These ones are not living knights, they're made of metal." Jaycub reaches over her and presses a button. "Try this one." The hornet slams onto its legs.

"Did you know about these metal knights?" Lorraine screams over at Jaycub.

"No, but I heard rumors through the castle before we left. That if we didn't fall into line, they'd replace us. I thought we'd just lose our jobs, not be entirely replaced by mechanical beings."

"You're saying Miles created robotic knights to do his bidding?"

"Him and the Richards." Jaycub points at the emblem on the hornet. The same strange emblem they've been seeing on the knights as well. It's the Richards' mark combined with Miles's face and Ronanbrands' crest.

Air catches in the back of Lorraine's throat when she sees it. Her mind swirling, but that only means they need to get to Malo's house now more than ever.

Lorraine pushes the lever forward and the hornet careens forward. She moves the lever right and forward. The hornet hurtles for the peninsula.

There's a large gate covered in vines where Elementropolis meets the protrusion. The gate knob is shrouded in shadows. Lorraine heads straight for it.

Overhead, the vibrations of the hornet wings fade to a soft hum in the distance. Two hornets drop on either side of Lorraine and Jaycub. Lorraine yelps, Jaycub holding her firm against the hornet's back. He leans into her ear. "Do you know how to fight at all?"

"I'm from the city," Lorraine squawks. She elbows him in the chest. "My shop is in the middle of the downtown. Stupid question, I know how to throw punches!"

"I'll take the right, you take left?"

Lorraine nods. Jaycub launches from the hornets back, unsheathing his sword. He swings at the knight's leg still mounted on the hornet. The knight crumbles to the ground, but not before a large metal stinger shoots from the hornet. It burrows straight into the hornet Lorraine is still mounted on. Her hornet hurls her to the ground. The second knight shoots another stinger at her, but it pierces the downed hornet.

Jaycub slams his sword into the knight on the ground. He races for Lorraine. She's already on her feet, crouching behind the broken mechanical hornet. As soon as he reaches her, she is launching herself onto the back of the second hornet. Pulling the knight down with his head locked in her elbow, the knight struggles to keep his grip on the hornet. She slams him down into the ground. Jaycub doesn't waste time. He wields the sword over his head and punctures the knight just as Lorraine rolls out of grip.

She leaps onto her feet, but she gasps. Jaycub points to the hornet. "Hurry up!" he yells

"My glasses." She spins around in search of her large round spectacles.

"Oh." Jaycub picks them up from the ground and hands them to her. "I think they're a bit broken."

She puts them on her face, but the arms are bent and one of the lenses are sheared into spiderwebs. "I can't see anything without them."

With the help of Jaycub, Lorraine leaps onto the back of the hornet. Jaycub mounts after her.

Reaching around her, he shifts the gears and pushes them forward. "Where am I headed? To the gate?"

"Yes," Lorraine answers. Her hand already holding the key.

As soon as he announces their arrival at the gate, she pushes off the hornet, and he guides her to the gate.

Jaycub carries Lorraine back onto the hornet, and he mounts it behind her. He charges forward.

"There's a house with a bridge," he describes.

Lorraine nods. "That's the place. Go make sure the gate's closed."

"You can't order me around," he answers despite the fact he's already leaping off the hornet to close the gate. Remounting, they take the path outlining the peninsula.

Jaycub stops them at the front of the bridge. Lorraine walks towards the bridge entrance, her hand extended out in front of her.

Quickly catching up behind her, Jaycub meets her at the front door on the other end.

Lorraine's hands fumble around the doorknob before the door finally opens. They both hasten inside.

The bag slides off her back into her hands. Opened, she sticks her head in and yells for Margaret, Odetta, and Presley. No response. She sticks her head in as far as her shoulders and gives another call. Silence follows her voice.

"I don't know how this shadow thing works." Lorraine tosses the bag aside. It lands onto the ground in front of the sofa in the living room.

Jaycub picks it up and sticks his head in. He pulls his head back out. "That's a unique experience." He sticks his head back in and yells for the Queen's ladies, prompting the same response. "Where are they?" His head now out of the bag.

Lorraine shrugs, her hands at her waist as she catches her breath.

"I can't see anything. All I see are blurred colors. On top of that, I don't have shadow elements, I'm Insectal." She turns to the direction she thinks is the kitchen. "Can you help me to the kitchen?"

Jaycub takes her arm and guides her out of the living room.

"Are you getting water? Can I have water?"

"It's not my house," she quips. "Cups are over in that cupboard...I think."

After downing two refills, Jaycub sets the cup down. "You are ballsy, and you know it."

Lorraine stares at him, her eyes narrowing. Against the white marble kitchen, Jaycub is a big, built knight. It wasn't hard to see him without her glasses. Her eyes narrow again anyways. "Tell me, knight. Are you loyal to Ospheria?"

"You're asking if I'm loyal to Aelyta or Miles." He nods. "You don't trust me because I'm a knight with no queen."

"You're a knight without a cause."

"I am loyal to the rightful throne. Worth is measured by the way one moves through difficulties." He steps closer to her.

"Aelyta or Miles?"

"You have to earn loyalty." He wraps an arm around her waist.

"Try again. Aelyta or Miles?"

"Aelyta—geez."

"And what if Aelyta can no longer hold the throne and crown? Who then?"

"Are you asking if I'd stay loyal to the crown no matter how wears it?"

She nods, gesturing her hand for him to answer.

"I think I might be loyal to you."

She rolls her eyes, but a smirk climbs her lips. He lets her go.

He watches her walk out of the kitchen only to hear her cry out for him.

Running around the corner after her, Lorraine asks him to help her out onto the terrace. The sun no longer on the edge of the horizon. The pink clouds ignite the sky.

He guides her outside. Her eyes are open wide. Her pupils are distant, but aware.

"I'm reading the winds," she explains. "Despite my eyesight, I can see the wind as clear as a crystal. But something is happening... The patterns are too unique to what I'm used to. Miles took the Minister of Elementropolis. He's occupying the city, but he's not in Elementropolis. Oh, where's Malo? Where's Aelyta?" Her eyebrows are knitted, eyes distant and wide.

Jaycub stands close. Lorraine gasps. "Aelyta's alive. Malo is on the edge of life." Lorraine blows into the wind as the ocean breeze brushes against her face. "Warn Aelyta of Elementropolis. If she doesn't listen, scream at her." Lorraine closes her eyes. "Thank you."

A wind blows, whistling past them. Lorraine turns towards Jaycub. "Does Edithe know?" The wind blows into a soft breeze. Lorraine nods another gratitude.

She turns and opens her eyes to find Jaycub closely pressed to her face. She gives a smile. "If you were trying to scare me—" she starts.

Jaycub shakes his head. "I have no idea what you are." Amusement in his voice.

"Insectal." She rolls her eyes again.

"Oh, with those big eyes," he returns with a smile of his own.

"You goof." She punches his chest. "Let's go find the other three in that stupid shadow bag. There is so much at stake here."

26

Helluo Librorum
A GLUTTON FOR BOOKS

The Library

IN THE LOWEST depths of Pyerre's Library, Luella, Edin, Malcolm, Maurene, and Ellsy scatter across the underground level of Pyerre's Library, attacking books. Malcolm isn't used to research, choosing books to read based on the covers. Edin can't keep from repairing the books as she scans its contents. But Kody, Luella, and Ellsy are active readers, their heads trapped inside the pages. Maurene tidies the books after the others have thrown them into a pile. Her arms full of books as she shuffles about the bookshelves placing each book back.

Luella squeals at the book she's reading. They all look at her. She doesn't glance away from the book, her finger keeping mark on a page. "Did you guys know the Goblin King was never a real thing? Yes, there was a goblin, but the stories have all been misconstrued—even the legend of the Bugnott Sword has been misinterpreted to Sword of Broken Winds." She reads aloud:

"There was a Butterfly Queen so beautiful, she became

known as the Fairy Queen. She gave birth to a son who was so devastatingly ugly, she called him a goblin and took away his wings as soon as he became of age. He was so wrought with revenge, he kidnapped a human from her world and brought her here into ours. Due to the human's involvement, the Mother Dragon brought forth the Great Flooding which birthed the uprising of the Floral and Fungal descendants."

"Well, that one isn't surprising to me," Ellsy says over her book. "Ospheria is a Crownship, not a kingdom. That's what makes the Goblin King a fairy tale, not history."

"That's what I was getting at. Why create a story of a king in a realm ruled only by the heads of women?"

"Your wording choice is ironic, Lue." Kody picks up his book. "There's a note here in Edithe's handwriting tucked in this book, *Human Powders: From Cut Flowers*. There's a list of flowers and one of them listed is Aelyta."

Luella, Ellsy, and Maurene peer over at Kody's book and the notes. Ellsy points to a paragraph on the page. "Is this why the harvest is happening? The Florals and Fungals are being used as resources? For what?"

Kody hands her the book, pacing back and forth. "I think this is nothing to do with Morphenum. Morphenum is used for enchantments. But this, spices—spices are used for cooking, for seasoning, for medicine..." His voices trails. "Within small doses, medicine is care. Medicine is cure. In a larger, exponential dosage, medicine can become poison. It can become a reckoning to the body and the body's system."

Maurene, who's been quietly hovering over the book, scoffs. They all turn to her. "Miles isn't that particularly intelligent. He can't even make a joke. I think the Richards are using Miles to get what they want. They are an ambitious bunch of men who only want nothing more than money."

"I agree for the most part," Ellsy responds. "But like father, like son. Kyanston and Julius are a reflection of the same person. They're spoiled, demanding brats. They would just demand what they want, not undermine to get there."

"If anything"—Malcolm yawns—"I think it's those old gasses who had always hovered over the late Queen Jane. Remember how they would snatch things out of her hands before the Queen would hand it over to Lyta? Aelyta hated them for that. She was adamant and crystal clear about those four." Malcolm doesn't wait for anyone else to respond as he continues. "Like that one day, the day after her Rite of Divinity. They summoned her for a meeting only to undercut her and have their own chitchat. She stormed their meeting and they told her off. I remember the look on her face when she came back to her chambers. Lyta didn't just look defeated, she was angry with those four."

"Who are the four we're talking about?" Luella glances at the Avelmore group.

Ellsy answers, "The four Royal Advisors. They're incredibly aged. I think they've been around for...two queens now?"

"Over the lifetime of three reigns," Maurene corrects. "Jane, Ruth, and the once counsel of queens."

Edin calls from the worktable. "I think you folks would find this useful." Edin hands them the booklet. "It hasn't been bound into a book yet. It looks like a conference reporting from the Philosopher's Academy."

Kody takes the book from her, skimming through the pages. "This is remarkable...outstanding..." He paces around with the booklet. "This is groundbreaking...It's...marked down one age ago. Two days after Jane's death?"

Ellsy snags the booklet from him and gasps. "That's the morning before Aelyta found her mother dead in their carriage." Ellsy glances to Maurene, who strides over with a hug.

Luella takes the booklet. "What's so groundbreaking?"

"Floral and Fungal Elements are used to heal Elementals. It's fascinating, but also grotesque. Of course, within the booklet, the Alchemadia Committee processed the substances from volunteers rather than taking them off the streets. The study used the Elemental substances to its full extent. Making materials like paper to medicine for the common blithe. The only thing they didn't do was test whether the Elemental substances can be used to make enchantments."

"But the new material to replace Morphenum," Edin pipes. "Do you think it's the Elemental...spices?"

"That's politics." Malcolm shrugs.

Ellsy and Luella gag at his comment. "How could you call this politics?" Ellsy yells. "This is pure deadly."

Kody nods. "This is unregulated use of the Alchemadia's philosophy. It's against all that the alchemists stand for. The thing is that someone in Ospheria, in a position of influence, got ahold of this information. This feeling isn't based on facts, but I can feel it's true."

Nodding rolls around the group.

"What are we agreeing to?" Edithe appears between Ellsy and Luella. Maurene and Ellsy jump back, stumbling into one another.

"Mom!" Luella cries. "Where'd you go this time?"

"I'm sorry, my sweet." Edithe pats her daughter with her ghostly hand. "I was stuck in the Liminal. It was like my soul couldn't pass back into this realm, and the souls couldn't get through to the other side. The vibration in the air was terrifying. And then Aelyta was there, in the Liminal with me. We met the goddesses of light and shadow. They sent her back to this realm, which is what caused the passing between realms to open again."

"You've met the goddesses?" Luella eyes her mom.

"I did, but it wasn't all what it seems. Things are happening."

"Of course, they already happened." Edin gestures outside. "There were Florals and Fungals executed in broad daylight on the streets. Their heads cut and harvested."

"Yes, yes, I know—well, no, not that part. That's what Aelyta was probably referring to. She called it the harvest. Her father is harvesting. But I think there's something more at play, the goddesses want Aelyta to 'bring to light.' Goddess Ko'nkiun referred to her as the child of the light...And Lyza, the child of stardust—that girl is as hard-headed as a rock. Strong-willed disguised as a delicate crystal."

Malcolm, Maurene, and Ellsy snicker. "That's Lyza."

Luella pushes her way towards Edithe. "What do you mean stardust child?"

Maurene explains, "Lyza was born from a rock found in Morf Mountain."

Ellsy adds, "She fell out of a chunk of rock."

Maurene reminisces, "I remember the day she was brought to Avelmore. The guards who brought her said it was as if she was from the mountains themselves, but the late queen said she came from the ocean of the sky."

"Lyza's arm"—Edithe nods to Maurene and Ellsy—"it's breaking open. Lyza believes it's doing so because the stars are spinning out of balance. There's something in the air that is spinning the atmosphere off its kilter. The Liminal is out of balance. The two have to be connected. It can't be simply a coincidence."

Malcolm hiccups. "I think I saw something in a book about stars and space."

"Well, that makes sense, the two would be together," Ellsy sneers.

"No, no, I mean there was something science related about the stars and space, but then there was something to do with the wind being alive..." He ruffles through the pile of books. Maurene hands him a book from the shelf.

"You only read through this one."

"Yes, yes, I think that's the one. There's a funny drawing on page something...oh, two hundred and eight. Here, look." He turns the book around to the group.

"Maybe there is some truth to Lorraine's forecasting." Edin and Luella share a glance.

Edithe rolls her eyes. "There's always some truth to what she sees."

"Well, of course, but this is major," Luella points out. "This is catastrophic."

"Is it something to do with Miles? Is there are ploy going on with Miles and all the rich and powerful?" Edin asks.

"That's possible," Luella starts. "But again, you lot mentioned Miles isn't smart. He isn't savvy. Could there be a mastermind controlling behind the scenes? Someone who is scientifically capable, but also in tune with Deneb has to be behind this."

Edithe barks, "I think I know!" They all turn to the ghost. Her eyes wide behind her round glasses.

"Let me explain first. The High Priestess was cut down at Marigold Temple," Edithe remembers. "And they've taken Pyerre to Morf Mountain, that's what Aelyta was worrying herself about in the Liminal."

"Who would kill the Hight Priestess?"

"That's the thing. I think the person, or people, behind the downfall of Deneb may be the same person who killed me." Edithe shrugs.

Every single one of them instantly pauses. Edin is the one to break the silence. "You said that you died by natural causes—that is was nothing nefarious."

Luella nods in agreement. Edithe glances at their faces. Her eyebrows collapse at the edges.

"I'm sorry, I didn't mean to lie."

"Do you know who killed you?" Luella asks. "For certain?"

Edithe sighs. "I was—you know, by someone when I was standing up there in one of the aisles of books. I was staring at that very book before—you know. He had a cloak over his head, the exact same one as the four cloaked men who killed the High Priestess."

"Four cloaked men?" Luella tenses. "What do you mean?"

"The Royal Advisors?" Malcolm implores.

"My heart is already stopped, but when I saw the cloaks coming down from their aircraft, I remembered the feeling in the back of my throat. My body remembered the way my heart stopped all over again. I thought I'd never see that cloak again, but then there it was. Four of them."

They all stare at the dandelion ghost, stunned at the confession. Edin and Kody both reach for Luella.

Luella's arms twist around herself as she glances back and forth between her mother and her aunt. "Mom, you lied to me about being murdered?"

27

A Hop and A Skip
THE INSECT

LORRAINE ROLLS HER SLEEVES, Jaycub pacing behind her. The two of them focus on the sack portal open in the middle of Malo's living room.

"Did you try sticking your leg into the bag?" Jaycub supplies.

Lorraine rolls her eyes. "Yes, and so did you."

"I don't know how this magic stuff works." His shoulders roll up.

"I don't know how this shadow magic works either." She crosses her arms and stares at the bag in front of her. A blurred, round plump of fabric nestles a swirl of distorted colors.

Jaycub snaps his fingers. "Maybe we just didn't open the bag big enough?"

Lorraine simply scoffs.

Quiet envelopes the room. Quiet, except for the sound of Jaycub's pacing, and the sound of an animal chomping.

Glancing around, Lorraine spots a black puffball gnawing against the wood floorboard.

"Misty." She rises from her spot on the floor. "Malo will be so mad if he finds out." She shoos the rabbit away.

The two of them watch as the animal scurries and leaps, disappearing into the backsack. Lorraine and Jaycub gawk at the sight, or more like the lack of the rabbit.

"What just happened—" Lorraine starts.

Misty's head pops out of the sack, and she bounds out of the bag.

Jaycub grabs Lorraine's hand and scoops the rabbit up with the other. They lunge for the bag and the three of them collapse into darkness.

"Are we...inside the bag?" Jaycub pads through the darkness.

"Stop grabbing my head." Lorraine brushes his hands away. "We're in the Shadow Realm."

"Don't let go of the rabbit." His voice quakes. "Whatever you do, please."

"I won't." Lorraine grabs his hand. "I won't let go."

She notices the white on Misty is glowing in the shadows. Lorraine puts her down and the rabbit hops forward once, then popcorns a couple times. When she stops moving, Misty's ears pivot like antennas.

Lorraine holds her breath as she follows the rabbit's white glow while holding onto Jaycub's hand. The rabbit prances in a direction. Lorraine keeps up, Jaycub following her lead.

The sound of whimpers and chattering softly in the darkness makes Jaycub gasp. "I hear something."

"Me, too."

Lorraine pulls Jaycub as she follows the rabbit through the shadows. "Margaret?" Lorraine cries out. "Presley? Odetta?"

"Who's there?" A voice cries out.

"Lorraine and Jaycub," Jaycub is the one to answer. "Oh, boy, are we so glad to find you three!"

"Are you all okay? Anyone hurt?" Lorraine keeps an eye on the white glow of the rabbit circling the three Florals.

"We're fine." Margaret stands. "We'd like to get out of here though."

"How do we do that?" Jaycub's shoulders drop.

Lorraine looks in the direction of Misty. "I have no clue, either."

"Great, so we're stuck here? In the dark? Forever?"

"Oh, Presley," Odetta tuts. "We just need to see things—"

"Do not," Presley cuts her off. "I don't need to hear you say 'in a brighter perspective' one more time."

"But it's ironic because there are no lights here in the dark." Odetta shrugs.

"We get it," Margaret and Presley snap.

Thunder rumbles through the shadows. A voice as thick as the shadows themselves. "Aelyta's been captured. I, too, am chained in Avelmore. Make sure to keep Misty fed. She likes strawberries."

"Malo, how do we get out of here?" Lorraine yells out.

Jaycub cries out, "Aelyta's in Avelmore, too?"

"If she's not dead yet." Malo's voice rumbles away like distant thunder. "Follow the light."

"What light? Wait, is that the light?" Jaycub pulls Lorraine's hand.

Margaret and Presley snap again, but their voices fall flat. Odetta giggles uncontrollably. Misty runs through all their legs before bursting forward. She saunters towards the small speckle of light ahead: one star twinkling all alone in the night sky.

The sparkling little light grows until it becomes as big as a door. Jaycub, leading the way, opens it. The shadows fall like a cloak and a room reveals itself, Misty prances around inside.

"Misty?" Luella cries. "Lorraine?"

Lorraine drops her hand out of Jaycub's as they enter the space. "Luella," she sighs. "Oh, Luella! I broke my glasses and my head is hurting from everything being blurry."

"Oh, I always carry a spare for you." Kody approaches. His transportable alchemist bag open in one hand. He hands her a large case.

Opening the large case, she shoves the overly large glasses onto her face. Nearly in tears, she gives Kody a dramatic thanks.

Lorraine turns to the three Florals with their eyes on the ghost in the room.

Edithe gives a little wiggle of her hand, a funny wave, to the Florals.

"You wanted us to meet your daughter, but you're already here?" Presley pipes.

"Yes, well, you guys took too long." Edithe shrugs.

Edin chimes, "To their credit, Miles is destroying all of Elementropolis."

"Even worse, Mom lied about her death!" Luella is the one in actual tears. "She was murdered." Luella hiccups.

Murmurs of agreement roll around the room. They all embrace little Luella.

"This is why I don't want to talk about...you know." Edithe cups her daughter's cheeks. Her ghost fingers can't wipe away the living tears.

Edin pulls out a small rag from the table she was working at. Handing it to her sister, Edithe uses it to dry Luella's tears.

"It's exactly why you tell us, tell me!" Luella cries out.

Kody, Lorraine, and even Ellsy patting the dandelion sprout as the mother and daughter embrace.

Ellsy turns to the ladies. "How are you guys even here?"

Approaching the three ladies, Ellsy gives them all hugs. Maurene coming over, not far behind her.

"Misty," Lorraine answers, proudly. "She's a shadow bun. But I have news from Malo, he's been captured and being held in Avelmore. We're not sure if Aelyta is dead or alive."

"Oh, she's alive," Edithe answers. "The goddesses made sure of that."

"We also have some news." Kody points to the pages they had just reviewed. "We might have some clue to who's behind the downfall of Deneb."

"Then we head to Avelmore to save Malo?" Lorraine suggests. "He's the last missing piece to saving the falling stars."

"Exchange information and let's get out of here." Malcolm pats Jaycub on the back.

Misty hops onto the table nearest Lorraine. "We'll have to use Misty to travel. I don't know how safe it is out there, but our safest bet is with this gal."

28

Those That Came Before
THE QUEEN

AFTER TESTING a few blows of Pyerre's water flames, the chains refuse to relent. A storm brews above them. Pyerre slumps against the chains. His two front legs clutched by shackles built just for him. Aelyta grumbles, leaning against the rock face. She's bleeding from the back of her head, but she hasn't told the old dragon yet.

Her hand pulls away from her wound. Unlike all the other times she's bled, Aelyta is bleeding gold. She won't be telling the dragon about her wound anytime soon.

Seeing how he's fuming his flames onto the cuffs on his two front legs, he knows she's more badly hurt than she's vocalized.

"You must recede to higher ground if I am not free in time for the flooding," he says, licking his arm where the metal skins him.

"I can manage water."

"It's not the water, Your Majesty. It's the current in which the water flows through these caverns. I don't know where they lead, and I fear the deeper the mountain we go, the darker our future may be."

He's right. The rain is already flooding up to her ankles, flowing somewhere into the depths of the mountain. "We need to get you unchained quickly." She wades the water towards the dragon. The cavern floods to her shins.

"Climb onto my back before the water gets too tall."

"But my weight..."

"Is only but a flower." He leans his tail for her. Aelyta grabs hold of his spine ridge and climbs to his neck. The rain pelts a curtain of crashing water from the clouds above.

Pyerre claws the rock face and climbs as high as the chains will allow. Pyerre clings to the side of the rock, while Aelyta clings to the back of his neck. Their grip tightens as the water rises. The current moves fast, causing a misty wind to pull against them. Pyerre climbs the rock face. His claws dig into the base of the chains, gripping as only a dragon can into a mountain.

Her grip tight, Aelyta grabs hold of her wrists around the dragon's neck. Her hand takes hold of the bells. The bells. She shakes her wrist, but the angle in which they're hanging defies gravity. Aelyta climbs around Pyerre's neck and shakes her wrist again. The bells glow gold and the gold climbs her arm.

"Breathe," Pyerre instructs.

With a blow, a bubble forms—small at first—from her lips. The more air she blows, the larger it grows. Aelyta blows up the bubble until it surrounds the dragon, pushing against the chains attached to the rock. A crackling, and the chains crumble from the rock face.

Aelyta gasps, and the bubble pops. They plummet into the roaring water below. The two of them are engulfed into the force of the current, Aelyta spinning underneath the surface. Pyerre gets tangled in the loose chains. She grabs hold of the end of the loose chain, pulling herself through the current up towards the dragon.

The bells on her wrist rattle against the metal. One flick of her wrist and she blows a bubble around her. With a rush of air into her lungs, she uses the chain to guide her to Pyerre. Blowing the bubble larger as she makes her way onto the dragon, she notices the chain is tangled around his two front legs and a rock. The bubble grows around the two of them as she works her hand at the links lodged in between the rocks.

Pyerre twists and turns behind her as she pulls the chain out from the rock. Her hands are still on the chain when the dragon is whipped into the current, pulling Aelyta with him. The two of them are carried into the depths of the mountain.

Darkness swallows them like a funnel of water. Aelyta screams as they drop straight down into the unknown. Before she could climb on top of Pyerre's back, they plunge into a large body of water. She clings to the chain attached to Pyerre's leg. As soon as she feels Pyerre's mouth grab hold of her, she lets go. He tosses her over the edge of the water. Tumbling, she rolls out onto her back, catching her breath. The dragon fumbles over the water's edge, still tangled in the chains.

Inside the mountain, dim lights flicker on the edge of the cavern. An old, abandoned factory of some kind used to take up the space here. Aelyta spies a set of tools on a wooden table near the rock face wall. She grabs large metal shears and clips the cuffs off the dragon's legs. Together, they untangle the chains. Pyerre shakes his wings and legs free at last.

Aelyta throws the shears aside. Large machinery lines the cavern in rows of three. Dangling down from above, tubes lined with a glittery substance attach to the machines below.

The glittering dust clings to the damp stones like pollen. The smell is pungent. Familiar. Aelyta nearly vomits at the realization.

The powder, the mountain, the machines. Aelyta sways at the sickness in her throat.

The Florals and Fungals turn to dust, and the water penetrates the powder into the mountainous rocks. The rain floods the bowls, and the water runs down into the mountains, soaked with the dead Elementals, pumped into the machines below the mountain. This is Morphenum. This is what creates the enchantments. This is the extra spice the Elementals have been using, ingesting, and consuming. The mountain is penetrated with years, probably even generations of Elementals, chained and bound until dust, only to become ingested by their kin.

"There's a tunnel," Pyerre grumbles by a large opening. "It may lead us out of the mountain."

"You can go ahead." Aelyta shakes her head. "I'm not leaving without the Elementals."

"How are you going to manage that?"

Looking around, there are more openings leading out of the cavern. The rainwater still flows into a large lake at the edge, the edge cutting into the opening.

"This body of water, where does this go? The bottom of the Muddy Bay deltas?"

"That is a possibility, Flower Queen. But what I can do is pull the rocks down from within." The dragon stands beside a large mechanism attached to the ceiling of the mountain above them.

"What does that do?"

Pyerre grumbles and flips the mechanism on. The

mountain rumbles from within. The ceiling crumbles atop of them. Aelyta ducks and Pyerre grabs hold of her, covering her with his wings. Screams ring through the cavern, echoing with the sound of the mountain caving in.

Heart-wrenching screams cut through her heart. Aelyta yells, her arms extend out to the Elementals falling through the mountain. Bubbles fill the cavern slowing down time. The rocks and Elementals frozen in descent.

"You're learning," Pyerre roars.

"I don't know how." Aelyta refuses to drop her arms. She lowers them gentle and slow, the bubbles following her command. Inside them, the Elementals are frozen and stunned. The bubbles land softly with a buoyant pop as they touch the debris littered ground. "Are any of you hurt?" She exclaims to the Elementals. They're sitting where they landed, confused and in disarray. All of them wet from the rain, which has now settled into a soft sprinkle of mist.

A soft whine of cries roll through them. Sproutlings. They're merely sproutlings. Not all of them, but most of them are. She looks up at Pyerre. "Can you check if the tunnel is clear? Lead them out of the mountain. I'll free the others."

"And there are many more mountains." Pyerre looks back at the other openings.

"I know." She sighs. "But I'll free as many as I can before the Richards come back after the harvest."

"Little ones, follow me." Pyerre nods to Aelyta. He leads the Elementals through the opening.

Aelyta runs farther into the caverns. With a jingle of her wrist, she blows a large bubble. Pushing it up to the mountaintop. One arm up to hold the bubble, the other flips the mechanism. The mountain crumbles into the cave, but the bubble secures the debris and Elementals. Aelyta floats them down gently. The bubble pops and the Elementals scurry.

"This way, everyone," Aelyta directs. "Follow the sproutlings and the dragon. They will lead you out of the mountains." She ushers them through. The surge of Elementals file out in a matter of minutes. Aelyta keeps running deeper into the mountains. Large bubble holding the ceiling of the cavern as she pulls the mechanism. The crumbling sounds through the cavern, but the orb holds the ceiling in place. Aelyta gently floats the ceiling and the Elementals down. Yelling the same instructions and waiting for everyone to file out.

Repeating, repeating, she doesn't stop. Even when the Elementals towards the back are dwindling and few in number, Aelyta refuses to give up. Except for the last two caverns, Aelyta pulls down the ceiling and carries down the Elementals into the cavern. Not one Elemental was alive to make the run out of the cavern, Aelyta leaves the last two caverns quietly and alone.

"May the goddesses guide your path to the Liminal," she whispers. A soft prayer for the forsaken.

It wasn't until she approaches the large, immense surge of the Elementals making their way through the cavern tunnels, that she realized her body was shaking, trembling.

At the head of the large crowd, Pyerre leads them through the tunnels. Aelyta squeezes through, diving between Elementals until she settles into a walking pace beside Pyerre.

No guards, no Richards, Aelyta scans for a clue that they were setup in some way. They migrate through the tunnels. Two large wooden doors to the outside greet them. The rain has stopped, and the sun is pointing towards the large entryway. The dark blue of the sky giving way to blue dawn. Not far, tall buildings make themselves known. They're near the Royal Philosopher's Academy.

Behind her, Aelyta hears the grumbles of disappointment. The Academy is the farthest location in Deneb away from Elementropolis. But it is a vast town that she is certain will be accommodating.

"Let's settle in the Royal Academy before moving onward for Ospheria," Aelyta suggests to Pyerre. The dragon groans his approval.

He turns to the other Elementals. "The Queen suggests we shall take rest at the Philosopher's Academy before setting forth to Ospheria. From Ospheria, you all may decide to move on to Elementropolis or Muddy Bay."

At first the people grumble, Aelyta makes note that they are tired, dehydrated. A ping in her heart. But the cheers soar from the back of the procession to the front of the crowd, yells of anger enraged and ready to fight.

"Let's go give them what they deserve." A Floral in the front line nods to Aelyta.

Turning to Pyerre. "I think we should give the people what they want." She turns back to the crowd. "Those who choose to fight, we must make a distraction to keep the knights busy from the others who choose to move on. At best, let us be rid of these torturers."

Cries of agreement ring from the Elementals.

As they approach the Academy, mechanical wasps line the path leading in. The facilities are empty of royal philosophers. And in their place, knights in unknown uniforms run amok.

"They're using the Academy as a form of bunker," Aelyta

whispers to the dragon. "We'll need to pass through quietly towards Ospheria."

No sooner than she's able to relay to the others, the knights catch sight of Pyerre and Aelyta. "Your Majesty, my back," he instructs.

Aelyta flings herself up onto his neck as he roars a stream of molten water towards the knights. Yelling to the other Elementals, "To Ospheria, go!" The crowd of Elementals rush through the Academy. Pyerre readies for another round. His chest glowing blue.

Knights mount their mechanical wasps, but Aelyta jingles her wrist, and the bells capture the knights in a bubble. She drops the bubble as Pyerre fires flames of water. "Is that all of them?" Aelyta scans the Academy from Pyerre's neck.

"There weren't many," Pyerre answers.

"They all must be at the harvest." A nasty taste fills her mouth. What have they done to the Academy? The studies? What have they done to the philosophers?

29

Song of the Old

ALL THE ELEMENTALS assist in clearing the grounds of Miles's knights. Those who chose to stay at the Academy made their farewells to Pyerre and Aelyta, and the rest of the Elementals who decide to move on to Ospheria.

Aelyta peers into the buildings, but they're empty and only used as storage by the knights. One glance back at the others and Pyerre, Aelyta slips towards the direction of the royal complex where she had visited for a conference with the philosophers merely a year ago alongside her mother.

The large conference hall is a grand lecture hall adorned in hallow wood touched by the many hands who have come here to learn. Where have all the philosophers gone? Were they chained and caged? Or, worse?

Roaming the grounds in search of any signs, any clues of where the previous residences have gone, Aelyta discovers the room. The facility has been wiped clean of any academic aesthetic. Turned into an elaborate laboratory, the large room is lined with shelves upon shelves of bottled powdered dust. Aelyta has found the stock of Morf Blue—the Richards' Morphenum.

Her hand runs along the shelf when the eruption of yells and screams ring from outside the building. Aelyta rushes out to find the Elementals running to her, clinking sounds and an uproar of smoke behind them. Aelyta steps aside and ushers the Elementals into the building. Reaching out her hand, the last Elemental grips it as she pulls the Fungal into the door. Aelyta grabs the door and notices the four white robes.

Without hesitation, she closes the doors before the hornet stingers hit with four thuds. Four stingers. Four white robes. Despicable white robes. Tension runs through her arms, her hands fist as she pivots her back against the door. Aelyta lets out an ire-filled scream. Panicked looks glance at her, but she doesn't care.

"I am angry of old, outdated men taking what is ours. I am angry of all of Deneb at the disposal of the men who believe they have all the power on this star-rock. We have been cut, reduced down to mere dirt. But Deneb is older and so are our roots, planted in these very soils. Our descendants are long. We may have been harvested like wild plants, but we are still Floral and Fungi of Deneb. We will grow stronger, heartier, because our roots have been implanted here far longer than the humans may want us to believe. We are a force of nature forced to grow in unwelcoming environments, but still we grow. And we will, our roots will hold us firm. Our stems will reach for the sun again and again. We will bloom in the harshest of storms. That is our greatest strength. The more we are cut, the stronger and more plentiful we'll become." Aelyta grabs the handles of the door and pushes them open. The sight of Pyerre slashing the mechanical hornets with his tail unfolds before them. Aelyta turns back to the Elementals inside the building. "Join me or not, but I am Aelyta Aurelianus, Queen of Ospheria. I will fight for all of you and for all of Ospheria, for all of Deneb."

Aelyta sprints for Pyerre, who catches sight of her. He leans in just in time for her to lunge up under his wing and swing herself up onto his back. She mounts the back of his neck. Pyerre lets out a thundering roar, his chest burning blue with a bolt of boiling flames of water readying.

Pyerre lifts his head before exhaling the flames onto the line of mechanical hornets in front of the pedestal floating the four Royal Advisors. Aelyta points her finger straight at the four white robes.

Elementals thunder from the buildings, charging towards the mechanical hornets.

The floating pedestal redirects to the direction of Avelmore Castle in the distance.

"They're retreating!" Aelyta exclaims. Pyerre's wings spread out. Two flaps and they're up in the air. Aelyta glances back at the Elementals pouring from the buildings, armed with chairs, desks, and books. "Let's take back Ospheria. Deneb is our home. Home should not be feared or threatened. Home is where we are welcomed and cherished. Home is where we feel safe. Miles has taken you from your home. It is time he descends from the throne." Aelyta's voice carries over the Elementals gathered at the edge of the Academy beneath Pyerre. Echoing over them, Aelyta cries out, "With our numbers, we are a mass to Miles's small cry. Let's set forth for Avelmore. Let us show Deneb our numbers. We are survivors of the mountains. We are survivors of the sun, the rain, the rocks. Let us set forth for the castle. In order to go home, we must take back our house. Let us set forth for Avelmore. Stand. Our. Ground."

Aelyta points to the east. Pyerre leans towards the

castle in the distance. The Elementals below march towards the wall of rock blockading Ospheria from all of Deneb. The sun is high above them, the air thick with pressure. A storm is brewing. The air is uncomfortable, but it is alive with song. The Elementals below sing the old songs of gold. A song as old as the Goblin King, the Butterfly Queen, the birth of the Goddess Ko'nkiun.

"We hold no weapons.
We yield our poison.
We sing the songs
that guide us to our freedom.
We are the Elements.
We are true to Deneb lands.
We are the Elements.
Together, hand in hand."

As they approach the wall of Ospheria, the singing only grows. Folks of Ospheria join the mass with Aelyta leading the way on the back of Pyerre. Their songs echo through the neighborhoods as they enter the line of Ospheria. Children run out from their houses to watch. There are Elementals who run into the march singing along. Elementals on the sidelines singing the song until the march passes by.

Like the supporters joining in masses, there are also the knights with the unique uniform riding in on mechanical hornets. Rows of mechanical hornets confront Pyerre and Aelyta at the head of the march. Pyerre roars a monstrous cry. "We do not come to harm!" Pyerre's voice booms. "Let us pass peacefully!"

The knights progress towards them. Their faces hidden behind their metal helms. Aelyta urges, "This is not a coup, but a protest. Elementals of all of Deneb refuse to live in fear. We do not wish to support a king who claims to be a king of all of Deneb. Deneb is, and shall always, remain kingless. Let us pass."

The mechanical hornets buzz frivolously before charging into the head of the snake. Pyerre's tail swings midair at the charging front. But their stingers do not aim for them, the hornets sling their stingers into the crowd below. Cries of pain and panic erupt. Aelyta looks down at the Elementals. Her eyes catch sight of the horrors. A mother clutching her sproutling screaming, "My baby!" Four Elementals help assist another injured Elemental. Three other Elementals with stingers protruding from parts of their body. It isn't right, and the sight below sickens Aelyta.

"We hold no weapons. We yield our poison. We sing the songs that guide us to our freedom. We are the Elements. We are the Elements. We. Are. The. Elements. Nature will take care of itself." Her voice rings against the sound of the mechanical hornet wings. "You use brute force, we want peace. You use weapons, we have none. You want power, we want freedom." Aelyta chants. Pyerre chants with her. The crowd below stands firm despite the injured and the dead. "We are the Elements. You use force. We want peace. You use weapons. We have none. You want power. We want freedom!"

The crowd moves forward. Pyerre bellows a round of roars. His chest glows blue, but he doesn't fire a single flame. His voice is as loud as the crowd below them. Another stream of stingers fires into the crowd. Screams of pain echo again, but the chants refuse to end. More stingers. More screams. More injuries. Aelyta's heart rips more, more, and more. But the chants still echo, the chants unrelenting. She dares to look down once more.

Her eyes lock onto the iridescent-blue skin of one of her ladies-in-waiting. She'd recognize the stardust child anywhere. Lyza is in the crowd, standing beside Cory, no less—but she's in the crowd. Lyza, a small petite figure, dressed in a royal maid's uniform. Aelyta catches the glint of metal in Lyza's hand. Flying above the crowd, Aelyta can hear the stardust Elemental screaming alongside the other's chants. Lyza's voice is faint against the backdrop of the many, but she's screaming, "Coward. Coward!"

Aelyta raises herself. Her voice loud, "Let us pass peacefully. I will give you one more chance to let us through."

One of the knights clinks the side of the mechanical hornet with his ankle in response to her request. The stingers pointed down at the ready. "One chance," Aelyta repeats. Pyerre's chanting stops, his chest warm and blue.

The knights fire another round of stingers at the Elementals. Pyerre ignites a blow of blue flames of water at the hornets. The crowd below surges forward. The march now at full speed towards Avelmore Castle.

Screaming at the top of her lungs, Aelyta cries out her rage. If they won't listen, if they won't reason, they'll have to learn the weight of the many. Aelyta claps her hands together, hard enough for the bells on her wrist to jingle. Pulling her hands away, she scoops the air. The jingle of the bells rustling as she pushes her palms towards the knights, the mechanical hornets, and the stingers. Repeating, the sound of the jingles. The dragon's roar. The chanting below. The air is thick with sound, thick with the weight of the many. Pulling and pushing the air, Aelyta's hand scoops and palms. The weight is there, she can feel it.

She doesn't pull hard, just scooping. She pushes, only to guide.

Her eyes narrow onto the castle behind the line of knights. Focusing, honing, she feels it. The drag and pull of the air, the wind, the shadows, and the Liminal. They're all intertwined like a braid of strings tied together by the sound of the bells jingling against her wrist.

Clouds quicken above the scene. Dark, swirling with speed, they veil the sun. The wind careens faster than the clouds can ride. The scream in the wind is the song of the old. With the chanting below, the bells on her wrist, Aelyta blows the wind into the direction of the hornets. The mechanical hornets roll like tumbleweeds. The knights struggle to stay mounted. Cries of their fall evokes cheers from the crowd below.

"Avelmore Castle, Pyerre." Aelyta points her hand to the castle. "Let's show all of Deneb how alive the Queen of Ospheria really is."

30

Exigo a me non ut optimus par sim sed ut malis melior

I REQUIRE MYSELF NOT TO BE
EQUAL TO THE BEST, BUT TO BE
BETTER THAN THE BAD

The Shadow

MALO HEARS the rumbling chaos in the distance. He glances up, his head sore from hanging in chains on the top of the cobbled roof. There are mechanical hornets firing into the landscape. He clearly sees Pyerre. Pyerre never uses his flames in violence. But in the distance, there he is. The dragon with water flames exerting himself. He doesn't fire at the line of the hornets. There's something moving on his back. Malo squints. A pull of his shadows, the tug in the darkness, an ache in his heart.

On the back of Pyerre's neck, Aelyta's learned to use the bells. From the moment he held the braided string in his hand, he knew it belonged to her. The bells ring with the forces of the wind. Edithe handed them to him, not Lorraine. From that singular action from Edithe, he knew: Aelyta must learn to use the bells.

"Good," Malo whispers. "She's coming home to herself."

From a distance, he truly feels like a thunderstorm evaporating away from her. A settling feeling softens in his shoulders. He has been given a second chance. The realization relaxes his body.

The night he made himself known to her with his dagger in hand, and the blade etched hilt deep in her heart, she was supposed to be dead. He had killed her, but this entire time, he was given a second chance.

Laughing into the breeze caressing his face, he says, "You all knew what was in store for us, didn't you?"

Malo curses the winds. Sighing, he continues, "Because real love doesn't truly leave even after they do." He looks up towards Aelyta, so far away, so small in the sky. "Whenever you're ready, Death, I am ready for my reaping."

He slumps into the chain ready for Death, a drift into the Liminal. He's hoping to greet Edithe as a bare soul, a spirit. Instead, the rooftop door creaks open. Malo's father climbs onto the flat of the roof next to Malo.

"Still alive are we?" Julius mocks. "I will free you from these chains. In return..." Julius levels his eyes with Malo, a glint shimmering in them. "In return, kill that girl and you will receive my highest honor. From her death, you will rise to take my place." Julius turns the key in the lock of the cuff. The metal falls from Malo's wrists and ankles.

"That's it?" Malo cracks his neck, arms, and knees.

Julius smirks. "That's it."

With a grunt, Malo leaps onto the flat of the roof in front of the trapdoor. He takes one last look at the dragon speeding for the castle. "Then, it's done." He disappears through the door.

A celebratory laugh bellows from his father behind him. "That's my son."

Shaking off the sentiment, Malo fires down the stairs. He grabs a small mechanical hornet from a knight's hip on the way out of the elaborate front door of Avelmore Castle.

Sauntering out, the stinger pointed at the ready for the queen.

Not a moment too soon, Pyerre drops with a quake of the ground. Rock and dirt flies like a tornado of dust and smoke. A cry from the dragon echoes through Avelmore. Malo doesn't move. His arm out, the stinger pointed at Aelyta. She moves for him, walking up to the stinger pointed to her forehead.

"I do not hold a weapon," she greets him.

Malo doesn't smile. "You have a dragon, the dragon of Deneb."

"And that means something? He's fighting for himself, like all Elementals are fighting for their lives."

"Speaking like a true queen, I see." He grabs hold of the back of her neck, pivoting her to face the front of Avel-more Castle. "You think you're coming home?"

"No," her voice soft. "No, I've come to finish the game."

"A game with your father?"

"A game set in play by the men who run from the face of justice!" she screams at the castle. "If you want me dead already, then do it."

She nudges the side of her temple to the point of the stinger. "They're all watching from inside. I can feel it. They want it that badly, then give them the show."

"Ready, are we?"

"Ready." Aelyta narrows her eyes at the front balcony where four white robes stand with two men standing off the side.

A click blasts next to her ear, but the stinger flies up to the balcony. Pyerre bursts a large flame of boiling water up into the balcony as the stinger pierces the neck of one of the Royal Advisors. The boiling flame floods the balcony. The tenants retreat into the castle.

"You thought I would truly kill you?" Malo caresses the back of her neck.

"Never."

"Good." He clicks the hornet in his hand for another stinger to appear. He grabs the back of her head and pulls her harder than he'd like, but he couldn't help himself. He engulfs his lips with hers.

She refuses to let go, but the sound of the march approaches.

"You're alive." She rests her head against his chin.

He cups her face. "Did they hurt you? Did they touch you?"

Aelyta's eyes darken. "I'll take care of them."

"No, I will." Malo steps away and turns to the dragon. "Come on, Pyerre. Let's bring down the roof."

Cheers and claps resound from behind Aelyta. She takes a few breaths before turning to look. The march of the Elementals amasses at the castle front.

Lyza at the front of the line, leading the chants and the march. Aelyta runs up to her.

"I never once thought you were dead." Lyza embraces Aelyta.

Aelyta chuckles. "Look at you! I'm so proud of you! You are quite the star."

"Oh, stop. I'm not a star, just stardust." She elbows Aelyta. "Let's go find those old gas-holes. I wanna watch them suffer." Lyza turns to Cory standing behind her. "Your turn to lead the people. You think you've got what it takes?"

Cory glances at Lyza, then turns to Aelyta. His eyes

soften at the sight of her. When his eyes land on the scarred shoulder, he diverts his gaze.

"It doesn't hurt anymore and it's pretty much healed." She shrugs her right shoulder.

"If I had known what you meant to Malo, I wouldn't have... Well, you see..." he stutters. "What I'm trying to say is that I'm sorry." His shoulders relax as the words flow. "I'm sorry I thought you betrayed me when you took back the plan. I'm sorry I lashed out when I should have internalized my own emotions. I didn't realize how much he loved you until I stabbed you. I didn't know, I swear."

"You care about Malo's feelings?" Aelyta's eyes go big.

Cory nods. "I do. I care a lot. He's taught me everything I know...music, art, and even the stars." He gazes upon Lyza's crackled skin.

"This." Aelyta gestures to the crowd. "Do you believe in this? Do you believe in them and their worth? Does their weight matter to you?"

"Yes, because I no longer feel like I am against them. I am one of them."

Lyza asks again, "You have all the information that they need to know. Can you rally them?"

"You want me to rally the Elements? To go against everything my dad built? Yes, I'll take your place," he answers Lyza. She gives him a nod and hooks her arm into Aelyta's. She skips off along Aelyta's side.

"You truly trust Cory?"

Lyza laughs. "He's like a puppy. He won't stop following me around. I threatened to kill him if he does anything stupid. And that makes me happy, because he is so stupid!" Lyza pats her arm. Aelyta lets out a howl of laughter.

"I would kill to see you threaten Cory, of all Elementals,

but I trust you. Whatever makes you happy. I love to see you happy."

"Entertained," Lyza corrects. "Just like how I'm going to watch you take down those cowards."

"Well, I'm actually going to go find old books that contain the answers to taking them all down. Every one of them down in one book."

Lyza gasps. "The ghost mentioned something about that. Aubree brought us all into your room searching for books with your mom's handwriting."

"Did you find my mother's old fairy tale books?"

"Fairy tale? Not the conference notes with the philosophers?"

"Well, that one, too. It seemed either the philosophers have resigned to giving my father full reign of knowledge and use of the Academy or my father had everyone removed...Either way, I need to go through those books again."

The two of them run through the large front entrance. The main room vast in height. They take the main stairs to the second floor. They pass the library doors and turn down the hall for the servants' door. Up the stairs, they march for Aelyta's chamber.

In the servants' hallway, the channel is wide enough for two servants to speed away. On the way up to the third floor, Aelyta runs face-to-face into Aubree. Lyza collides into her back. Boreas, Briley, and Branson tumble Aubree into Aelyta. "You're here!" Aubree exclaims.

The men behind her all cry out, "Lyta!"

Lyza pops her head from around Aelyta. "We're headed for the books."

"We just came from your chamber. Boreas, here, told us you flew in on a dragon."

"Pyerre," Aelyta corrects. "And yes, I do need those books." Rumbles of the dragon's roar shakes the castle walls. "We need to hurry." Aelyta gestures up the stairwell.

Together, they all jog up the steps for the third floor. Throughout the castle, the sounds of running footsteps thunder from all directions. When the group reaches the exit towards Aelyta's chamber, the sound of men yelling can be heard from behind the servants' door.

Boreas, at the head of the line, turns to the group behind him. His finger raises to his lips. They weren't talking before and they remain silent now.

With a small creak, Boreas peers through the small gap of the door. Swinging the door wider, he ushers everyone out of the stairwell. They all run for her chamber door. Aelyta is the last, ensuring Boreas makes it inside.

From the bottom of her spiral staircase, she can hear Lyza and Aubree upstairs in her studies. Running up her little corner of the castle, she doesn't have time to linger.

Aelyta runs into the studies and claps her hands. "We're looking for fairy tales, philosopher conference notes, philosopher contracts, and any infrastructure or developmental projects that occurred within the last year before Mother's death."

She clears the table, moving the piles of books onto the floor. The group begins organizing a new pile on the table, growing into two, then five. Aelyta skims through the books as fast as she can, Lyza scanning the pages beside her. A small scribble on the margin with a sum amount catches Aelyta's eye.

"Wait, everyone stop. I've been going at this all wrong. Follow the money trail. The Richards care only about the money. My father only cares about the money. I absolutely stand by the fact that the advisors care about the money. Find anything to do with finances. Find the receipts."

A pen in her hand, Aelyta grabs a notebook. Her hand quick at work. *3.4M: Donations to the Academy marked from R&R.* Aelyta grabs a page Lyza leaves for her. Aelyta continues in a list. *2.8M: R to R.* She scans for more. With no other information, she moves onto the next page left open for her. *5.9M: To Miles, plus his allowance.*

In her mother's handwriting, a scribble reads: *Where is it all going?*

Where indeed?

"Aubree," Aelyta calls. She's scanning the other pages open in the queue. "Can you continue recording all these down?"

Lyza turns to Aelyta. "Where are you going?"

"How do you know..." Aelyta shakes her head. "I'm going to the library. The advisors must have kept their own accounts of their whereabouts. Their offices are in the back of the library."

"You're not going anywhere."

The entire room gasps at the sight of the large group stepping out from the shadows. Lorraine and Jaycub first, before Kody, Luella, Ellsy, and Maurene. Then Edin, Malcolm, Margaret, Presley, and Odetta. The study shrank in size by the amount of bodies unable to fit in the room.

"How are you all here? And all at once?"

A little rabbit leaps onto a chair, chewing the leather from the wood.

"Misty!" Aelyta exclaims.

"That's a whole lot of time we don't have a whole lot of." Edin pats the rabbit's head. "But Misty belongs to Malo, and the two share shadow routes."

"But, how?" Lyza grips Ellsy with her whole body.

Ellsy pulls away. "I guess it started off with Margaret, Odetta, and Presley getting stuck in the Shadow Realm. Then Lorraine and Jaycub tried to get in through a backsack, but Misty helped. They somehow found us—oh, Kody, Edin, Luella, Maurene, and Malcolm were under Pyerre's Library. The ghost was pulled into the Liminal for a second time. Misty brought us here. And we all have abhorrent news to bring you." Ellsy sucks in air afterwards. "But yes, we sure have more important things to discuss."

"Muddy Bay"—Lorraine steps forward—"is completely annihilated."

"And the knights your father rallied, their numbers are large." Jaycub adds.

Luella chimes in, "The worst piece of all is that we know who the mastermind behind all of this is."

"Or masterminds, plural," Aelyta corrects.

"One of the four advisors killed my mother in Pyerre's library." Luella nods. "He may as well be on a team with the other advisors."

"Oh, I do not doubt that one bit. They keep offices in the back of the library here in the castle. We need evidence that they are behind all this. The best thing we can do for Ospheria, for all of Deneb, is to provide due process. But before we go, let me say that I am beyond thrilled you all are alive and here. Unless, I'm dead again."

"Dead...again?" They all provide a blinking stare her direction.

"That, too, is a long story," Aelyta chucks aside. She doesn't wait for a response. Aelyta whirls down the stairwell. She pauses for a moment when she opens the door. There's no one standing guard. Lyza runs into her back.

Inside the castle, it's quiet. There are no other footsteps. No movements except for theirs. Outside the castle reflects differently. Pyerre's rumbles and roars pound the walls. Screams like sirens in the sea of chants.

A tug pulls in the air. Aelyta grabs Lyza's arm. "I think we should go back out to the front."

"But the library is just right there." Lyza points.

The large entrance is at the bottom of the stairs of the landing leading to the library. With an urge to head outside, Aelyta's eyes are trained on the main doors. "Taking down all these men requires evidence, proof. But there's something in the wind and it's calling for me."

"What do you mean?"

"I'm not sure, but..." The bells on her wrist jingle. Her wrist frozen in place, not a single draft in the air. The bells chime together. A glow climbs in jagged lines up Aelyta's arm.

Bursting down the stairs, Lyza following swiftly behind, Aelyta leaps through the main hall and bounds out the door. Pyerre turns to see her run from the doorway. "He's coming for you," the dragon warns at her approach.

Pyerre kneels his neck for Aelyta. She swings her leg over him. The dragon gives one crumbling roar. The Elementals fall silent as they turn to Aelyta high on Pyerre's back, bells on her wrist restless in the wind. The crowds fall to their knees, row by row.

Prickles of nerves climb the sides of her neck. Her ears burning from the heat. "He's coming." Her voice small. She places a hand over her chest. "And I'm not ready." She looks around at the Elementals gathered on their knees in front of Avelmore Castle. "We're not ready."

31

Dum spiro spero
WHILE I BREATHE, I HOPE

The Queen

ELEMENTALS BOW on bended knee as Aelyta looks over them on the back of Deneb's dragon. They left the remains of the knights and their mechanical hornets where they have fallen. The injured are being attended to off to the side, away from the front lines. Despite the odds, the Elementals still stand against the knights and their metal. Metal against the Elements.

With one inhale, Aelyta speaks with every force of her body. A vibration from the bottom of her ribs.

"We are unique equations of the ancient descendants. The Elementals are made of the soil, the air, the fire, and ocean's deep. And as our limbs reach the light, we grow towards a better future. May we interlock our vines together. May we grow from the dirtied soil newer, richer, and stronger than those that came before. I don't demand anything from you. I simply ask you to join me.

"Miles is on his way here with his knights of metal hornets. This isn't a war as we know it. This is an extermination of all Elemental-kind. Miles is turning our people into Morf Blue, and calling it order, lawful. We must rise against it, plant our roots and stand strong together to fight this tyranny!

"I ask that you join me as we stand firm and steady to protect what is left of Ospheria, what is left of Elementropolis, of Muddy Bay, and all Deneb.

"We must stand as the forces of nature, together. We are a tidal wave of Elements against a small rock in the ocean. Together, we are the Elements of Deneb. We are the forces of nature.

"The fight will not be an easy one.

"But I will give you, each and every one of you, I will give my fight. I will give you all my light. I will not let my father take Deneb down just so he can sit on a throne made of our very essence. I will not allow it.

"I will withstand my father's efforts and the men who believe they have the upper hand to push everyone down. I will stand as your armor.

"Not as Queen of Ospheria, no. I will stand for you all as Aelyta Aurelianus, a Floral descendant, a Floral who resides in Deneb like all of you. Ospheria is my home. I ask that I may guard your journey home. Are you ready for home?"

The crowd cheers. Pyerre lifts his wings as he lets out a dragon's cry. His wings beat, lifting him into the sky, sending waves of wind into the ground.

Cory, at the front of the line of Elementals, leads the large mass towards the rock wall of Ospheria. Lyza catches up to him. Briley and Branson clasp hands before separating. Branson following after Lyza and Briley running back into the castle. Aelyta looks out at the pull of the clouds. A spiral of clouds circle high and in the distance. It's not a storm that is brewing. The tension so strong, the air feels almost stagnant.

"Do you feel that?" Aelyta asks Pyerre.

Pyerre flaps his wings. "Tornadoes on the horizon. We have a race with destiny."

Rising into the air from the mountains behind Avelmore, metallic spores eject, flying towards the Elementals below. Blue fog gathers above Ospheria like a looming cloud.

"What is that?" Aelyta gasps. She looks down at the Elements. The blue fog swallows them. "Run." she warns. "Run!"

More spores puff into the air. Pyerre flaps his wings as they make their way for the wall of Ospheria. The Elementals are frantic movements of color shifting like an ocean wave.

With his mighty wings, Pyerre flies towards another cloud moving faster than any cloud in all of Deneb. Aelyta braces herself as she knows who this cloud belongs to. Her heart pounding with the pulsing in her ears.

Like sandpaper grinding down the back of her throat, Aelyta is anxious. What is the best move here? The Elementals can't fight the metallic knights. Pyerre is a powerful beast. But alone, will the metal knights conquer one singular beast? What if she pushes everyone to their death? What if she rallied the people to meet their end?

Screams ring from below. The two of them look down, but the blue fog is too thick. "I don't think we can go up against my father," Aelyta's voice shakes. "He's built a metal army with enough knights to back him."

"Hush, little flower. Look."

She stares down into the fog. "I don't see anything."

"Wait, and keep watch."

Her eyes scan the blue clouds below. She hears the screams of the Elementals, then silence. The quiet is jarring. Straight into the air, winged creatures burst up towards them in the sky. Aelyta nearly jumps. Recognition settles when she realizes what's surrounding them in the air are winged Insectals.

"You all have wings!" she cries with laughter. "Wings!"

Screams still come from the fog.

Pyerre scoops down. His wings fan the fog clearing the scene. Pyerre softly lands.

Florals and Fungals lay wilted on the ground. The sound from the depths of Aelyta's chest echoes along with the roar of the dragon.

Her eyes scan the wilted garden before her. Flowers and Fungals cut down and wilted. Her eyes refuse to blink. They refuse the denial of the landscape.

She doesn't notice Lyza gripping her arms, her shoulders, then up to her cheeks. It wasn't until Malo pardons himself, his electricity zipping along her skin, her magnetic energy dancing across his. Her eyes finally rip away from the wilted and pour into his bright-white eyes. His hair a small tug of nostalgic familiarity. He came to her in the form of Itzal.

"Whenever you're ready," he starts.

But she doesn't let him finish, she cries. "Where are they? Where is the destruction of Deneb? As long as I breathe, as long as I am standing, I will continue forward. This only fuels the ire, the poison within me brewing." Goosebumps climb her arms. A breeze cuts through the fog, clearing more of the Florals and Fungals lying wilted on the stone path leading to Avelmore Castle.

Lorraine pulls Aelyta towards her. Insectal eyes bore into Aelyta behind the even larger glasses. The voices of the wind swirling around them. They're not screaming. They're singing. The winds are singing the song of the old.

First, Aelyta follows the wind just as Lorraine follows along with Aelyta. Malo picks up the song, then Jaycub. Pyerre bellows the words. The song carries through the last breath of the Florals and Fungals wilting on the stone path. The Insectals land their flight, singing the songs. Together, united, the song of the old is sung from every body, from every breath.

"We hold no weapons.
We yield our poison.
We sing the songs
that guide us to our freedom.
We are the Elements.
We are true to Deneb lands.
We are the Elements.
Together, hand in hand."

Aelyta sings and she walks. She walks for the stone wall that encloses Ospheria from all of Deneb. She walks for the Florals and Fungals who have lost their limbs, their Elements. She walks, and she sings. And the Elementals, any who can and will, are too. No fog fills the air now, only the song of the old and the winds that barrel through.

As the Elements walk for the edge of the city, the wind picks up speed. Pushing the bodies in every direction, the Elementals do not relent as they continue their onward force. The buzz of distant numbers of metal wings vibrates against the wind, a warning.

32

The Forces of Nature
THE TYRANTS

"THIS IS A GOOD DAY," Miles yells. "Celebrate today, no one shall remember today as the Butterfly Festival. No, that's old news. This is the day we conquer the parasites that take and take and take. Their mere existence is criminal. All must hail me now, King Miles!"

With the press of a trigger, a long line of whips crash into the metal hornets flying in formation. He turns in his chair to face the other men. A large screen glaring behind him. He sticks out his hand like a toddler to the four advisors. "I want to see the Goblin Sword, again."

"Your Highness," one of the advisors answers. "We must save it to kill the Queen."

"She's not queen." Miles snaps to his feet. The chair crumbles to the ground.

Julius coughs a laugh. Miles spins his gaze to Julius. "I doubt Malo will lose sight of what he wants, what he truly wants. No girl will make him give up years, decades, of pandering and slaving in the guild."

"What are you saying?" Miles stalks closer to him.

"I'm saying"—Julius smiles—"he'll have her dead. It won't be long now."

"You trust that bastard?"

"No, he's a bastard. But I do trust his need to prove himself to me."

Thelonius scoffs. "Entrusting a bastard instead of your real son?"

"And yours is dead," Miles points out.

"Men." The Royal Advisors stand in a line. "We must stay focused on the main goal at task."

"We don't have to focus on killing when we have others doing it for us." Miles turns back to the screen. "We have made killers of metal. It's a good day to celebrate. We're ridding Deneb of all these parasites!"

The screen displays the view of metal knights flying on mechanical hornets. Man-made warfare for man-made purposes. The formation breaks as they drop to the ground. The screen shakes from the impact. The view displays the cries and screams of surviving Elementals.

Miles chuckles. "Just like Elementropolis. Except we killed the Prime Minister, and we'll kill their 'Queen.' Today, we become gods." The men all clap, patting Miles on the back.

The sound of buzzing grows louder and louder. The ground shakes and screaming ensues. Malo turns to Aelyta. "I can't be seen."

"Are you going to hide?"

"No, I'll attack them from behind."

Jaycub chimes, "I shall join you, but I need to do something first." He removes his armor, helm first, and hands it to Lorraine. Before long, he stands before her in his plain tunic and pants. "It won't fit you well, but it's better than dying in a fight that was never meant to be yours."

"You're giving me your knight armor?"

"I'm giving you my protection." He steps closer. "All of my protection is yours."

"But this uniform... You worked hard to obtain it. Your title, your position..."

"Are in your hands, yes. You have stripped me bare and I cannot think of anyone more worthy than you to do so."

"You do know how much I hate this uniform."

"And everything it represents, yes. But you are worth protecting, that should mean so much more."

She steps up to him. Her eyes look up at his. "It means so much." She greets his lips with one long kiss before he tears away from her. Jaycub gives Malo a nod. Jaycub's eyes trained on Lorraine as the shadows engulf the two of them.

Aelyta takes Lorraine's hand. Lorraine turns to Aelyta. "Your chambermaid and your ladies-in-waiting, they found something in their search up in your chamber. There have been funds going to your father for renovations to the castle. He's been accepting money from the Richards for something to do with the departure from Deneb?"

"Departure from Deneb? What does that mean?"

"I don't know, but you should go inside and see for yourself."

"Not before I fight alongside the Elementals."

Pyerre kneels his wing. "You may fight with me, Your Majesty."

Aelyta turns to Lorraine. "I yield my place to you, if that's okay with Pyerre."

"A privilege to fight alongside a longtime friend."

Lorraine places a hand to her heart and gives him a quirk of a smile. Pyerre chuckles as she climbs onto his back. Aelyta waits for her to settle before yelling, "Let's raise hell for gerontocracy, the oligarchy, and the patriarchy!"

Pyerre takes off with a burst of wind into the sky. Aelyta rushes forward with the rest of the Insectals. No weapon in her hands but poison coursing through her veins. Aelyta's never been a physical fighter. No, she's a strategic fighter. Her attacks are indirect and with purpose. Time is of the essence and effort must be maximized.

She pulls her poison to her hands, feeling the thick richness heat within her fingers. A familiar feeling flutters under her skin. It's unlike what she's felt before, awakening her very essence as deep as her bones.

Kneeling next to the closest wilted flower, she presses her fingers to the Floral. Purple and green flow through the Floral's veins before their eyes pop open. Pupils dilated in the color of bright purple, skin veined with neon green. Aelyta grins as she moves to the next wilted Elemental.

One by one, wilted Florals and Fungals rise from their decay. Eyes bright with purple and skin lined with green. Their petals no longer crumbling to dust. As they reach the metal knights, their limbs snap into long vines ensnaring anything and everything in front of them. The numbers of risen Elementals tangle the metals, their Elemental numbers growing, and the metal crunching at the weight of the many.

Malo and Jaycub reappear from the shadows covered in bruises, sap, and wounds. Aelyta gasps, but they barely notice. They're both stunned by her magic. Reviving the dead is not a common capability.

Jaycub drops to his knees. "Blessed Divinity."

Malo grabs Aelyta. "Forgive me." He turns to the nearest metal knight. "Come out here and watch the rest of the show, you cowards. You're going to watch this last bit in person."

He turns to Aelyta. Shadows engulf his head. His eyes glowing lightning-white, especially now that the sun has set. Light zaps cut across their skin.

"What are you doing?" Her eyebrows knit.

He pulls her tight and close. "My job."

Jaycub stands confused. The sound of footsteps and claps come from the entrance of the castle.

She looks out towards the others. Her father is standing awkwardly with the Goblin Sword propped against his leg. Julius and Thelonius standing beside him. The four advisors wearing their winning grins. The Elementals in an entangled mess behind her. She can't see where Pyerre and Lorraine are in the sky.

"You have ruined all of Deneb!" Aelyta shouts.

Miles laughs. "You think you have all the power? You think you're special because, what?" He points at Malo. "He assisted the killing of your mother. And you trusted him? I hired him to kill you, and he didn't even accomplish that." Miles spits at Malo's shadowed face.

"I'm confused, I thought you *were* the assassin that killed my mother." Aelyta looks to Malo. "Wasn't that the hit job you took before killing me?"

"I covered the job..." Malo starts.

Miles answers instead, "I killed her. Don't you take credit for it." He turns to Malo. "How dare you take credit for that! I killed your mother, and I should've done it sooner. All he did was use his 'shadows' for cover. His father was so pleased with the results that we asked him to kill you." Miles laughs. "You trusted Julius's bastard son. You naive little child."

"Ahh, I see... What you don't seem to understand is the difference between men like Malo and men like you." She steps towards her father. "I'm no fool. In fact, I'd leave it to the soil of the earth and the wind of the sky to judge who I am." A flash of lightning before the sound of thunder rumbles over their heads. "But you." She points to the men standing as if they have the right to conquer mountains. "You all can be judged by me."

Another lightning ignites the night sky displaying a large twister barreling in no particular direction.

33

Death's Third Impression

FLASHES OF LIGHTNING illuminate the dark. A large twister growing bigger. It's not moving left or right, which means it's moving for the castle.

The four advisors turn to Malo. "Kill her, kill her now."

"Yes, kill her or I will." Miles struggles to lift the Goblin Sword. The hilt alone wider than his shoulders. He barely lifts it midway before dropping the tip of the sword to the ground.

The sword crumbles into pieces. Ansaldo, one of the advisors, falls to his knees. Picking up the pieces, stone and dust seep through his fingers.

"The sword is made of stone?" Menecrates points to Constantine.

Scoffing at the advisors fight, Julius pushes Miles aside. He grits his teeth at Malo. "I will claim you as my son if you just kill her, now."

If anyone could see Malo's head, it would be Aelyta. From how close he's gripping her, she can see his shadowy, dark head distinctly in the night. He's not moving and his expression is placid.

The wind is picking up speed. Aelyta places a hand on Malo's hand gripping her shoulder from across her chest.

Before she could say anything, Malo erupts first. "The Elementals have been enslaved to you for too long. The queens have played by your rules, and they paid the price to play your game. I will never be a slave to you again, nor will any Elementals. Long live the Queen!"

Releasing Aelyta from his grip, he kneels onto one knee. "My Queen!" He cries.

Jaycub nearby, falls to his knees just the same. "My Queen!" He cries.

In the dark of night, voices cry out. "My Queen!"

She glances back at the others. Although she cannot see them, she can feel their eyes and their knees rooted to the ground.

With a flick of her wrist, the bells jingle into the sword nestled in her hand.

"You wanted the Bugnott Sword so badly, you couldn't tell the difference between the real sword and a fake. You all have chosen the fake sword, and it suits you. All of you." She points the sword towards her father and the men gathered around him. "You're all fake. Performative and in denial with the lack of knowledge of what truly makes Deneb great, what Deneb truly beholds. So, if you want to kill me"—Aelyta smirks—"I've been waiting!"

"No," Malo gasps.

"Lyta." Jaycub steps forward.

She doesn't glance to them behind her. "It's okay. I have greeted death before." A smile dances across her face remembering the first time she met Malo. "I can be cut down into small pieces, but my pieces will remain who I am. They hold the truth of what you have done and will continue to do. I am not afraid."

Malo's face relaxes at the sight of her. "You are the light of my life. I will step into the light for you no matter the cost. Wherever you go, I will follow. Whenever you're ready, I am here."

Aelyta raises her hand to his cheek. "I love you," she whispers before planting a kiss on his lips.

She can feel his smile on her lips. "What? Bad kiss?"

"No." He laughs. "You knew where my lips were. So, you can see through my shadows?"

A soft chuckle sneaks out of her before she shakes her head. She reaches for his hand. He grips it gently, and he pulls it to his lips, planting a kiss on the back of her hand.

Aelyta turns to the men. She stares daggers at her father, his companions, and the four Royal Advisors. "The forces of nature are pulled out of balance. You shall pay the price of the chaos you have caused."

She swings the sword towards the men.

Another barreling wind comes from the opposite side of the tornado. Avelmore Castle sits directly in the middle of two careening vortexes.

Thunder roars. A flash of lightning engulfs Aelyta in white light. Darkness-blinking blindness. Two glittering orbs where Aelyta stands. Lines of light glowing from her skin.

She turns to her father. "I wonder, what's heavier—the Goblin Sword or my power?"

Her hand twirls and a lightning bolt jumps from her hand, wrapping around Miles's body. Down the line she goes, lightning binds the men as they attempt to run. And one by one, they tumble to the ground like fallen trees.

Lyza and Cory are entangled in the vines among the other Elementals. Lyza is gripping the head of a metal knight while Cory is crushing its chest. Edithe appears next to Lyza. "Come with me, Stardust." The ghost holds a hand out for Lyza.

"You're leaving me? Please, don't leave me. I'll go with you. Wherever you go, take me with you."

"I can't guarantee you'll live," she says.

"I don't care," he answers. "As long as you're not dead."

With her free hand, she reaches for Edithe's outstretched hand. Edithe bursts them towards Aelyta. Lyza and Edithe grab hold of Malo. He steadies himself in the chaotic winds.

"If I touch Aelyta, lightning sparks," Malo tells Edithe.

"Exactly." Edithe nods. "Lyza is stardust, and I am a spirit of the afterlife. Aelyta has ancient magic we do not have the understanding of. She is also the Beacon Queen. If she combines all our magic together, we can prevent the stars from being sucked into her vortex."

"These tornadoes are because of Lyta?" Lyza exclaims, her head swivels from Aelyta to the two tornadoes barreling towards them.

"What if we kill her in the process?" Malo looks to Lyza and Edithe.

Edithe's eyes soften behind her round glasses. "We don't know about that, but we do know that this may help save us all and all of Deneb. You know the forecast. Lorraine hasn't quit talking, warning about this. But time and again, Lorraine has provided the same thing. Aelyta is the answer to the problem."

Edithe grabs hold of Aelyta's hand, pulling her towards them. Aelyta screams like the roaring winds around them.

Malo touches her cheek, and Lyza gives her a hug with one of her arms.

Aelyta bursts into flames, and gray clouds shoot from her mouth. Black veins spread from her golden glowing eyes, down her face and neck, spreading around her body. The pull of the wind is stronger now.

The lightning strikes. Not from the sky. They're shooting out from Aelyta. And in a blur of wind and lightning, the two tornadoes collide.

34

Beacon Queen

ALL OF TIME has come to a pause. Aelyta chases the darkness. Waiting, hoping, she hones her eyes into the void. Her eyes do adjust, barely though. Silhouettes surround her. She can't tell what, who, or where she is. "Malo? Lyza? Edithe?" Aelyta cries out. Her voice mutes into the blankness. "What is going on?"

With every ounce of effort, she moves her feet beneath her. As if walking through muck and mud, her feet don't move as fast as she wants. She pushes through with her arms. It doesn't help. Time stopped, and she is unable to walk. Even turning her head around moves slow, slow, pause. Shift, slow to the other side. Slow moving. Ever so slowly.

She opens her mouth, breathing in. With an exhale, she screams. Into the darkness, a quiet wail barely makes it out of her. She slams onto her knees, or at least she attempts to. The fall doesn't satisfy the slam she feels as she barely drifts down to her knees. Frustration builds within her, a growing wrath forming within. An ire building for a release that can't seem to gratify. Leaning as hard forward as she can push, her hand finally lands onto something. Her fingers squeeze, gripping. Another scream forming in her chest. She exhales another scream.

A flash of light flares. Aelyta shuts her eyes from the burning glare. A hand touches the back of her head. She squints at the blaring light above her. A face looks down at her. A face she has seen once before. It smiles back at her. "You did once see me." Her voice doesn't match the movement of her mouth.

"Goddess Ko'nkiun." Aelyta's voice moves faster than the movement of her lips.

The goddess nods, grinning as she settles herself in front of Aelyta. Her hair flowing into the void as if the void itself. "There are many who are waiting to see you," the goddess speaks. "But I wanted to bring to light what you have done."

"What have I done?" Aelyta's heart drops into her stomach. "I caused this, didn't I? Instead of helping, I broke the universe. All the stars are dead because of me."

The goddess chuckles. She laughs as Aelyta lifts her head to the golden woman. "With the help of your friends, you have caused a ripple through the aether. A ripple so great, all of time itself has come to a staggering halt. You, my dear, are a product of the universe and the universe listened. Come with me." The goddess rises and reaches her hand out for Aelyta.

With movements slower than her thoughts, her arm moves up, up. She touches the hand of the goddess, and the goddess grabs hold. Pulling her up, she guides Aelyta through the darkness. A ray of light flares above from the goddess and engulfs them into glaring brightness.

Two familiar voices bring tears to her eyes. Like plugs pulled from her ears, she turns to the sound of the familiar voices. The High Priestess stands beside Edithe, both waiting. As Aelyta approaches, they embrace her with open arms. The two of them free her from their grasp. The High Priestess gently pats her cheeks dry of tears. They gesture towards the goddess. But Aelyta doesn't look to the golden being, her eyes overflowing with new tears as she runs for her mother.

Her mother pulls her in and squeezes her tight. "I missed you," her mother whispers into her ear. "I am so proud to see how much you have grown without my help." She pulls away enough to look into Aelyta's face. "But there is still so much to be done, my child." Her mother wipes her face. "We're not done yet."

Her mother steps away from Aelyta and stands beside the High Priestess and Edithe. Goddess Ko'nkiun ascends next to her; an arm wraps around Aelyta. She looks up at the goddess. "Are all the stars dead?"

"Not quite," the goddess answers.

"Your soul is what keeps the aether from dying," the High Priestess adds.

Edithe states, "When Malo, Lyza, and I held onto you, your soul took hold of all the stars of the universe."

"Why is it so dark? It's like death itself." Aelyta scans their faces.

"That's correct," Edithe remarks, "the stars went out on impact of the collision."

"You behold the universe," Aelyta's mother joins in. "You must be the one to guide the universe back into place."

"The only problem is"—the High Priestess shifts a look towards the other women—"your soul has dispersed in the process."

"Pieces of your soul have scattered across the stars," Edithe adds. "It was the price you paid to halt all of them from dying. I don't think you'll be able to make it back to Deneb."

"I won't be able to return to Ospheria?" Looking to Edithe, then turning to her mother. "I won't be able to sit on the throne of Avelmore?"

Her mother shakes her head. The High Priestess gently holds Aelyta's arm. "It's a big ask, but you will save all those you love back at home."

"And all those you met along the way." Edithe holds onto her other arm.

"Won't I anger the goddesses?"

The goddess laughs. "Don't you worry about that. Guide the souls and stars, my dear."

"How do I do that?"

"You were born from the flesh of your mother and through the magic of my light." The goddess catches her chin. "You are a reflection of all the magic you have surrounded yourself with on Deneb."

Edithe holds her hand. "We will be by your side. Even if you can't see us, we'll be here as much as you are for the souls that need you to guide them home."

"Even Lyza and Malo?"

Gripping her hand in both of hers, Edithe's earnest eyes enlarge behind her ghostly glasses. "I get to decide who stays and who goes."

"That's your power, isn't it? Reading dust and judging lifelines?"

Edithe nods with a shrug. "I'm a ghost who can give anyone I want stomachaches." She giggles. "I didn't find out until I died. I didn't want to leave Luella, so I kept myself tied to the souls. It's what you probably replicated when you halted the stars and the universe from imploding."

Aelyta takes one more scan of the faces around her. "I

think I get it now." She grips Edithe's hands. "Thank you." Releasing Edithe, she hugs her mother. "Is this the last time I'll see you?"

"I don't know, but I can only hope we can meet again one day." Her mother kisses her head. "My sweet baby girl. I have loved you since the day you came into my life and you have changed my very essence, my very being. I am truly, so proud of you. Not because of your sacrifice, I am proud of how much you have learned and grown, how much you have loved. I will be waiting for you, however long it takes. I will be waiting for you."

The High Priestess reaches out her hands to Aelyta. Reaching her hands out in return, the High Priestess doesn't embrace her. She holds firm the bells tangled around Aelyta's wrist. A rhythm of incantations pour out of the priestess. The bells glow in a soft light. The glow climbs Aelyta's arm, spreading throughout her body. Goddess Ko'nkiun's hands form a globe of golden rays. She presses the orb into Aelyta's forehead. Aelyta gives them all one last goodbye before darkness engulfs her, leaving her all alone in a ringing silence.

A warmth grows within the center of her chest. Aelyta's eyes shoot open. A glow runs down her arms to her hands, illuminating the bells tangled around her wrist. There's a hand pressed within hers. Malo floats limply beside her. And around her waist, Lyza's arms grip tightly. Aelyta glances over to see Lyza is unconscious too. She turns back to her glowing arms and now legs. She jingles the bells. A soft light rings around the top of her head.

Pulling Malo towards her, Aelyta presses two fingers to his forehead. A white glow absorbs into his skin. His eyes burst open, emitting a golden light. A large gasp for air before he turns to Aelyta. She plants a kiss on his forehead before releasing him. "Can you use your shadows?"

"I can try," he gasps.

She nods. Aelyta pulls Lyza up and around, placing two fingers to her forehead. Just like Malo, a white glow sinks into the skin of her forehead before her eyes blink open, glowing a golden light. She gapes her mouth at Aelyta.

"Take your time," Aelyta's voice soft. She waits as Lyza adjusts to the void around them.

"Are we dead?"

Aelyta shrugs. "Want to help me gather the stars back to the sky?"

"Divine goddesses, yes I do!"

Aelyta chuckles as she untangles the bells around her wrist and ties them to Lyza's arm, double knotting the bow. Lyza rings the bells and her already luminescent blue-and-yellow skin glows in a vein-like spiral around the illuminating sparkles dotted across her skin. Lyza roars into a hearty laugh. She bursts up into the air. She zooms back down towards Aelyta.

"Wanna help lead the way?" Her arms reach out towards Aelyta.

Aelyta smiles, taking them. "Let's give these souls somewhere to go home to."

They ascend towards the sky. Aelyta's halo a beacon in the dark. Beside her, Lyza's glittering-blue glow pulses as the bells on her wrists ring, leaving a trail of petals behind her. With each ring of the bells, Lyza's glow brightens. Aelyta slows, crossing the trail behind Lyza. Leaving a small piece of herself to the petals, Aelyta tightens the ripples. She ushers Lyza to wrap through the constellation, Deneb. She sews herself through the petal trails as she closes the stars together. As they return back to Ospheria,

Aelyta's breathing thins. Lyza asks her if she's alright, but Aelyta nods her head with a smile. "We still have a lot of work to do."

Malo makes his way over to her. "Many have found your lights." He looks between Aelyta and Lyza. "Both of your lights."

Aelyta's flight no longer strong enough to hold her up. "Good." She nods. "They may find their way home."

"Some, though," Malo starts. "Some couldn't see the lights at all."

"Good," Aelyta stutters, "then our lights are working."

Malo wraps an arm around Aelyta's waist to hold her up, but upon contact, her body fails her. She plummets down, deep into the void. Lyza screams, but Malo dives, racing for her. His hands reach out for her. Her light slowly dying as she falls deeper into the darkness. He attempts to pull the shadows at his will, but the shadows can't reach him here.

"Aelyta!" he yells as he hurries towards her.

Her eyes fly open at his voice. Her hand reaches out for him. He pushes for her, pulling her hand, lunging her up towards him. They come to a staggering halt in the abyss of darkness. They both expected lightning to burst from their contact, but nothing flashes in the Liminal dark.

Clutching one another, Malo grips her as he asks, "What's going on? Something is happening and I don't know what it is."

"The stars must be sewn back together. Lyza gathered the stars"—Aelyta takes a sharp breath—"and I was the thread that tied the stars back."

"You'll feel better once we get back to Ospheria." Malo cups her cheek. "I'll have Kody take a look at you."

Aelyta shakes her head. She returns his gesture by cupping his cheek also. "I don't know if I can make it back."

"What do you mean?"

"I gave up pieces of my soul to sew the stars back together." She holds his face against hers, bearing her eyes deep into his.

"Why? I can't understand." Malo pulls her tighter into his embrace.

"Fall was upon us." She struggles to chuckle. "The solar seasons were ending."

"This isn't a time to joke." He shakes his head.

"I did it, so you all could have a place to return to." She rubs her fingertip against his cheek. "Like the flowers awakening in the spring. Ospheria has a beautiful history because of beautiful people. Not because of all their colors, but because of all their forms. Even yours." She gives him a deepened kiss. "I love yours the most."

"You'll be able to see Ospheria again. Don't lose hope, we just have to get to Kody, okay? You'll see." He returns her kiss.

Pulling away from her lips, Malo looks up to see Lyza's glow blinking like a small star in the sky. He carries Aelyta in his arms as he moves towards her. As they fly up, Aelyta's eyes heavily blink close. Malo frantically pecks kisses against her head as he staggers up towards Lyza.

"Did you know about this?" he cries to Lyza. "Did you know she has sacrificed herself?"

Lyza's eyes widen.

"You didn't know either?"

Lyza shakes her head as she pulls Aelyta's face up towards her.

"Aelyta? Is that what's happening?"

Aelyta's head flops back, eyelids rolling up. Malo shakes her limp body, but she doesn't react. Her hands fade into the darkness creeping up her arms until her whole body no longer exists in Malo's arms.

"Aelyta?" Lyza cries.

Malo's eyes refuse to blink. He refuses to move his arms despite the lack of weight that was once there. His mouth gapes open, then closes. He tries to scream but nothing comes out.

"I don't—I don't know what to do," he manages to mutter. Without blinking, he turns to Lyza. "I don't know what to do now." Tears overflow the edge of his eyes. He doesn't stop them. He doesn't fight them. The tears freely run down his face. He turns back to his arms, still empty.

35

Blessed Be the Divine Descendants

EDITHE LOOKS to the golden glowing goddess. The spirit stands patiently beside the High Priestess, and together, their eyes calmly set upon the golden goddess. The High Priestess smiles as the spirit turns her head to and from the two of them.

"All in due time," the High Priestess says to Edithe. "Divine timing."

"I have a feeling that we'll be waiting an eternal time for the Queen's arrival," Edithe returns.

"You're right," the goddess speaks. The two spirits turn their heads back to her. She continues, "We'll be waiting for Aelyta's arrival for an eternity. But there is someone who we're waiting to meet, all in divine timing."

Not a moment later, Malo erupts before them, followed beside a dazed Lyza. He maneuvers towards the goddess, leaving Lyza staring at the spirits she believed to be long dead.

"Where is she?" Malo points to the glowing being. "Is she here?"

The goddess shakes her head, her flowing, glowing hair glimmering behind her. "My child, she is not."

"Then?" Malo stutters. "Where could she be?"

"Where are we?" Lyza whispers.

Edithe and the High Priestess wrap their arms around her as they answer together, "You're in the Liminal space."

"Where the souls meet before moving on," the goddess proceeds. "My son"—she turns back to Malo—"she has guided the souls back to their stars."

"She's your mother?" Lyza exclaims.

Malo doesn't acknowledge her. "Julius still has you trapped here?"

"Your father trapped me, but he does not know that I can free myself wherever I please. I travel the stars whenever I like."

"You chose to stay here than with me, as my mom?"

"I chose to be a part of the universe. The same way Aelyta chose to be the hold between the stars."

"She didn't make it back to Ospheria?"

The goddess and the two spirits shake their head at him. "That was not the plan," the goddess answers.

"She was to return here once the souls have been guided back," Edithe remarks. "That was the plan, at least."

Lyza gasps. They all swivel their heads to her. "I think I know what happened," she rasps.

Waiting for her to continue, Lyza looks down at her hands. When she looks up, her eyes catch sight of the goddess. "Her soul split into the stars, so they may glow again. Is that possible?"

"That can't be possible," the High Priestess cries. "She'll never return to the Liminal, meaning..."

"Which means, she'll never return at all," Edithe gasps.

"It's my fault, isn't it?" Lyza's hands tremble. "I touched her last. It was because of me."

Malo puts a hand up. "No. Don't do that. You know that this is what she would do. Aelyta would choose to do this over saving herself. If she had the chance to change course, she would choose to guide the souls back to the stars no matter the cost."

"There is a way to retrieve her, though." The goddess gleams over to Malo. "Lover's Lighthouse..."

"If I can get Kody to create something to use the lighthouse as a portal..." Malo's eyes widen.

"You can split yourself between the stars also." The goddess nods.

"Retrieve the pieces of Aelyta's soul," Lyza exclaims.

"And return her back to the Liminal state." Edithe claps her hands.

"That's if the alchemist can complete the task," the goddess reminds them. "It's not an easy feat to create a portal."

"If he won't do it, then I will." Malo tightens his fist.

"Motivation is one thing, my sweet boy." The goddess smiles down at him. "You'll need a lot more than mere motivation."

"I know." Malo nods once. "I know what it'll take." He turns to Lyza. "Ready to head back to Ospheria?"

"Yes." Lyza sighs. "This place is giving me goosebumps."

The goddess enlarges. With the glow of her being, spirits line a path. "Follow the divine descendants," the goddess instructs.

"Blessed Be." The High Priestess bows to Malo and Lyza.

Edithe turns to Malo. "I'll see you soon."

"I'll check on Luella for you." Malo pats her shoulder.

With a smile, Edithe thanks him. They follow a line of spirits they both recognize and those they don't. The path leads down like a spiral staircase. At each step, a spirit glows. A descendant to guide them back.

Lyza remarks, "Aelyta gave them the beacon glow?"

"I think you did that." Malo points to the bells entangled around her wrist.

"I like the idea of her and I working together to do that." Lyza nods a firm nod of approval. "One last roundup before she left."

Malo sighs with a smile. They walk the rest of the way down in silence. "I see something." Malo points to the center of the spiral.

A house embedded into a large rock off the edge of a cliff attached by a covered bridge. He breaks into a sprint. Lyza picks up her arms and pushes into a run after him. Speeding down, down until the spiral opens to a rippling picture of the house. They both leap through and tumble into a wall. Not a wall, a door. A voice can be heard from behind the door. "Took you both long enough." The door opens to an iridescent haired large bug eyes behind even larger glasses.

Malo scoffs as he rises to his feet. "Did the wind tell you?"

Lorraine laughs. "No, Edithe made it back before you both did. Come on, she's inside with everyone else."

"Are we back at my place?" Malo steps through the door.

"No, Silly! You're in Aelyta's chambers." Luella answers. "Glad to see you're both alive."

"But I thought I saw my house—"

"Where's Aelyta?" Aubree rushes for them.

Malo and Lyza exchange a glance. Lyza turns to

Aubree, her lips in a tight line and gives two shakes of her head.

Aubree drops to the floor, as Briley and Branson run to help her. Boreas slides down the wall. The ladies-in-waiting reach for each other's hand. Lyza joins them.

Jaycub and Malcolm kneel. Lorraine, Luella, and Edin hold each other close.

"She has now joined the Blessed Descendants," Aubree cries out. Her voice cracking with agony.

"No, actually." Edithe appears out of thin air.

Malo jumps at the sight of Edithe.

Edithe chuckles but continues, "I do not sense her in the Liminal, nor has she greeted the goddesses in the afterlife. She has become the very entity holding the stars from falling."

36

Weight of a Soul

"CAN you forecast anything from the winds?" Malo questions Lorraine.

"The wind has been silent since their wrath." Lorraine hesitates. "I'll find out what I can." Lorraine gives Jaycub's arm a pat-pat before leaving out the front door. Jaycub awkwardly grumbles at them before following her out the door.

Boreas remarks, "There's food in the kitchen if any of you are hungry."

"Starving." Lyza lunges for the door at the same time as Malcolm.

"Glad the death of the stars hasn't changed you." He smiles at her.

Malo turns to Edithe. "They're all trying to regain peace again. How can I ask my friends to help me find Aelyta when they've all lost something in this destruction?"

"As someone once said"—Edithe tilts her ghostly head at him—"mere minutes ago for me, probably hours ago for you—but it was stated that things occur in divine timing."

Days turn into weeks, the trials begin and progress. The four advisors are stripped of their titles. All four men, as well as Miles, Thelonius, and Julius, are charged for treason. The seven guilty for treason have been sentenced to death. The goddesses of justice shall decide their fate. The trial has been finalized for six months after the day Aelyta saved Deneb.

A ceremony, a processional walk from Avelmore Castle to the peninsula gate, transpired for the lost queen. In her place, a congregation of ladies naming themselves The Queen's Lace, have proceeded with cleaning and clearing the cities of structural debris, bodies, and metal.

With the help from Jaycub and Aubree, Lorraine established a museum in Elementropolis. She has displayed collections belonging to Aelyta and the queens before her. A demonstration of history that was almost erased by Miles and his men.

Luella worked under Pyerre, with assistance from her spirit mother, to upkeep records of Deneb, Ellsy training alongside her.

Kody has been reviewing the advanced technology the Richards had kept hidden away from the public. A few lost philosophers and alchemists joining the pursuit to protect the future from any advantages that could destroy Deneb again. They work together alongside Luella's work at Pyerre's Library.

Communities are forming, coming together to rebuild the cities across Deneb.

One Elemental though, has been buried in darkness and shadows, unable to see a bright future ahead. Malo lingers around his house, meandering from room to room. The empty sitting room. The silent library tucked under the stairs. The breeze passes through the open doors that lead to the large entertaining terrace.

Malo walks up the steps of the stairs. He takes a turn at the landing and opens the door to the bedroom strewn with what is left of her. The bed messy just as she left it. The door to the bedroom terrace welcomes the sounds of the ocean and seagulls' cries. The closet door is left open.

Malo runs his hand across the many fabrics hung for her to wear. A tug pulls him to sit onto the carpeted floor. A zap calling to him from the bottom drawer. He pulls the drawer open to find the coronation dress in the state in which he created. His hands run across the large gaping rip where his dagger cut through the bodice. Her scent still lingering between the threads of the dress.

Pulling the dress to his chest, engulfing himself in the remains of what is left of her. Something heavy drops onto his lap. Rummaging around the fabric, he finds the Queen's crown entangled with a delicate watch.

Malo lifts the watch up closer to his face. He remembers this very watch on Aelyta's wrist the first morning of his false assignment, pretending to be a low-ranking knight assigned to be Aelyta's personal guard under his pseudo name. As he sits on the floor of her closet, that false life feels like a lifetime ago.

"You know she's not really passed." Edithe breaks the silence from the doorway.

"I just have to find her," Malo mutters without looking up.

"You also have to build a mechanism that will open portals to other stars before you can do that." She laughs.

Malo gives her a look with knitted brows.

She hands him a canvas. "Lorraine found this in the boat when we couldn't find you guys after 'the fall of the winds,' as she calls it."

He takes the canvas, flipping it over. The figure is sitting on a wingback chair against the backdrop of golden curtains, sunlight peeking through the gap gracing her foot as she reads a book. Malo returns the canvas. Edithe takes it in both her hands. Lorraine walks into the bedroom, with a quiet sigh.

"Come on." Lorraine kneels beside him. "Everyone is waiting for you downstairs. Did you not hear us? We knocked on the door. You've always wanted us to knock, right?" She nudges him up to his feet. "There you go. Edithe mentioned that you have a task to finish. And that task involves Kody, yes? He's downstairs. And you know who's cooking for us downstairs?"

"Is Kody in my kitchen?"

"Uh, well, yes—but also Boreas is here, too."

Malo nods as Lorraine and Edithe walk him down the stairs.

37

Smiles of the Moon

THE WORLD MOVES FAST around him. Time forgetting the Queen who lost herself to save the stars.

In the twenty years that have passed, Deneb has gone through a transformation. The abandoned citadel that the ladies-in-waiting have all sheltered away with Malcolm and Jaycub has now been rebuilt. It appears on the map now as Salamander Citabell. Leading the new formation of Citabell, Maurene and, ironically, Malcolm. Malcolm, who once hated being in the old, abandoned citadel found it the perfect place to settle down after Aelyta's loss. Helping refurbish the old greenhouse buildings of the city, Malcolm and Maurene have opened the new citadel to those who lost their homes in Muddy Bay.

Restoration to Muddy Bay is still ongoing, but the Bay will not regain the same population it once had beside Elementropolis and the Cygni Sea. But the people love the ocean, and the Elements love their home, the process is stubborn and unrelenting. Muddy Bay must start from the beginning, topsoil of it all. During the tornado storm, the entire bay area had been flooded. Pyerre has found a home in the ruins. The flooding bringing back an ancient river that once divided Deneb. Pyerre resides in Muddy Bay in hopes that his presence in the geographical division does not lead to political divide as well—especially not after the destruction Miles had caused.

In Elementropolis, the city is thriving as the only last surviving evidence. Luella and Ellsy have taken over Pyerre's Library since his departure from his collection. Luella heavily focused on the protection of information, while Ellsy heavily determined to restore the knowledge of Deneb to its rightful objective truth.

The coastal city has also welcomed a new facility. Lorraine and Aubree's museum thrives after twenty years of opening. Jaycub and Lyza help as much as they can while splitting their time between the city and Avelmore Castle. Jaycub has been reforming the knighthood to protect the people. He married Lorraine, and together, they had three children. Jaycub has been prominent in the reformation of the Ospherian ways. As is Lyza, she has been reforming the laws of Ospheria alongside Odetta, Presley, and Margaret.

Margaret and Presley had discovered Miles's war room had been turned into a room covered in technology the two of them had never seen before. Kody has been splitting his limited time studying the war room, restoring Elementals, and supporting Malo. The creation of that very room was the winning evidence used against Miles and the other tyrants.

As for Ospheria, Margaret, Lyza, Odetta, and Presley have taken charge in the loss of their queen. With two other ladies in the heart of two existing cities, all six of them interlaced through all of Deneb. This is the reason to why they've been named, The Queen's Lace.

Lyza remains in contact with Cory, who had been in trial alongside his father. Unlike Julius, Cory was found not guilty of treason because of his intent behind his actions—or lack of. After his trial, Cory has kept away from the public eye. He has found solace in music history, recrafting the songs of the old and reemerging them from the darkness. He's created newer versions for the children, like nursery songs, as a way to preserve the history and the old songs. In this way, he tells Lyza that the constant revisit of the old songs is an atonement for his guilt despite the trial's results. That, despite the trial finding him innocent in the tyranny of his father, Cory still felt at fault for the loss of Aelyta and the destruction of Deneb.

The ANP has returned to Avelmore as well. The news press has been focused on objective truth and literary journalism. They no longer report on the news in just Avelmore, expanding their reaches to report on the refurbish Salamander Citabell, the rebuild of Muddy Bay, and the preservation of Elementropolis. Their new motto has become reports to unify and encompass all and every community of Deneb.

Since Aelyta's departure, Deneb has never been more grounded in community. Each Elemental has deeply relied on one another. Deneb is slowly, like the force of nature that it has always been, self-correcting.

The only person stuck in a wheel of grief and struggle is Malo. The past twenty years, Malo has been adamant about creating the mechanism to return Aelyta back to Deneb. And the past twenty years, he has created failures upon failures. From breaking mirrors to rebuilding large clocks, Malo could not create a portal to obtain Aelyta. Even with Kody's help, he became lost in his own head and shadows. Being entrapped in shadows, not a single part of him resembles a body anymore, but a mass of dark swirling shadows.

One day, Malo hovers over a book from one of Aelyta's collection. Her notes still tucked away in the pages. Pulling one of her writings loose, his finger traces her penman-ship. The way her letters swirl together, curving into the words. An ache in his chest bursts into a solemn yearn. The way she would form her thoughts on the paper in his hand are the only connection he has left, the only evidence he has left of her existence.

The book still smells of her. He lifts the tome to his face and takes in the scent of her.

A gentle cough sounds behind the book in front of him. Peering over the top, Malo quickly readjusts himself. "How long have you been standing there?" Malo closes the book and quietly places it down on the table in front of him.

Kody's chuckles echo in the library's study room. The room that held them all for the last time together. Kody's head tilts. "I'd say long enough. I saw enough. Is this how you're searching the books for answers?"

Malo gives him a sideways glance. "I'm not giving up, if you're here to talk me out of it."

"It's been almost twenty years," Kody states. "If you do manage to find a pathway, it will take you much longer to bring her back. And then what? Ospheria is moving on without her."

"I can't move on without her," Malo cuts him off. "I can't. Move on. Without...her."

Kody sighs as he slumps into a chair in front of the large cylindric lens. Malo slumps against the side of the table next to him. Sitting in silence, Malo picks up the collection of crystals spread in front of him. The only sound filling the room between the men is Malo playing with the crystals. At first, he places the crystals in circles atop the backlit tabletop under the lens. The crystals light up in a soft glow. He moves more crystals into the light.

Kody leans forward and plays with the little square mirrors. One mirror, he places between the rocks watching the glow ignite brighter. Another mirror against another rock. He chuckles at their kid-like play. Kody sits up. "Wait!" he yelps. He leans into the lens and gasps. Glancing around the lens at Malo. "Kaleidoscope."

Malo blurts, "What?"

"That's the answer." Kody jumps from the chair. "Splitting yourself into stars, but you're not splitting yourself like Aelyta did. You'll be reflecting yourself, like a kaleidoscope."

Malo's mouth agape, and his head shakes. "I don't understand."

"You dumb-wilted plant...shadow." Kody waves at his face. "We just need a large light, you'll be the crystal. And mirrors, all the mirrors, and, and..." Kody pats his pockets. He pulls out a notepad and pen, scribbling away. "I need to call a few people."

Running in circles behind Kody, Malo is counting the items needed with his hand. "Light?" he says aloud.

"Yes, a large one." Kody still paces with a notepad and pen.

Malo stops, and Kody bumps into his back. "The lighthouse?" Malo turns to Kody, and Kody grins widely back at him.

"I have to make some calls, but I'll meet you there." Kody pats Malo's shoulder and rushes out the doorway into the central library.

Malo grips his forehead, pulling his hair back. His breathing turns into a laugh. "I'm going to bring her home." His hands fall to his chest where the ache once was. His heart pounding like the horses thrumming against the ground as they run.

Leaping from the boat, Malo lands on the dock that juts from the lighthouse island. He ties the boat and makes his way inside. Dropping his bag on the floor as he enters the towering building, the sound echoes the pillar lighthouse. He beats his forehead with his fist. He should have given Aelyta a tour of the lighthouse, but instead he showed her the firefly flowers. The firefly flowers.

Malo walks down the path and out towards the fire pit. The firefly flowers are tall this time of year. He runs his hand through the tall grass and flowers. He sits himself down where they once laid under the stars. Looking out towards the ocean, Malo watches the setting sun. Nearly twenty years ago, he was laying right here next to Aelyta watching the same sun rise.

"Soon," he murmurs to himself. "She'll be here soon. This time, I'll show her the inside of Lover's Lighthouse."

The sound of voices brings Malo back. He turns to the dock where the voices are coming from. Rising from the grass, he brushes his pants and hands. Waving to the group climbing onto the dock from their boat, Lyza is the first to wave to him. Luella, seeing her waving, looks to Malo and waves also. The rest of the group bounds up the dock towards the lighthouse.

Malo meets them at the pathway leading to the front door. They all collide into a large hug. Kody's the first to break away. "Come on, folks! We've got work to do."

"Thank you all for coming out here. It's been almost a year since I've seen you all together. I know I've been distant ever since Aelyta...but I'm glad some of you have found the time to visit Lover's Light with me." Malo yells for them all to hear. Lyza tucks under his arm. Edithe floating beside them, rubbing his back as they pile into the first floor of the lighthouse.

Malo opens the bag full of groceries. Kody digs in, Luella's husband gives a hand. Aubree and Lorraine's children play on the floor in front of the fireplace. Lorraine and Jaycub help carry in more stuff from the boat. Lorraine yells to the kids about playing properly and minding themselves as Aubree is no longer a young age, which causes Aubree to laugh a wicked screech.

Edithe boils water in the kitchen and starts up a large pot of wilted fiddlehead. Lyza yells over all the chaos at Luella, who almost bent down to grab some bags to carry. "Don't you dare!" Lyza screams from across the room.

"Luella, dear," Lorraine pats her arm. "You go sit down."

Scoffing, Luella replies, "Just cause I'm pregnant doesn't mean I can't help."

"You're here for your brain, not for brawns," Kody reassures a grumpy Luella.

"You're trying to tell my daughter what to do?" Edithe floats in through the wall. They all frown at themselves. "Yeah, good luck with that. You all know she doesn't listen." Edithe goes back to the kitchen through the wall.

The next few weeks, Malo relishes in the banter that never seems to cease. Kody directs the group with his knowledge in alchemy with a drawn-up plan of what they're making at the top of the lighthouse.

It took a full month for them to finish the star-scattering kaleidoscope. Luella and her husband are the first to leave, taking Malo's smaller boat back to the main coast. But before their descent, they both give Malo their goodbye's, and he sends them off with well wishes. Both his hands cup Luella's plumped face. He gives her one last look. Time is moving onward. Her face, once a child. Twenty years really has passed and that's evident in her face. "I'll miss you, kid." He pulls her into one last hug. Letting her go, he pulls her husband into the same embrace.

"I know, I know." Luella's husband pats Malo's back.

"I know you know," Malo returns.

He watches their boat leave the dock and tails for the coastline. Malo turns back to the lighthouse where the rest of the group are bantering away with each other. Leaving is going to hurt.

Edithe pops up beside Malo. "You're not leaving, you sap."

Malo jumps at the sudden appearance of the ghost. "Every time." He grasps his chest.

"You're saying goodbyes like you're about to give your last breath." Edithe steps in front of him. He sidesteps and attempts to go around her, but she pops in front of him. He groans, but Edithe shushes him. "Just like Aelyta. You're not dying. She's not dead. You're just being reflected into the universe, across the universe."

"What if I can't come back? What if she can't come back?"

Edithe rolls her eyes. "You move on. We move on. Time moves on."

"Exactly." Malo sighs.

"No, you don't get it. Time moves differently for me, because..." Edithe gestures to her ghostly presence. "Time moves differently for Ospheria. Time also moves differently for Aelyta."

"You don't know that." Malo waves her away.

"You're right, I don't. But I do know that because her soul is broken into the universe, time must move differently for her."

"So, I shouldn't be sad that everyone is moving on?"

"What I'm saying is that we're all flowers in the seasons. Bloom in the spring, wilt in the fall. But even when the flowers sleep in the winter, the birds and the deer are still awake. They don't sleep when the flowers do. Some die in the winter, but others are birthed from the cold."

The soft sliver of the moon rises into the night sky. Malo leans against the back wall of the second floor where the group is gathered. Kody and Edithe sit closest to the fireplace. Aubree and Lorraine curl up together under their own furry blankets. Jaycub and his three children are roughhousing in the middle of the room. Lyza sits against the large window seat.

Tomorrow night is the night he'll step into the large kaleidoscope. But as he nestles into the shadows, tonight might be a better time than any. Malo hears Lorraine remark a tone at her kids. Her eldest daughter sticks her tongue at her mother. The room erupts in laughter. Aubree waves a finger at the girl.

His eyes meet Edithe's. She stares at him intently. He gives her a soft shrug. And in that moment, he catches Lyza staring at him wide-eyed. He hesitates a moment, but gives her a nod.

Lyza's legs swing over the edge of the bench seat. She barely makes a sound, but her eyes fill to the brim. Not to bring attention, she scuffles her way to Malo, who has slipped through the door. Lyza follows him up the stairs to the top of the lighthouse.

"You're leaving tonight," she doesn't ask. Her voice firm.

"I think I am." Malo helps her up at the top landing.

Edithe appears behind him. "It's because the moon smiles tonight."

Malo jumps, grabbing hold of the railing at the edge of the lighthouse. Edithe laughs, but it doesn't reach her eyes. She turns to the chamber door that leads into the bulb. Malo gives her a half-grin. "I'll see you guys soon."

The light swirls above their heads. At every turn of the beam, Malo's heart beats a little bit faster. He turns to Lyza behind him. "She's among the stars," Lyza reassures. "I know it."

"If you're worried, I'll wait for you in the Liminal space," Edithe chimes. "Just in case."

Lyza takes a step forward. "Are you sure you don't want to say goodbye to the others before you go?"

"The others have already said their goodbyes, to me and to Aelyta. To them, I've already become lost in the shadows. I've fallen deep into my own darkness. Grief has swallowed me whole," Malo confirms. "You both know this also."

Edithe nods. But Lyza firmly answers, "At least take this." She hands Malo a ring.

"What's this?" Malo rolls the ring carefully in his hand.

"It's Aelyta's supposed wedding ring. Cody gave her options, but she didn't take his offers. She wanted the ring from her grandmother's collection. This is the ring she was planning on marrying with." Lyza points to Malo's hand.

He closes the ring in his fist. "Thank you for keeping it safe all these years." He nods to Lyza.

Tears rolling down her face, Lyza shrugs. "It's what I do best. I miss her so much."

"Me too." He pulls her into a hug. "I'll bring her back."

Malo catches a glance of Edithe floating beside the chamber door. She's also sniffling. "Whenever you're ready," Edithe says.

Letting go of Lyza, Malo straightens himself. He places the ring over his pinkie. The size of it is smaller than his, stopping at his pinkie knuckle. He grips his hand and lifts his head. "Ready."

He pushes the chamber door open and glides into the bulb chamber. Edithe and Lyza somberly smile at him from behind the door frame. They give him one last wave before Edithe closes the chamber door.

The light spins in the chamber. Within the enclosure, mirrors are built around the bulb in varying angles that resemble a snowflake. The light stops spinning, signaling either Edithe or Lyza pulled the switch. The two light beams lift upward towards one another atop the bulb, shooting up towards the sky.

Behind the beam of light, the smiling moon shines in the night. Malo watches the moon as the light beams split amongst the mirrors. The chamber fills with light until Malo's vision goes white. His hands feel for the platform in the center under the light bulb.

Stepping up onto the platform, Malo's head is the first to feel the pull. Tension pulls his arms next. His legs crumble. Grinding his teeth, the warmth of the bulb burns his face, his hands, his neck. The blinding light combusts and the cold air hits his skin. Goosebumps trickle across every part of his body, glittering his skin like the stars in the night sky.

Epilogue

STARING at the lighthouse bulb from outside, Lyza watches a blink in the light. Standing beside Edithe, they watch as the lights fill with color. An aura borealis streams the night sky.

Edithe turns to Lyza. "I must go." The ghost leaves Lyza standing in the wind at the top of the lighthouse. Tears stream down her face. She's alone. She's truly alone.

Wiping her eyes, Lyza heads down the stairs back to the second floor. Gently sneaking back into the flat, she slinks along the wall.

Jaycub and his three children are still roughhousing in the middle of the room. She tries to make it to back to the window seat.

Glancing at her from across the room, Lorraine rises from her chair. Lyza freezes in her tracks. Before Lorraine could ask, three knocks pound on the door beside Lyza. The room falls silent. They all pause to turn towards the door.

The doorknob jiggles. Lyza reaches for the door. "Malo?" Lyza swings the door open.

Stepping through the doorway, a Floral with the browning signs of age edging her petals smiles at them. "You all look just as you were."

Lyza, closest to the Floral, leans into her, squinting. "Aelyta?"

The Floral nods as she shivers in the doorway. "It's pretty cold outside."

Aubree rises from her chair. "Come to the fireplace." But before she could reach the fire, Aubree embraces Aelyta. Aubree's hands on both Aelyta's cheeks. "Oh, you've become a flower."

Aelyta's eyes soften as she embraces Aubree. Aubree releases Aelyta as she warms up by the fire.

"Whose kids are these?" Aelyta gestures to the children sitting patiently on the floor.

"Mine," Lorraine and Jaycub raise their hands. "Ours." They say together.

Her chest tightens—not from exhaustion, but from expectation. Like something should be here already. Something that should've been familiar. Someone who should be waiting for her. Her eyes settle on the empty space near the window seat, her heart sinking. Where's Malo?

Aelyta laughs. She scans the room. "Where's Malo?"

Acknowledgments

I am descendant-blessed to be surrounded by an amazing group of women. From writing peers to editors, I cannot fathom how truly spectacular these women are and to be a part of this project.

Lauren, and Tea and Tales Publishing, your thoughts and contribution are what kept the ship afloat. I wouldn't have seen the light through the shadow realm without you.

Sabrina, and Inkfall Editing, your astute attention to detail are phenomenal. You are the best cheerleader a novice novelist could ever ask for.

Kate, Meghan, and friends; I am forever grounded but free to roam the limitless skies with you all. Thank you for the safe space to explore my writing, imagination, and wine-intake.

Erin and the local library writing group, another safe place to shake off the imposter syndrome with others who feel the same way. I truly appreciate the space you have provided. A library is a very special place, indeed.

My family, husband and son, your patience—and, no shortage of support—gave me the push to finish a project I never thought would ever see the light of day.

You, the reader, thank you for taking a chance on this book. I hope it leads you the shadows, whatever that may be. May you conquer evil kings. May you go forth and live among the Elements.

About the Author

Photograph by Tilly & Tuck Photography

Theophany Juhn grew up in Northern California. She has a history of studying everything under the sun and moon from linguistics to politics. She settled on a degree in English where she utilizes her past studies in her writing. Forsaken Flowers is Theophany's debut novel.

www.ingramcontent.com/pod-product-compliance
Lightning Source LLC
Chambersburg PA
CBHW012038140726
47991CB00011B/3186